WELCOME TO
MASTODONIA

Out of the rose clump, a face stared fixedly at me—a cat face. The whiskers. The owl eyes. The grin.

Entranced and frightened, I moved forward slowly, the gun at ready. I was close now. Closer, something told me, than I should be. But I took another step, and on that step I stumbled.

Recovering, I noticed the rose bush was no longer there and neither was the hen house. I stood on a little slope that was covered with short grass. It was no longer night. The sun was shining, but with little warmth. The cat face was gone.

Then suddenly from behind me I heard a shuffling, thumping sound and I pivoted around. The thumping, shuffling thing stood ten feet tall. It had gleaming tusks and a long trunk. A mastodon, I told myself.

A mastodon!

And it was coming straight toward me . . .

MASTODONIA

CLIFFORD D. SIMAK

A Del Rey Book

BALLANTINE BOOKS • NEW YORK

ONE

A dog's high kiyoodling brought me up in bed, still half asleep, barely functional. The first light of dawn lay within the room, showing in its ghostliness the worn carpeting, the battered highboy, the open closet door with its array of hanging clothes.

"What is it, Asa?"

I turned my head and saw Rila sitting there beside me and I asked myself, for the love of Christ, how come—that after all these years Rila should be here. Then I remembered, in a sort of blur, how come she was here.

The dog cried out again, closer this time, a cry of anguish and of fright.

I began scrambling out of bed, grabbing for a pair of trousers, feet scuffing to find the slippers on the floor. "It's Bowser," I told Rila. "The damn fool never came home last night. I thought he had a woodchuck."

Bowser was hell on woodchucks. Once he started on one, he never would give up. He'd dig halfway to China to get one out. Ordinarily, to put an end to all his foolishness, I'd go out to get him. But last night, when Rila had shown up, I'd not gone hunting Bowser.

When I reached the kitchen, I could hear Bowser whining on the stoop. I opened the door and there he stood, with a wooden shaft dragging behind him. I stooped and put my arm around him and hauled him to one side so I could see what was going on. Once I'd done that, I saw that the shaft of wood was a lance and that the stone blade attached to it was embedded in Bowser's back leg, high up. Bowser whined piteously at me.

1

"What's the matter, Asa?" Rila asked, standing in the door.

"Someone speared him," I said. "He's got a spear in him."

She came swiftly out on the stoop, moving around the two of us, and went down the steps to the sidewalk.

"The blade is only halfway in," she said. "It's only hanging there."

Her hand reached out and grasped the shaft, then gave a twitch and pulled it free.

Bowser yipped, then whined. He was shivering. I picked him up and carried him into the kitchen.

"There's a blanket on the davenport in the living room," I told Rila. "If you would get it, please, we can make a bed for him over in the corner."

Then I turned to Bowser. "It's all right. You're home now and it's all right. We'll take care of you."

"Asa!"

"Yes, what is it, Rila?"

"This is a Folsom point." She held up the spear so that I could see. "Who would use a Folsom point to spear a dog?"

"Some kid," I said. "They are little monsters."

She shook her head. "No kid would know how to mount the point on the shaft—not the way this one is mounted."

"The blanket, please," I said.

She laid the lance on the table and went into the living room to get the blanket. Back with it, she folded it and knelt to put it in one corner of the kitchen.

I lowered Bowser onto it. "Take it easy, boy, we'll fix you up. I don't think the cut's too deep."

"But, Asa, you don't understand. Or didn't hear what I said."

"I heard," I said. "A Folsom point. Ten thousand years ago. Used by paleo-Indians. Found associated with the bones of prehistoric bison."

"Not only that," she went on, "but mounted on a shaft shaped by scraping—that's the earmark of prehistoric technology."

"Yes, I know," I said. "I hadn't meant to tell you

right away, but I might as well. Bowser, it seems, is a time-traveling dog. Once he brought home some dinosaur bones . . ."

"Why should a dog want dinosaur bones?"

"You miss the point. Not old bones. Not fossilized. Not weathered. Green bones, with shreds of flesh still hanging onto them. Not the bones of a big dinosaur. Small one. From an animal the size of a dog or maybe just a little larger."

Rila did not seem curious. "You get scissors and trim off the hair around that wound. I'll get some warm water to wash it out. And where's the medicine cabinet?"

"In the bathroom. To the right of the mirror." As she turned to leave, I called, "Rila."

"Yes," she said.

"I'm glad you're here," I said.

TWO

She had come out of the past—at least twenty years out of the past—only the evening before.

I had been sitting in front of the house, in a lawn chair under the big maple tree, when the car turned off the highway and came up the access road. It was a big, black car, and I wondered, just a little idly, who it might be. To tell the truth, I wasn't particularly happy at the prospect of seeing anyone at all, for, in the last few months, I had gotten to the point where I appreciated being left alone and felt some mild resentment at any intrusion.

The car drew up to the gate and stopped, and she got out of it. I rose from my chair and started walking across the yard. She came through the gate and walked toward me. She was well up the path before I recognized her, saw in this svelte, well-dressed woman the girl of twenty years before. Even then, I could not be sure that it was she; the long years of remembering might have made me susceptible to seeing in any beautiful woman that girl of twenty years before.

I stopped when she was still some distance off. "Rila?" I called, making it a question. "Are you Rila Elliot?"

She stopped as well and looked at me across the dozen feet that separated us, as if she, as well, could not be absolutely sure that I was Asa Steele.

"Asa," she finally said, "it is really you. I can see it's really you. I'd heard that you were here. I was talking with a friend just the other day and he told me you were here. I had thought you were still at that funny little college somewhere in the West. I had thought so often of you . . ."

4

She kept up her talk so that she would not have to do anything else, letting the talk cover whatever uncertainty she might still feel.

I crossed the space between us and we stood close together.

"Asa," she said, "it's been so goddamn long."

Then she was in my arms and it seemed strange that she should be there: this woman who had stepped out of a long, black car in this Wisconsin evening across two decades of time. How hard it was to equate her with the gaily laughing girl of that Mideastern dig, where we had slaved together to uncover the secrets of an ancient tumulus that, finally, turned out to be of slight importance—I digging and sifting and uncovering, while she labeled and tried to somehow identify the shards and other prehistoric junk laid out on long tables. That hot and dusty season had been far too short. Laboring together during the day, we slept together on those nights when we could elude the notice of the others, although, toward the end, I remembered, we had ceased being careful of the others, who had not really seemed to care or to take notice of us.

"I had given up ever seeing you again," I said. "Oh, I thought of it, of course, but I couldn't bring myself to break in on you. I told myself you had forgotten. I told myself you wouldn't care to see me. You'd be polite, of course, and we'd exchange some silly, stilted talk, and then it would be the end, and I didn't want to end it that way. I wanted the memories to stay, you see. I had heard ten years or so ago that you'd gone into some sort of import-export business, then I lost all track of you. . . ."

She tightened her arms around me and lifted her face to be kissed, and I kissed her, perhaps not with the excitement I might once have felt, but with deep thankfulness that we were together once again.

"I am still in business," she said. "Import-export business, if you want to call it that; but shortly, I think, I will be getting out of it."

"It's a little silly, standing here," I said. "Let's sit down underneath the tree. It's a pleasant place. I spend a lot of evenings here. If you'd like, I could rustle up some drinks."

"Later on," she said. "It's so peaceful here."

"Quiet," I said. "Restful. The campus, I suppose, could be called peaceful, too, but this is a different kind of peace. I've had almost a year of it."

"You resigned your university post?"

"No, I'm on sabbatical. I'm supposed to be writing a book. I've not written a line, never intended to. Once the sabbatical is over, it's possible I'll resign."

"This place? Is this Willow Bend?"

"Willow Bend is the little town just up the road, the one you drove through getting here. I lived there once. My father ran a farm-implement business at the edge of town. This farm, this forty acres, was once owned by a family named Streeter. When I was a boy, I roamed the woods, hunting, fishing, exploring. This farm was one place that I roamed, usually with friends of mine. Streeter never minded. He had a son about my age—Hugh, I think his name was—and he was one of the gang."

"Your parents?"

"My father retired a number of years ago. Moved out to California. My father had a brother out there and my mother a couple of sisters up the coast. Five years or so ago, I came back and bought this farm. I'm not returning, as you may think, to my roots, although this place, Willow Bend and the country hereabout, has some happy associations."

"But if you're not returning to your roots, why Willow Bend and why this farm?"

"There was something here I had to come back and find. I'll tell you about it later, if you're interested. But about yourself—in business, you say."

"You'll be amused," she told me. "I went into the artifact and fossil business. Started small and grew. Mostly artifacts and fossils, although there was some gem material and some other stuff. If I couldn't be an archaeologist or a paleontologist, at least I could turn my training to some use. The items that sold best were small dinosaur skulls, good trilobites and slabs of rock with fish imprints. You'd be surprised what you can get for really good material—and even some that is not so good. Couple of years ago, a breakfast cereal company came up with the idea that it would be good promotion to enclose little cubes of dinosaur bone in their packages as premiums. They came to me about it. Do you know how we got the dinosaur bone? There was a bed out in Arizona and we mined it with bull-dozers and front-end loaders. Hundreds of tons of bones to be sawed up into little cubes. I don't mind telling you I'm a bit ashamed of that. Not that it wasn't legal. It was. We owned the land and we broke no laws, but no one can ever guess how many priceless fossils we may have ruined in the process."

"That may be true," I said, "but I gather you have little use for archaeologists or paleontologists."

"On the contrary," she said, "I have high regard for them. I would like to be one of them, but I never had a chance. I could have gone on for years, the way you and I went out into that godforsaken dig in Turkey. I could have spent all summer digging and classifying and cataloging, and when the dig closed down, I could have spent more months in classifying and cataloging. And in between times, I could have taught moronic sophomores. But did I ever get my name on a paper? You bet your life I didn't. To amount to anything in that racket, you had to be at Yale or Harvard or Chicago or some such place as that and even then, you could spend years before anyone took any notice of you. There's no room at the top, no matter how hard you work, or how you scratch and fight. A few fat cats and glory-grabbers have it all nailed down and they hang on forever."

"It worked out pretty much that way for me as well," I told her. "Teaching in a small university. Never a chance to do any research. No funds for even small-time digs. Now and then, a chance to get in on a big one if you applied early and were willing to do the donkey work of digging. Although I'm not really complaining. For a time, I didn't really care too much. The campus was safe and comfortable and I felt secure. After Alice left me—you knew about Alice?"

"Yes," she said, "I knew."

"I don't think I even minded that much," I said. "Her leaving me, I mean. But my pride was hurt and, for a time, I felt I had to hide away. Not here, I don't mean that, and now I'm over it."

"You had a son."

"Yes, Robert. With his mother in Vienna, I believe. At least, somewhere in Europe. The man she left me for is a diplomat—a professional diplomat, not a political appointee."

"But the boy, Robert."

"At first, he was with me. Then he wanted to be with his mother, so I let him go."

"I never married," she said. "At first, I was too busy, then, later, it didn't seem important."

We sat silently for a moment as the dusk crept across the land. There was the scent of lilacs from the misshapen, twisted clump of trees that sprawled in one corner of the yard. A self-important robin hopped sedately about, stopping every now and then to regard us fixedly with one beady eye.

I don't know why I said it. I hadn't meant to say it. It just came out of me.

"Rila," I said, "we were a pair of fools. We had something long ago and we didn't know we had it."

"That is why I'm here," she said.

"You'll stay a while? We have a lot to talk about. I can phone the motel. It's not a very good one, but . . ."

"No," she said. "If you don't mind, I'm staying here with you."

"That's okay," I said. "I can sleep on the davenport."

"Asa," she said, "quit being a gentleman. I don't want you to be a gentleman. I said stay with you, remember."

THREE

Bowser lay quietly in his corner, regarding us with accusing, doleful eyes as we sat at the breakfast table.

"He seems to have recovered," said Rila.

"Oh, he'll be all right," I told her. "He'll heal up fast."

"How long have you had him?"

"Bowser has been with me for years. A sedate city dog to start with, very correct and pontifical. Chased a bird sedately every now and then when we went out for a walk. But once we came here, he changed. He became a roustabout and developed a mania for woodchucks. Tries to dig them out. Almost every evening, I have to go hunting him and haul him out of the hole he's dug, with the woodchuck chittering and daring him from deep inside his burrow. That's what I thought Bowser was doing last night."

"And see what happened when you didn't go to find him."

"Well, I had more important things to do, and I thought it might do him good to leave him out all night."

"But, Asa, it was a Folsom point. I can't be mistaken. I've seen too many of them and they are distinctive. You said some kid might have got hold of it, but I know no kid could mount it on the shaft the way that it is mounted. And you said something about dinosaur bones."

"I told you he was a time-traveling dog," I said. "Impossible as that sounds."

"Asa Steele, you know that's impossible. No one can travel in time, least of all a dog."

9

"All right. Explain fresh dinosaur bones."

"Maybe they weren't dinosaur bones."

"Lady, I know dinosaur bones. I taught paleontology at the college and dinosaurs became a sort of hobby for me. I read all the papers I could lay my hands on and one year we picked up some dino bones for the museum. I mounted the damn things. I spent one entire winter stringing all those bones together and making artificial skeletal details that were lacking, coloring them white so no one could accuse us of faking anything."

"But, fresh!"

"Shreds of flesh still clinging to them. Some gristle and tendons. The meat was getting high. So was Bowser. Apparently, he had found a decaying carcass and had rolled in it, picking up all that lovely scent. It took three days of scrubbing him to get the stench out of him. He was so high there was no living with him."

"All right, then, if you say so. How do you explain it?"

"I don't. I've gotten so I don't even try. For a time, just to show you, I toyed with the idea that maybe a few smallish dinosaurs had survived into modern times and that Bowser had somehow found one that had died. But that doesn't make any more sense than a time-traveling dog."

There was a knock on the door.

"Who is there?" I yelled.

"It's Hiram, Mr. Steele. I came to see Bowser."

"Come on in, Hiram," I said. "Bowser's in here. He had an accident."

Hiram stepped inside, but when he saw Rila at the table, he started to back out. "I can come back later, Mr. Steele," he said. "It was just that I didn't see Bowser outside."

"It's all right, Hiram," I told him. "The lady is Miss Elliot, a friend of mine I haven't seen for a long time."

He shuffled in, snatching off his cap, clutching it with both hands to his chest.

"Pleased to meet you, miss," he said. "Is that your car outside?"

"Yes, it is," said Rila.

"It's big," said Hiram. "I never saw as big a car. And you can see your face in it, it shines so nice."

He caught sight of Bowser in the corner and hurried around the table to kneel beside him.

"What's the matter with him?" he asked. "He's got all the hair off one of his hams."

"I cut it off," I told him. "I had to. Someone shot him with an arrow."

The explanation wasn't exactly correct, but it was simple enough for Hiram to understand and not start asking questions. Arrows he knew about. A lot of kids in town still had bows and arrows.

"Is he bad hurt?"

"I don't think so."

Hiram bent and wrapped an arm around Bowser's shoulders. "That ain't right," he said. "Going around and shooting dogs. There ain't no one should shoot a dog."

Bowser, inviting sympathy, beat the floor feebly with his tail and lapped at Hiram's face.

"Especially Bowser," said Hiram. "There ain't no better dog than Bowser."

"You want some coffee, Hiram?"

"No, you go ahead and eat. I'll just sit here with Bowser."

"I could fry you up some eggs."

"No, thank you, Mr. Steele. I already had breakfast. I stopped at Reverend Jacobson's and he gave me breakfast. I had cakes and sausages."

"All right, then," I said. "You stay with Bowser. I'm going to show Miss Elliot around the place."

When we were in the yard and out of earshot, I said to her, "Don't let Hiram bother you. He's all right. Harmless. Wanders around. The town sort of takes care of him. Drops in and people give him food. He gets along all right."

"Hasn't he anyplace to live?"

"He has a shack down by the river, but doesn't spend much time there. He goes around visiting friends. He and Bowser are great friends."

"I gathered that," said Rila.

"He claims he and Bowser talk together—that he talks to Bowser and Bowser talks back to him. It's not only Bowser. He's a friend of all the animals and birds. He sits out in the yard and talks to a crazy, cockeyed robin and the bird stands there, with its head tilted to one side, listening to him. You'd swear, at times, it understands what he is saying. He goes out into the woods to visit the rabbits and the squirrels, the chipmunks and the woodchucks. He gets after Bowser for hasseling the woodchucks. Says if Bowser let them alone, the woodchucks would come out and play with him."

"He sounds simpleminded."

"Oh, there's no doubt of that. But there are people like him all over the world. Not just in little villages."

"You sound as if you like him."

"More accurately, I don't mind him. There's no harm in him. As you say, he's a simple soul."

"Bowser likes him."

"Bowser dotes on him," I said.

"You said—I think you said—forty acres here. What in the world would a man like you want with forty acres?"

"Look around you," I told her. "Perhaps you'll understand. Listen to the birds. Look at that old apple orchard over there. Filled with blossoms. No great shakes at producing apples. Most of them are small and wormy. I could spray them, I suppose, but that's a lot of bother. But small and wormy as they may be, there are apples here most people have forgotten, if they ever knew. There is one old snow apple tree and a couple or three russets. You haven't tasted anything until you bite into a russet."

She laughed. "You're making fun of me," she said. "You always made fun of me. In your nice, soft-spoken, gentle way. You're not here for bird song or for some long-forgotten apples. That may be part of it, of course, but there is more than that. You said last night, you came here to find something, then you never told me what it was."

I took her by the arm. "Come along," I said. "I'll give you the tour."

The path went around the weather-beaten barn with the sagging door, across one corner of the orchard with its scraggly trees and then along the edge of a long-neglected field overgrown by weeds and bordered by woods. At the end of the field, the path stopped at the edge of a depression.

"This is a sinkhole," I told her. "Or, at least, it is thought of as a sinkhole."

"You've been digging here," she said, looking at the trenches I had excavated.

I nodded. "The natives think I'm crazy. At first, they thought I was treasure hunting. I found no treasure, so now they are agreed I'm crazy."

"You're not crazy," she said, "and that is not a sinkhole, either. Tell me what it is."

I took a deep breath and told her. "I think it's a crater where a spaceship crashed God knows how long ago. I've been finding bits of metal. Nothing big, nothing that really tells me anything. The vehicle, if that was what it was, didn't crash at any great speed. Not like a meteorite. Otherwise, even the kind of metal I am finding would have not survived except as molten chunks. It came in hard enough to dig a hell of a big hole, but there is no sign of plasma reaction. Down deeper, I am confident, lies the greater part of the mass of whatever it was that hit here."

"You knew of this hole before, when you lived here as a boy?"

"That is right," I said. "This country is laced with so-called mineral holes. There is a lot of lead in this country. At one time, there were mines—nothing big, of course, but small, operating mines. In the old days, more than a hundred years ago, prospectors swarmed all over this county and the next. They dug exploratory holes all over the landscape, hoping to uncover strikes. In later years, every hole came to be regarded as a mineral hole. A lot of them, of course, weren't. My pals and I, when I was a boy, were sure this was a mineral hole and off and on, of summers, we did some digging here. The old codger who farmed the place didn't seem to mind. He used to joke with us about it, calling us miners. We found some strange metallic fragments, but they weren't ore and were in no way spectacular. So, after a while, we lost interest. But, through the years, I kept thinking back on it and the more I thought about it, the more I became convinced that what we'd found had been the debris of a spaceship. So I came back, pretending just to be coming back to the scenes of my childhood. When I found the farm had been put up for sale, I bought it, sort of on the spur of the moment. If I had taken time to think about it, I don't suppose I would have. In retrospect, at times, it has seemed a sort of silly thing to have done. Although I have enjoyed the months I've spent here."

"I think it's wonderful," said Rila.

I looked at her in surprise. "You do?"

"Think of it," she said. "A spaceship from the stars."

"I can't be sure of that."

She moved closer, reached up and kissed me on the cheek.

"It doesn't matter if it's true or not," she said. "The point is that you can still dream, that you could convince yourself it could be here."

"And you, a hard-headed business woman."

"Being a business woman was a matter of survival. At heart, I'm still an archaeologist. And all people in that line of work are pure romantics."

"You know," I said, "I was torn between two emotions about showing this to you. I wanted to share it with you, but I was afraid as well—afraid you'd think me irresponsible and silly."

"How sure are you? What evidence do you have?"

"Chunks of metal. Strange alloys of some sort. I sent some chunks to the university for testing and the report shows that there are no known alloys of that sort. The university people got uptight. Asked me where I'd found the stuff. I told them I'd picked it up in a field and had got curious about it. That's the way the matter stands now. It's still my show for a while. I don't want the university horning in on it. Some of the pieces are just chunks of metal. A few show some machining. No sign of rust, just a faint blurring of the surface, as if the metal is showing some slight reaction to long exposure. Hard and tough. Metal almost as hard as a diamond and still not brittle. Terrific tensile strength. There may be other explanations, but an alien spaceship is the best, the most sensible, that I can come up with. I tell myself that I must be scientific and objective, that I can't go riding off on a hobbyhorse . . . "

"Asa, forget it. You're not riding a hobbyhorse. It's all hard to accept, the hypothesis that you have and the evidence you have found, but the evidence is there. You can't simply overlook it."

"In that case," I said, "there is something further. On this one, there is no evidence at all. Just the evidence of my eyes and the feeling that I have. A strange neighbor—I guess that's the best way to describe him. I've never really seen him, never got a good look at him. But I've felt him looking at me, and I've caught glimpses of him, not really seeing him, but a certain outrageous configuration that makes me imagine he is there. I say imagine because I'm still trying to be scientific and objective. On a purely observational level, I'm sure that he exists. He hangs out in the orchard, but he's not there all the time. He wanders quite a bit, it seems."

"Is there anyone else who has seen him?"

"Others, I would guess, have seen him. Periodically, there is a panther scare—although why people should be afraid of panthers, I don't know. But in rural communities, bear and panther scares seem to be a favorite pastime. An atavistic fear, I suppose, that still hangs on."

"Maybe there are panthers."

"I doubt it. There has been no authentic mountain lion sighting for forty years or more. The thing about it is that this creature I am talking of does leave a cat impression. There is one man who knows more about it than anybody else. He's sort of a cross between Daniel Boone and David Thoreau, and he's spent his life out in the woods."

"What does he think about it?"

"Like me, he doesn't know. I've talked to him a few times and we've agreed we don't know what it is."

"You think there is some connection between this creature and your spaceship?"

"At times, I'm tempted. But it seems a bit far-fetched. The implication would be that it's an alien creature that escaped the crash. That would mean it is impossibly long-lived. Also, it would seem unlikely anything could have survived the crash, if there was a crash."

"I'd like to see some of the metal you dug up," she said.

"No problem," I told her. "It is in the barn. We'll have a look when we go back."

FOUR

Hiram was perched on one of the lawn chairs in front of the house with Bowser laid out on the grass beside him. The front-yard robin stood impertinently a few paces off, eyeing their intrusion of its territory with perky belligerence.

Hiram explained, "Bowser said he didn't want to stay in the house, so I carried him out."

"He used you," I told him. "He could have walked himself."

Bowser beat an apologetic tail.

"The robin feels sorry for him," said Hiram.

The robin had no look of sorrow.

"I ain't got nothing to do," said Hiram. "You go about your business. I'll watch over Bowser till he's well. Day and night, if you want me to. If he wants anything, he can tell me."

"All right, then, you watch over him," I said. "We have things to do."

At the barn, I had a hell of a time getting the sagging door open again. Someday, I promised myself, I would get it fixed. It wouldn't take more than a few hours work, but somehow I had never quite gotten around to it.

The interior of the barn, redolent of ancient horse manure, had a pile of junk stacked haphazardly in one corner, but was mostly filled by two long tables I had set up with boards laid across sawhorses. Ranged on the tables were all the pieces of metal I had found or dug out of the pit. At the far end of one of the tables lay two hollow hemispherical pieces of bright metal I had found when I had cleaned out the barn.

Rila walked over to one of the tables and picked up

a jagged piece of metal. She turned it over and over in her hands. She said, in some amazement, "Just as you said, there isn't any rust. Just some slight discoloration here and there. There's some iron in it, isn't there?"

"Quite a lot," I told her. "At least, that's what the university people said."

"Any ferric metal rusts," she said. "Some alloys will stand up for a long time, but they finally show some rust. When oxygen gets to them."

"More than a hundred years," I told her. "Probably, a great deal more than that. Willow Bend celebrated its centenary several years ago. That crater was formed before the town was founded. The crater has to be much older than that. There are several feet of loam in the bottom of it. It would have taken some time for that loam to form. It takes a lot of leaves over many years to form a foot of soil."

"Have you tried to fit some of these fragments together?"

"I've tried, and there are a few pieces that can be fit together, but they don't tell you anything."

"What do you do next?"

"Probably nothing. Keep on with the digging. Keep quiet about it. You're the only one I've told. If I said anything to anyone else, all I'd get would be ridicule. Suddenly there'd be all sorts of instant experts who could explain everything away."

"I suppose so," she said, "but here you have at least tentative evidence that there is, at least, one other intelligence in the galaxy, and that Earth has been visited. This would seem important—important enough to face up to some ridicule."

"But, don't you see," I argued, "that any sort of premature announcement would blur, if not kill off, any significance. The human race seems to have a strange, instinctive defensiveness against admitting there is anyone but ourselves. Maybe that's because we are afraid, deep down inside of us. We may have a basic fear of any other kind of intelligence. Maybe we are afraid that another intelligence would show us up as second rate, make us feel inferior. We talk, at times, about the loneliness of our situation in the universe, voicing a fear that we are alone, but sometimes, it seems to me that that is no more than philosophical posturing."

"But if it's the truth," Rila said, "sooner or later, we'll have to face up to it. There would be some advantage in facing facts early. Then we'd have some time to get used to the idea, to get our feet planted more firmly under us if the time ever comes when we have to meet them."

"A lot of people would agree with you," I said, "but not that faceless mob, the public. We may be intelligent and fairly level-headed, but collectively we can be pig-headed in a lot of different ways."

Rila moved down the table and stopped opposite the two shiny hemispheres. She tapped one of them with her fingers. "These? They came out of the dig?"

"Not out of the dig," I said. "I don't know what they are. They fit together to form a hollow sphere. The skin is about an eighth of an inch thick and extremely hard. At one time, I was going to send one of them along with the metal I sent the university, then decided not to. For one thing, I'm not sure they tie in with any of the rest of this mystery. I found them here, in this barn. I wanted to set up the tables, but there was a pile of junk in the center of the floor. Old pieces of harness, some odds and ends of lumber, a couple of packing cases, a few worn-out tires, things like that. I moved everything into that stall over there. That's when I found the two hemispheres at the bottom of the pile."

Rila lifted one of the hemispheres and fitted it over the other, running her hand around the area where they came together.

"They do fit," she said, "but they can't be fastened back together. There is no thread arrangement, nothing. A hollow ball that came apart somehow, sometime. You have the slightest idea what it is?"

"Not the faintest."

"It could be something fairly simple, something in relatively common use."

I looked at my watch. "How about some lunch?"

I asked. "There is not too bad a place about twenty miles up the road."

"We can eat right here. I could cook up something."

"No," I said. "I want to take you out. Do you realize that I never took you out to eat?"

FIVE

The manhattan tasted good. I realized that it was the first civilized drink I had had in months; I'd almost forgotten how a decent drink could taste. I said as much to Rila. "At home, I guzzle beer or slop some Scotch over a couple of ice cubes."

"You've been sticking close to the farm," she said.

"Yes, and not regretting it. It's the best money I ever spent, buying that place. It's given me almost a year of interesting work and a sense of peace I've never had before. And Bowser has loved it."

"You think a lot of Bowser."

"He and I are pals. Both of us will hate going back."

"I thought you said you weren't going back. You said when the sabbatical was up, you would resign."

"I know. I say that every now and then. It's a fantasy, I guess. I have no desire to go back, but I haven't much choice. When I think of it, I come up against the hard fact that while I'm not exactly destitute, I'm not in a financial situation to become a non-wage-earner for any length of time."

"I know how you must hate the thought of leaving," she said. "It's not only the peace you speak of, but the chance to continue the dig."

"That can wait. It will have to wait."

"But, Asa, it's a shame."

"Yes, I suppose so. But if it's waited for God knows how many centuries, it can wait a little longer. I'll come back each summer."

"It's strange," said Rila, "what long-range views archaeologists can take. I imagine that is a viewpoint that goes with the profession. They deal in long-time phenomena, so time has less importance to them."

21

"You talk as if you never were an archaeologist."

"Well, I never really was. That summer with you in Turkey and then, a couple of years later, a fuddy-duddy dig in Ohio, excavating an Indian campsite. A year or so at Chicago, mostly spent in cataloging. After that, it was easy to decide being an archaeologist was not what I wanted."

"So you went into the fossil-artifact business."

"Small at first," she said. "A little shop in upstate New York. But apparently I came in at about the right time. Collectors were beginning to get interested and the business grew. There were more and more shops springing up each year and I could see that the real money was as a supplier, so I scraped together some money and floated a loan and again started out in a small way. I worked hard. I got a perverse satisfaction out of it. Here I was making a living out of something that was a rather despicable offshoot of a profession I had failed at—perhaps, rather, had been too impatient to try to succeed at."

"You said last night you are considering selling out."

"I took in a partner some years back. He wants to buy me out. He's willing to pay more than the business is worth. He has become somewhat upset at some of my ideas and my methods. If he buys me out, I give him three years before he goes broke."

"You'll miss it. You like being in business."

She shrugged. "Yes, I do. There's a ruthlessness about it that appeals to me."

"You don't look the ruthless type to me."

"Only in business," she said. "It brings out the worst in me."

We finished our drinks and the waiter brought the salads.

"Another round?" I asked.

She shook her head. "I limit myself. One drink at lunch. Long ago, I set that rule. At business lunches, and there were a lot of them, you were expected to lap it up, but finally I refused to do that. I'd seen what it could do to people. But have another if you wish."

"I'll go along with you," I said. "After we finish

here, if you're willing, we'll go see our old Daniel Boone."

"I'd like to, but it may run us late. How about Bowser?"

"Hiram will take care of him. He'll stay with Bowser until we get back. There's a cold roast in the refrigerator and he will split it with Bowser. He'll even go out and collect the eggs. He and Bowser will talk it over first. He'll say to Bowser, it must be time to pick up the eggs, and Bowser will ask what time it is, and Hiram will tell him, and then Bowser will say, yes, let us go and get them."

"This pretense about Bowser talking. Do you think Hiram really thinks he does or is the whole thing just make-believe?"

"I don't honestly know," I said. "Probably, Hiram thinks so, but what difference does it make? It's funny with animals. They have personalities and you can set up routines with them. When Bowser is out digging at a woodchuck hole, I go out to get him and drag him out of the hole, caked with mud and dirt and about worn out. Even so, he doesn't want to go home. He is committed to that woodchuck. But I grab him by the tail and say, 'Git for home, Bowser,' and he goes, trotting ahead of me. But I've got to grab him by the tail and I have to say the words. Otherwise, he'd never go home with me. I couldn't coax him home and I couldn't chase him home. But when I go through that silly business, he always heads for home."

She laughed. "You and Bowser! Both of you are crazy."

"Of course we are. You can't live with a dog for years . . ."

"And chickens. I remember I did see some about. Have you pigs and horses and . . ."

"No. Chickens are all. Eggs to eat and an occasional fryer. I considered buying a cow, but a cow is too much bother."

"Asa, I want to talk business with you. You said you didn't want the university horning in—I think is the way you put it—on this dig of yours. What would you think of me horning in?"

I had a forkful of salad halfway to my mouth and now I put it down. There was something in the way she said it that was almost a warning. I don't know what it was, but all at once, I was a little scared.

"Horn in?" I asked. "What do you mean?"

"Let me share your work with you."

"What a silly thing to ask," I said. "Of course you can share it with me. Haven't I already shared my discovery with you, telling you about it?"

"But that wasn't what I was talking about. I wasn't asking for the sharing as a gift. I meant a partnership. You don't want to go back to teaching. You want to keep on with the dig and I think you should. You are onto something important and it shouldn't be interrupted. If I could help a little so you wouldn't have to leave . . ."

"No," I said harshly. "Don't go any further. No, I wouldn't have it. You're offering to finance me and I won't have it."

"You make it sound so terrible," she said. "As if I had proposed something horrible. I'm not trying to take you over, Asa. It isn't that. I have faith in you, is all, and it's a shame that you have to . . ."

"It's big business offering to bail out the underprivileged," I said angrily. "Damn it, Rila, I will not be patronized."

"I'm sorry, then, that I mentioned it. I had hoped you'd understand."

"Goddamn it, why did you have to mention it? You should know me better than that. It all was going so fine and now . . . "

"Asa, remember the last time. The horrible fight we had. It ruined twenty years for us. Let us not let that happen again."

"Fight? I don't remember any fight."

"I was the one who was angry that time. You had gone off with a couple of the men and got plastered, neglecting me. You tried to explain, you tried to say you were sorry, but I wouldn't listen. It was the last day at the dig or the next to the last day and I never had the time to get over being angry. We can't let some-

thing like that happen now. At least, I don't want it
to. How about you?"

"No," I said, "neither do I want that to happen. But
I can't take money from you. No matter how well
off you are, how little you would miss it."

"Not well off," she said. "And, again, I'm sorry.
Can't we just forget it? And can I stay around for
another little while?"

"As long as you wish," I told her. "Forever, if you
want to."

"How about your friends and neighbors—will they
talk about us?"

"You're damn right they'll talk about us. A place
like Willow Bend hasn't much to talk about; they grab
at any little thing."

"You don't seem concerned."

"Why should I be? I'm that nutty Steele kid, who
came back to the old hometown, and they're suspicious
of me and resentful of me and the most of them don't
like me. They're friendly, certainly, but they talk about
me behind my back. They don't like anyone who isn't
bogged down in their particular brand of mediocrity.
It's defensive, I suppose. In front of anyone who left
the town and came back short of utter defeat, they
feel naked and inferior. They are acutely aware of
their provincialism. That is the way it is. So, unless
you are concerned about yourself, don't give it another
thought."

"I am not at all concerned," she said, "and if you
are thinking of making an honest woman of me . . . "

"The thought," I told her, "has not crossed my
mind."

SIX

"So you want to know about the coon that isn't any coon," Ezra Hopkins said to Rila. "It took me, God knows, long enough to find out that it wasn't any coon."

"You're sure it's not a coon?"

"Miss, I'm sure of that. Trouble is, I don't know what it is. If old Ranger here could only talk, maybe he could tell you more than I can."

He pulled at the ears of the gaunt hound that lay beside his chair. Ranger blinked his eyes lazily; he liked to have his ears pulled.

"We could bring Hiram here some time," I said. "He could talk with Ranger. He claims that he can talk with Bowser. He talks with Bowser all the time."

"Well, now," said Ezra, "I won't argue with that. There'd been a time I would have, but not any more."

"Let's not talk about Hiram and Bowser now," said Rila. "Please go ahead and tell me of this coon."

"Boy and man," said Ezra, "I have ranged these hills. For more than fifty years. There have been some changes other places, but not many of them here. This land isn't fit for farming. It mostly stands on edge. Some parts of it are used to run cattle in, but even cattle don't get no farther into the hills than they have to go. Time to time someone tries to do some logging, but it never amounts to much, because they lose money trying to get the timber out of here once it has been cut. So, all these years, these hills have been my hills. Them and the things that are in them. Legally, I own the few useless acres that this shack stands on, but, in another way, I own it all."

"You love the hills," said Rila.

"Well, I suppose I do. Loving comes from knowing and I know these hills. I could show you things you never would believe. I know a place where the pink lady's slippers grow and the pink ones are wild for sure. The yellow ones will stand some tampering with, although not very much; the pink ones won't stand tampering at all. Turn some cattle into a place where the pink ones bloom and in a couple of seasons, they are gone. Pick more than a few of them and they are gone. People say you don't find them any more, that there are no more in these hills. But I tell you, miss, I know where there is a patch of them. I don't tell no one where and I don't pick them and I don't tramp around among them. I let them strictly be. I just stand off a ways and look at them and think of the pity of it—that once these hills were covered by them, but not any more. And I know where a she-fox has her den, hidden well away. She has raised six litters there, and once the cubs are grown a bit, they come out and play around the den, little awkward things that fight among themselves, play fighting, that is, wrestling and tusseling, and I have a place where I can sit and watch them. I think the old she-fox must know that I am there, but she doesn't seem to mind. After all these years, she knows I mean no harm."

The shack crouched against the steep hillside just above a stream that dashed and chattered down its rocky bed. Trees crowded close and a short distance up the hill from the shack, a rocky outcropping thrust out of the sloping earth. The chairs in which we sat, in front of the shack, had their back legs sawed short to equalize the slope. A pail and washbasin stood on a bench beside the open door. Against one wall of the shack was ranged a pile of firewood. Smoke streamed lazily from the chimney.

"I am comfortable here," said Ezra. "Being comfortable comes from not wanting much. Folks up in town will tell you that I'm worthless and I suppose I am, but who are they to measure worth? They say I do some drinking and that is the honest truth. Couple of times a year I go off on a bender, but I never hurt no one. I never cheated anyone that I can think of.

I've never told a lie. I have one real bad failing. I talk too much, but that comes from hardly ever seeing anyone to talk with. When someone does come visiting, it seems that I can't stop. But enough of that. You came to hear about Ranger's pal."

"Asa never told me that creature was Ranger's pal."

"Oh, he's Ranger's pal all right."

"But you and Ranger hunt him."

"Maybe at one time, but not any more. In my younger days, I was a hunter and a trapper. But I haven't done any of either for several years. I hung up my traps with a feeling of shame that I had ever used them. I still knock over a squirrel every now and then for stew and a rabbit or a grouse. I still hunt some, but only as the Indians hunted: for meat to fill the pot. There are times when I don't even do that, when I stay my hand. I suppose that as a predator, I have the right to hunt—at least, that is what I tell myself—but I do not have the license to kill, without cause or reason, my brothers of the woods. Of all the hunting, I liked coon hunting best. Have you ever hunted coon?"

"No, I never have," said Rila. "I've never hunted anything."

"You hunt coon only in the fall. The dog runs the coon until he puts him up a tree, then you try to locate him in the tree and shoot him. Mostly for his pelt, or, what is worse, for the sport of it—if you can call killing sport. Although when I killed coon, I killed not for the pelt alone, but for eating, too. There are people who believe that coon are not fit to eat, but, I tell you, they are wrong. It's not the hunting though; it's the crispness of the autumn night, the sharp briskness of the air, the smell of fallen leaves, the closeness that you feel with nature. That and the thrill of the hunt; for I do admit there is a thrill in hunting.

"But there finally came a time, when Ranger was a pup—and he's an old dog now—that I quit killing coon. I did not quit the hunting, but I quit the killing. Ranger went out of nights and we hunted coon. When he put one up a tree, I would hunt it out and aim the gun at it, but I did not pull the trigger. Hunting without shooting, without killing. Ranger didn't understand at first, but finally he did. I thought that not killing, I might ruin him, but he understood. Dogs can understand a lot if you are patient with them.

"So we hunted without killing, Ranger and I, and, in time, I became aware that there was one coon which led us a sterner chase than any of the others. He knew all the tricks of the hunted and many nights, Ranger was unable to bring him to a tree. Oftener and oftener we ran him, as if he delighted in the chase as much as we—an old buck coon that had become our equal or more than our equal and who was using us as much as we were using him, laughing at us all the while, playing games with us. I admired him, of course. You are compelled to admire a worthy opponent who plays the game as skillfully, or perhaps more skillfully, than you do. But I became a bit angry at him, as well. He was just too good; he was making fools of us. So, finally, not by any conscious decision, but by degrees, I found myself ready, in regard to this particular coon, to abandon my rule to never kill another coon. If Ranger could tree and hold him and I could find him in the tree, I'd kill him and prove, once and for all, which was the better, he or us. You understand that coon hunting is done only in the fall, but that was not true with this particular coon. Many times, in other months of the year, Ranger ran him alone, and there were nights when I'd go out as well. It became a never-ending game between Ranger and the coon, and occasionally I joined in, no matter what the season."

"How are you sure it was a coon?" asked Rila. "Ranger might have been running something else—a fox, a wolf."

Ezra said stiffly, "Ranger would never have hunted anything but a coon. He's a coon hunter; he comes of a long line of coon dogs."

I said to Rila, "Ezra's right. A coon dog is a coon dog. If he runs a rabbit or a fox, he's worthless as a coon dog."

"So you never saw this coon," Rila said to Ezra, "and you never killed him."

"But I did. See him, I mean. It was one night, several years ago. Ranger put him up near morning, four o'clock or so, and I finally spotted him, a shape against the sky, crouched on a limb near the top of the tree, making himself flat against the limb, hoping he'd not be seen. I raised the gun, but I was breathing so hard from my run that I couldn't take good aim. The muzzle just kept going around and around in little circles. So I lowered the gun and waited until I was breathing easier and he stayed there, crouched on his limb. He must have known that I was there, but he never stirred. Then, finally, I raised the gun again and the aim was steady. I had my finger on the trigger, but I never pulled it. It must have been a minute that I had him in the sights and my finger on the trigger, ready to pull, but I didn't pull. I don't know what happened. Looking back on it, I imagine I thought of all the nights of running and how it would be all gone if I pulled the trigger. How, instead of a respected opponent, I'd have no more than a furry body, and how neither one of us again could have the fun of hunting or of being hunted. I don't remember thinking this, but it must have been what I thought, and when I was at the end of thinking, I brought the gun down. When I put the gun down, the coon up in the tree turned his head and looked at me.

"Now, here's a funny thing. The tree was tall and the coon was well up in its top. The night was not exactly dark—the sky was brightening with the coming dawn—but the coon was still too far away and the night still too dark to see distinctly the face of any coon. And yet, when he turned his head, I saw his face and it was not a coon's face. It was more like a cat's face, although it was not a cat's face, either. It had whiskers like a cat and even from the distance where I stood, I could see the whiskers. Its face was fat and round and still—this is awful hard to tell and make it sound reasonable—and still it was a sort of bony face, like a skull that was fleshed out. Its eyes were big and round, unblinking, like an owl's eyes. I should have been scared out of my britches. But I wasn't. I just stood there, looking back at this catlike face, surprised, of course, but not as surprised as I might have been. I believe that all along, without admitting it to myself, without saying it out loud, I had known this thing we had been chasing wasn't any coon. Then it grinned at me. Don't ask me how it grinned or how I knew it grinned. I saw no teeth, I'm certain, but I knew it grinned. It had the feeling of a grin. Not a grin at having beaten me and Ranger, but a grin of good fellowship, a grin that said, 'Haven't we been having an awful lot of fun?' And so, I tucked my gun underneath my arm and headed back for home, with Ranger following me."

"There's one thing wrong," said Rila. "You said that Ranger is a coon dog and will hunt nothing but a coon."

"That puzzled me, too," said Ezra. "There were times when I wondered an awful lot about it. That's why, I suppose, I wouldn't admit to myself that it wasn't any coon, even when I must have known it wasn't. But since that night I told you about, Ranger has run him many times, and sometimes I've joined in for the simple fun of it. I've seen old Catface around the place, peering at me from a bush or tree, and when he knows I see him, he always grins at me. A grin of good fellowship; nothing mean in it. You have seen him, Asa?"

"At times," I said. "He hangs around in my apple orchard."

"Always just a face," said Ezra. "That grinning face. If there is a body there, it is indistinct. No sign of how big or what shape it is. There have been times when I've come upon Ranger and this creature —the creature peering from a bush at Ranger and Ranger just standing there, companionable. You know what I think?"

"What do you think?" Rila asked.

"I think that Catface comes around and talks to Ranger to set up a run that night. It says to Ranger, how about running me tonight? And Ranger says, it's okay with me. And Catface asks, do you think you can get Ezra to come along? And Ranger says, I'll talk to him about it."

Rila laughed gaily. "How ridiculous," she cried. "How beautifully ridiculous."

Ezra said sourly, "Maybe to you. It's not ridiculous to me. It seems quite right to me. To me, that seems entirely logical."

"But what is this thing? You must have some idea. You must have thought about it."

"I've thought about it, sure. But I don't know. I've told myself maybe it is something that has survived out of the prehistoric past. Or the ghost of something from a prehistoric age. Although it doesn't have a ghostly look to it. What do you think, Asa?"

"Sometimes it appears a little faint," I said. "A little fuzzy, maybe. But not in the same way a ghost would be faint or fuzzy. It doesn't have a ghostly look to it."

"Why don't the two of you stay for supper," Ezra suggested. "We could sit and talk the night away. I ain't talked out by any means; I got a lot of things stored up to say. I could ramble on for hours. I got a big kettle of turtle stew on the stove, five times as much as Ranger and I can eat. I caught a couple of young snappers down by a little pond not far from here. An old snapper can be moderate tough, but a young one is downright toothsome. Couldn't offer much else than turtle stew, but when you got turtle stew, you don't want nothing else."

Rila looked at me. "Could we?" she asked.

I shook my head. "I'm tempted, but we should be getting back. It's two miles out to the road where we parked the car. I wouldn't want to try those two miles in the dark. We better start now so we'll have some light to follow the trail."

SEVEN

Back in the car, heading for home, Rila asked, "Why didn't you tell me about this Catface?"

"I did mention him," I told her. "I didn't elaborate on what kind of thing he is. You wouldn't have believed me."

"And you thought I'd believe Ezra?"

"Well, don't you?"

"I'm not sure if I do or not. It sounds like a backwoods tall tale. And Ezra—a philosophical hermit. I never dreamed there were people like him."

"There aren't many. He's a bitter-ender of a died-out breed. When I was a boy, there were a few of them around. At one time, there were a lot of them. Old batches, my grandmother used to call them. Men who never married, who tended to pull away from society and live by themselves. They batched it—cooked for themselves, washed their clothes, grew little kitchen gardens, kept a dog or some cats for company. They lived by hiring out, working for farmers during busy seasons, perhaps doing some wood cutting in the winter. Most of them did some trapping—skunks, muskrats, things like that. To some extent, they lived off the land, hunting, fishing, gathering wild edible plants. Mostly they lived hand-to-mouth, but they got along, seemed generally happy. They had few worries because they had shucked responsibility. When they grew feeble and were unable to fend for themselves, they either were committed to the old-time poorhouses, or some neighbor took them in and kept them for the chores they could still manage to do. In other cases, someone dropped in on their shacks and found them dead a week. They were mostly shiftless and no account. When they got a little extra money together, they would go out on a drunk until their money was gone, then go back to their shacks and then, in another few months, they'd have scraped together enough for another drunken interlude."

"It sounds like a singularly unattractive life to me," said Rila.

"By modern standards," I told her, "it is. What you are looking at is a pioneer attitude. Some of our young people have picked up the idea. They call it living off the land. It can't be all bad."

"Asa, you say you have seen this creature Ezra was telling us about, and you talked about panther scares. So other people may have seen it, too."

"That's the only way I can explain the panther stories. It does look faintly catlike."

"But a grinning panther!"

"When people see a panther, or something they think is a panther, they're not too likely to notice any grin. They're scared. The grin, in their interpretation, could become a snarl."

"I don't know," she said. "The whole thing is so fantastic. And yet, so is your dig. And Bowser wounded by a Folsom point. And the green dinosaur bones."

"You're asking for an explanation," I said. "Rila, I'm out of explanations. There is a temptation to tie everything together. But I can't be sure all these mysteries tie together. I can't be sure at all. I wouldn't blame you if you walked away. It's not a pretty thing to face."

"Perhaps not pretty," she said, "but exciting and important. If anyone else had told me, I'd consider walking away. But I know you. You'd be honest in your thinking if it killed you. But it is a little frightening. I have the feeling that I'm standing on the brink of something I don't understand, perhaps some great reality that will force us to take a new look at the universe."

I laughed, but the laugh came out a little forced. "Let's not take ourselves too seriously," I said. "Let's go one step at a time. It's easier that way."

"Yes, let's do that," she agreed, sounding relieved. "I wonder how Bowser is getting along."

When we arrived home a few minutes later, it became apparent that Bowser was getting along quite well. Hiram was perched on the back stoop, with a stretched-out Bowser plastered close against him. Seeing us, Bowser beat his tail in welcome.

"How is he?" Rila asked Hiram.

"Bowser is okay," said Hiram. "Me and him had a good day. We sat and watched the robin and we did a lot of talking. I washed out the place where the arrow hit him and it looks good. There ain't no more bleeding and the wound is beginning to scab around the edges. Bowser was a good dog. He lay still when I cleaned it out. He didn't even twitch. He knew I was helping him."

"Did you find something to eat?" I asked.

"There was a piece of roast in the refrigerator and Bowser and me shared that. There was a little left and I gave that to Bowser for supper and fried some eggs for myself. We went and got the eggs out of the nests. There were eleven of them."

Hiram got slowly to his feet, seeming to unfold as he arose. "Since you are here," he said, "I'll go on home. I'll be back in the morning to take care of Bowser."

"If you have something else to do," I said, "there isn't any need. We'll be here. We'll take care of him."

"I got things to do," Hiram said with dignity. "There are always things to do. But I promised Bowser. I told him I'd take care of him until he was all well."

He came down the steps and started to go around the house, then stopped. "I forgot," he said. "I didn't shut the chicken house. It should be shut. There are a lot of skunks and foxes."

"You go on," I said. "I'll shut up the chickens."

EIGHT

The noise brought me straight upright in bed.

"What's the matter?" Rila asked sleepily from her pillow.

"Something's at the chickens."

She stirred protestingly. "Don't you ever get a night's sleep here? It was Bowser last night and now the chickens."

"It's that goddamn fox," I said. "He's got three of them so far. The chicken house isn't much better than a sieve."

Through the night came the squalling of the frightened birds.

I swung my feet out of bed, found the slippers on the floor and shoved my feet into them.

Rila sat up. "What are you going to do?"

"This time, I'll get him," I said. "Don't turn on any lights. You'll scare him off."

"It's night," said Rila. "You won't be able to see a fox."

"There's a full Moon. If he's there, I'll see him."

In the broom closet in the kitchen, I found the shotgun and a box of shells. I clicked two of them into the chambers of the double-barrel. Bowser whined from his corner.

"You stay here," I told him. "And keep quiet. I don't want you messing around, scaring off the fox."

"You be careful, Asa," Rila cautioned, standing in the doorway of the living room.

"Quit worrying. I'll be all right."

"You ought to put something on," she said. "You shouldn't be running around out there, just in your slippers and pajama pants."

"It's warm," I said.

"But it might be dewy. You'll get your feet wet."

"I'll be all right," I said. "I won't be out long."

The night was almost as bright as day; a great golden Moon shone directly overhead. In the softness of the moonlight, the yard had the haunting quality of a Japanese print. Lilac scent hung heavy in the night air.

Frantic squawking still came from the hen house. A clump of cabbage roses stood at one corner of the structure, and as I went pussyfooting across the wet, cold grass, heavy with dew, as Rila had said it would be, I got the impression, somehow, that the fox was not in the chicken house at all, but hiding in the rose clump. I stalked the rose clump, gun at ready. It was silly, I told myself. The fox either was still in the chicken house or had left; he would not be hiding in the roses. But the feeling persisted that he was in the roses. Thinking this, almost knowing it, I wondered how I knew, how I could possibly know.

And at the moment I was thinking this, all thought and wonderment were knocked out of me. Out of the rose clump, a face stared fixedly at me—a cat face, the whiskers, the owl eyes, the grin. It stared at me, unblinking, and never before had I seen it so clearly as at that moment—so clearly or for so long a time. Most of my sightings had been no more than fleeting glimpses. But now the face stayed on, hanging in the bush, the softness of the moonlight highlighting the details of the face, making each whisker stand out clearly. And this was the first time, I was sure, that I had actually seen the whiskers. Previously, I had gotten impressions of them, but had never really seen them.

Entranced and frightened, but more entranced than frightened, and with all thoughts of a fox knocked out of my mind, I moved forward slowly, the gun at ready, although now I knew I would not use it. I was close now, closer, something told me, than I should be, but I took another step, and on that step I stumbled or seemed to stumble.

When I recovered from the stumble, the rose bush

was no longer there, and neither was the hen house. I stood on a little slope that was covered with short grass and moss, and up the hill a ways was a clump of birch. It was no longer night; the sun was shining, but with little warmth. The cat face was gone.

From behind me I heard a shuffling, thumping sound, and I pivoted around. The thumping, shuffling thing stood ten feet tall. It had gleaming tusks, and a long trunk hanging down between the tusks was swinging slowly from side to side like a pendulum. The thing was only a matter of a dozen feet away and coming straight toward me.

I ran. I went up that slope like a scared rabbit. If I hadn't run, sure as hell that mastodon would have run over me. He paid no attention to me; he didn't flick a glance at me. He just went shuffling along, for all his bulk stepping daintily and with deliberate precision.

A mastodon, I told myself. For the love of Christ, a mastodon!

My mind seemed to catch and stay upon the word— a mastodon, a mastodon, *a mastodon*—there was room for nothing else, just that one repeating word. Backed against the clump of birch, I stood transfixed, the stuck needle of my mind repeating that one word, while the beast went shuffling across the landscape, turning now to head downhill toward the river.

First, it had been Bowser, I thought, yelping home with a Folsom in his rump, and now it was me. I had somehow traveled, ridiculous as it might seem, the selfsame trail as Bowser.

Here I stood, I thought, a ridiculous figure dressed in pajama pants and a pair of worn slippers, clutching a shotgun in my hand.

A time tunnel had brought me here—or a time road or a time path, whatever one might call it—and that goddamn Catface was mixed up in my predicament somehow, as, undoubtedly, he'd been mixed up in the time traveling that Bowser had done. The funny thing was that there had been no sign of the time path, nothing to warn me that I was putting a foot upon it. What kind of sign, I wondered, would a man look for

—a sort of shimmer in the air, perhaps, although I was sure there had been no shimmer.

And while I was thinking of that, I thought of something else. When I had reached this place, I should have marked it so that I'd have at least a fighting chance of getting back into my own time again. Although, I told myself, that probably wasn't as simple as it sounded—just marking the place where you came out might not mark the path. Nonetheless any chance of marking the spot now was gone. I had run scared, and with reason, when I'd seen the mastodon. Now there was no way I could find the original spot.

I comforted myself by thinking that Bowser had traveled in the past and had come back. So it was not impossible, I told myself, for a person to get back. If Bowser could get back, so could I. Although the moment that I thought of that, I was not too sure. Bowser might have a way to smell out a time tunnel that no man could ever have.

Just standing there and worrying about it, however, would not solve the problem, would not give the answer. If I couldn't find the road back to the present, I might have to stay a while, and I told myself I'd better take a look around.

Looking in the direction the mastodon had gone, I saw a herd of mastodons, a mile or so away, four adults and a calf. The mastodon that had almost run over me clumped steadily to join them.

Pleistocene, I told myself, but how deep into the Pleistocene, I had no way of knowing.

While the lay of the land remained unchanged, it had a vastly different look, for there were no forests. Instead, there was a stretch of grassland that looked somewhat like a tundra, dotted here and there with clumps of birches and some evergreens, while along the river, I could make out misty yellow willows.

The birch trees in the clump next to me were leafed out, but the leaves were small, the immature leaves of spring. On the ground beneath the trees was a carpet of hepaticas, the delicate, many-hued flower that came to bloom shortly after the snow was gone. The hepaticas lent an air of familiarity, almost of identity. In my boyhood, on this very land, I had ranged the woods to bring home in grubby hands great bouquets of the flowers, which my mother would put in a squat brown pitcher, setting it in the middle of the kitchen table. Even from where I stood, it seemed to me that I could smell the exquisite, distinctive, never-to-be-forgotten odor of the tiny flowers.

Spring, I thought, but it was cold for spring. Despite the sun, I was shivering. An ice age, I told myself. Perhaps just a few miles to the north reared the shining ramparts of the glacial front. And here I was, with no more than pajama pants and slippers, and a shotgun in my hand—a shotgun with two shells in its barrels. That was all. That was the sum total. I had no knife, no matches, nothing. I glanced toward the sky and saw that the sun was edging up toward noon. Noon and chilly as it was, it could be freezing by nightfall. A fire, I thought, but I had no way to make a fire. Flint, if I could find some flint. I racked my brain to recall if there was flint to be found in the neighborhood, although even if there were, what could I do with it? Flint struck against flint would produce sparks, but not hot enough to start a fire. Struck against steel, the sparks would be hot enough to start a fire in tinder. The gun was steel, but there wasn't any flint—for now I remembered that in this area there wasn't any flint. Perhaps I could take a shell and open it, extracting the shot charge, then pour out some of the powder to be mixed with tinder, and fire the opened shell into the tinder. Theoretically, the burning powder expelled from the barrel would fire the tinder if it was mixed with powder. But what if that didn't work, I asked myself. And where would I look for tinder? In the heart of a rotten log, if I could find a rotting log and could tear it open to get at the dry, pulpy inner wood. Or bark peeled off a birch tree and shredded finely. Maybe that would work. I wondered whether it would, but could not be certain.

I stood defeated, exhausted with my thinking and the fright that was creeping in. Now, for the first time, I became aware of birds. First the flowers and now the birds. I'd been hearing them all the time, but my brain, roaring with its problems, had rejected them. There was a bluebird perched on a winter-dead stalk. A mullen stalk, perhaps. I tried to remember if the mullen was native or had been imported, in which case, it could not be a mullen stalk. Anyhow, the bird clung to the swaying stalk and sang. A meadowlark leaped from the grass and soared into the air, spraying its trill of excited happiness behind it. In the birch trees, little birds that must have been some sort of sparrow hopped cheeping from branch to branch. The place simply crawled with birds.

The lay of the land, once I had gotten myself oriented, began to look more and more familiar. Naked as it might be, it still was Willow Bend. The river swung out of the north and curved toward the west, then veered east again. All along the bend, the stream was lined with yellow willow trees.

The mastodons were moving off now, down the valley away from me. Other than the mastodons and birds, I could detect no sign of life. But there could be other life, I thought: sabertooth, dire wolf, maybe even cave bear. I could take care of myself for a time, I knew, but only for a time. Once the two shells had been fired, I would be without a weapon, defenseless, the gun no better than a club.

Watching carefully for any sign of life, I walked down the slope toward the river, which I saw was wider and flowing more rapidly than I had ever seen it. Melt water from the glaciers to the north, perhaps.

The misty yellowness of the willows came from pollen-laden pussy willows, great fluffy caterpillars covered with a golden dust. The stream was clear—so clear that I could see the pebbles rolling on the bottom and the flashing shadows of fleeing fish, darting schools of them. Here was food, I told myself. Without a hook or line, I still could weave a net of withelike willow branches, stripping off pieces of the willow bark to hold the woven branches in place. It would be a crude affair and an awkward business, but it could be done; I could weave the net and use it to catch fish. I wondered how raw fish might do as a steady diet and gagged a little at the thought.

If I had to stay here, I told myself, if there was no way of getting back to my own time, then somehow or other, by some hook or crook, I must rediscover fire— fire to keep me warm, fire to cook my food.

Standing there beside the river, I tried to get the facts sorted out. Looking at the situation realistically, I had to reconcile myself to the idea that my chances of getting back to Willow Bend were small. That meant that there were a lot of things to do. First things first, I told myself. Shelter at the moment was more important than food. If necessary, I could starve for a little while. But before the fall of night, I had to find someplace where I would be sheltered from the wind, some small hideaway that might conserve my body heat. The important thing, I knew, was not to panic. I had not panicked so far; I could not afford to panic.

Shelter, food and fire—those were the three things that I needed. Shelter came first, after that, food; fire could wait a little while. Fish, once I had rigged a net, would supply food, but there would be other food as well. Probably tubers and roots, even leaves and bark, although I had no way of knowing which of these would be safe. Perhaps I could find out by watching what bears and other animals ate, take a chance that what they ate was safe. There would be, as well, slow game, small game, but for these, I'd need a weapon, a club. If I could not find another kind of club, the gun would work, but it would be heavy and awkward to handle. A stick would be better. Surely, somewhere, I could find a proper stick that would fit my hand—a well-seasoned piece that would not break at the first blow. A bow and some arrows would be better and, in time, I probably could come up with such a weapon. I'd have to find a sharp stone or a stone that could be broken to form a cutting edge. With it, I could cut down and shape a sprout into a bow. When I'd been a lad, I remembered, I'd been hell let loose with a bow and arrow. I'd need a cord, and fine roots—fine, tough roots—would serve. Was it cedar roots that the Indians had used to sew canoes? It had been years since I'd read "The Song of Hiawatha" and there was something in it, I was sure, that told about cedar roots being used to make canoes. Probably some of the ever-greens that grew here were cedars and I could dig down and get the roots.

While I was thinking all of this, I had turned away from the river and was walking back toward the birch clump. I turned to the right and climbed the small slope above the clump, for it had occurred to me that I had better start right now looking for someplace to spend the night. A cave of some sort would be ideal. If nothing else, if no cave were available, I might make out by crawling into a grove of evergreens. The branches of most evergreens hung close against the ground, and while they might not afford much protec-tion from the cold, at least they would keep out the wind.

I reached the top of the little rise and began to angle down it, looking for some ground formation that might lead me to shelter. Thus it was that I was almost on top of it before I saw it—the hole gouged in the ground. Stopping at its edge, I looked down into it. But it was some seconds before I realized what I had found.

Then, suddenly, I knew. This was the pit where I had been digging. It was old. There was no freshness to it. A bit bigger than when I had first come upon it, but still old; its walls were overgrown with grass and a small birch tree thrust out of the far wall, the tree tilted at a crazy angle.

I squatted down and looked at it and a curious wave of terror came over me. A terrible sense of time. If only the gouge could have been new and raw, I thought, I might have derived some strange comfort from it. But for some reason I could not understand, the oldness of the pit stirred a deep depression in me.

A cold nose touched my naked back and, instinc-tively, I leaped straight up, letting out a squall of fright. I came down on the slope of the pit, rolling to the bottom, the gun flying out of my hand.

Sprawling on my back, I stared up the slope at the thing that had touched me with its nose. It wasn't a sabertooth or a dire wolf. It was Bowser, looking down at me with a silly grin on his face, his tail waving frantically.

On hands and knees, I scrambled up the wall of the pit, threw my arms around the dog and hugged him while Bowser washed my face with a slobbering tongue. I staggered to my feet and reached out to grab his tail.

"Git for home, Bowser!" I yelled at him, and the limping Bowser, one back leg stiffened by the Folsom wound, headed straight for home.

NINE

I sat at the kitchen table, wrapped up in a blanket, trying to get the frost out of my bones. Rila was busy at the pancake griddle.

"I hope," she said, "that you didn't catch a cold."

I shivered; I couldn't help it. "It was cold back there," I told her.

"The idea of running out with nothing on but pajama bottoms."

"There was ice north," I said. "I could practically feel the ice. I bet I wasn't more than twenty miles from a glacial front. This is a driftless area. The ice came down, time after time, moving south on each side of us, but never crossing this area. No one quite knows why. But twenty or thirty miles north, there could have been ice."

"You had a gun," she said. "What happened to the gun?"

"Well, when Bowser over there came up behind me, he close to scared me witless. I jumped and dropped the gun and when I saw Bowser, I never stopped to pick it up. The only thing that I could think of was that he could get me home."

She brought a platter stacked with cakes to the table and sat down opposite me.

"This is ridiculous," she said. "Here we are, talking about your going back in time as if doing so were an everyday affair."

"Not to me," I said, "but it is to Bowser. The thing about it is that he must go to many different times. He wouldn't have been stabbed in the rump with a Folsom point at a time when he could have found dead dinosaurs to drag home."

"To tangle with a Folsom point," she said, "he couldn't have traveled back much more than twenty thousand years. Perhaps, a great deal less than that. You are sure you saw no signs of man?"

"What kind of signs? Footprints? Broken arrows lying around?"

"I was thinking of smoke."

"There wasn't any smoke. The only solid time clue that I have is a mastodon that damn near ran me down."

"You're sure you did go back? You aren't having fun with me? You didn't just imagine the whole thing?"

"Sure. I went out in the woods and hid the gun, then whistled Bowser to me and grabbed him by the tail . . ."

"I'm sorry, Asa. I know. Of course, you didn't. You think that cat-faced thing has something to do with it? Here, get started on those cakes before they get cold. Drink some of the coffee. It is hot. It will warm you up."

I forked cakes onto my plate, buttered them, poured on syrup.

"You know," said Rila, "we just might have something."

"That's right. We have a place where it isn't safe to go looking for a fox."

"I'm serious," she said. "We may have something big. If you have discovered time travel, think of what you could do with it."

"Not on your life," I said. "I'm not fooling around. I've had it. When I see Catface again, I'm going to turn around and walk rapidly away. You could get trapped back there. I couldn't count on Bowser to come back every time and get me."

"But supposing you could control it."

"How could you control it?"

"You could make a deal with Catface."

"Hell, I can't even talk to Catface."

"Not you. Hiram, maybe. Hiram could talk with Catface. He talks to Bowser, doesn't he?"

"He thinks he talks with Bowser. He thinks he talks with robins, too."

"How do you know he doesn't?"

"Now, goddamn it, Rila, just be sensible."

"I am being sensible. How can you be so sure he doesn't talk with Bowser? As a scientist . . ."

"A scientist of sorts."

"All right, even as a scientist of sorts, you know very well you can't take a position, either negative or positive, until you have some evidence. And remember what Ezra said about Catface coming around and making arrangements for Ranger to run him."

"Old Ezra is crazy. Very gently crazy. But crazy just the same."

"And Hiram, too?"

"Hiram's not crazy. He's just a simpleton."

"Maybe it takes gently crazy people and simpletons and dogs to do things we can't do. Maybe they have abilities we don't have. . . ."

"Rila, we can't turn Hiram loose on Catface . . ."

The screen door creaked and I swung around. Hiram came bumbling through the door.

"I heard you," he said. "You was talking about me and Catface."

"We were wondering," said Rila, "if you ever talked with Catface. Like you do with Bowser."

"You mean that thing that hangs around the orchard."

"You have seen it, then."

"Lots of times. It looks something like a cat, but it isn't any cat. It's just got a head. You don't never see a body."

"Have you ever talked with it?"

"Times I have. But it doesn't make no sense. It talks about things that I don't understand."

"You mean it used words that you don't know."

"Maybe. Maybe some words. Ideas mostly. Ideas I never heard of. Funny thing, it doesn't move its mouth and it doesn't make no sound. But I hear the words. Come to think of it, that's the way with Bowser. He never moves his mouth and there isn't any sound, but I hear the words."

I said, "Hiram, pull up a chair and have some breakfast with us."

He shuffled in embarrassment. "I don't know if I should. I already had my breakfast."

"There's batter left," said Rila. "I can make some hot ones."

"You never pass up breakfast with me," I said. "No matter how many other breakfasts you have had. Don't change because of Rila. She's a friend who came visiting. She'll be around, so get used to her."

"Well, if it's all right," said Hiram. "I'm partial, Miss Rila, to cakes with lots of syrup."

Rila went to the stove and poured more batter on the griddle.

Hiram said, "Truth is, I can't feel friendly with this cat-face thing. At times, I'm a little scared of him. He's a funny-looking jigger, with just that great big head and no body you can see. That head of his looks like someone had up and painted a face on a big balloon. He never takes his eyes off you, and he never blinks."

"The thing is," I told him, "that Rila thinks it might be important for us to talk with him, but we can't talk with him. You're the only one who can."

"You mean no one else can talk with him."

"No one but you can talk with Bowser, either."

"If you should agree to talk with Catface," said Rila, "it must be a secret. No one but the two of us must know that you have talked with him, or what you talked about."

"But Bowser," protested Hiram. "I can't keep any secrets from Bowser. He is my best friend and I would have to tell him."

"All right, then," said Rila. "I guess it would do no harm if you told Bowser."

"I promise you," said Hiram, "that he will never tell a soul. If I ask him to, he'll never breathe a word of it."

Rila looked at me, unsmiling. "Is it all right with you," she asked, "if he lets Bowser in on it?"

"Just so long," I said, "as it is understood Bowser will tell no one."

"Oh, he won't," Hiram promised. "I'll warn him not to." And having said this, he turned his full attention to the stack of cakes, shoveling up great mouthfuls of them, leaving a smear of syrup clear across his face.

Nine cakes later, he was ready to resume the conversation.

"You said there was something important I should talk to this Catface about?"

"Yes, there is," said Rila, "but it's a little hard to explain it exactly right."

"You want me to talk to him about this thing you have in mind, then tell it back to you. Just the four of us will know . . ."

"The four of us?"

"Bowser," I said. "You are forgetting Bowser is the fourth."

"Oh, yes," said Rila, "we must not forget old Bowser."

Hiram asked, "It will be a secret just with the four of us?"

"That is right," said Rila.

"I like secrets," Hiram said, delighted. "They make me feel important."

"Hiram," Rila asked, "you know about time, don't you?"

"Time is what you see," he said, "when you look at a clock. You can tell if it's noon or three o'clock or six."

"That's true," said Rila, "but it's more than that. You know about us living in the present and that when time goes by, it is known as the past."

"Like yesterday," Hiram suggested. "Yesterday is past."

"Yes, that's right. And a hundred years is the past and so is a million years."

"I don't see what difference it makes," said Hiram. "All of it is past."

"Have you ever thought how nice it would be if we could travel to the past? Go back to the time before the white men came, when there were only Indians. Or back to a time before there were any men at all."

"I have never thought of it," said Hiram. "I have

never thought of it because I don't think it can be done."

"We think Catface may know how to it. We'd like to talk with him to find out how to do it or if he'll help us do it."

Hiram sat silently for a moment, struggling visibly to let it all sink in.

"You want to go into the past?" he asked. "Why would you want to do that?"

"You know about history?"

"Sure, I know about history. They tried to teach me it when I went to school, but I wasn't any good at it. I never could remember all them dates. It was all about the wars they fought and who was president and a lot of stuff like that."

"There are people," Rila said, "called historians who make it their business to study history. There are a lot of things they are not sure about because people who wrote about it wrote it wrong. But if they could go back in time and see what happened and talk to people who were living then, they would understand it better and could write better histories."

"You mean we could go back and see what happened a long, long time ago? Actually go and see it?"

"That's what I mean. Would you like to do that, Hiram?"

"Well, I don't rightly know," said Hiram. "Seems to me you could get into a lot of trouble."

I broke in. "As a matter of fact," I said, "you wouldn't have to go unless you wanted to. All we want you to find out, if you can, is whether Catface really knows how to do it and if he can show us how."

Hiram shrugged. "I'd have to prowl around at night. Probably out there in the orchard. He shows up sometimes in the daytime, but it's mostly at night."

"Would you mind doing that?" I asked. "You could sleep daytimes."

"Not if Bowser could go with me. Night is a lonesome time, but if Bowser was with me, I wouldn't feel so lonesome."

"I suppose that would be all right," I said, "if you put a leash on Bowser and keep him close beside you.

And another thing: when you see the Catface, just stand there talking to him. Never walk toward him."

"Mr. Steele, why shouldn't I never walk toward him?"

"I can't tell you that," I said. "You've just got to trust me. We know one another fairly well and you know I'd never tell you wrong."

"I know you wouldn't," Hiram said to me. "You don't need to tell me why. If you say so, it's all right. Me and Bowser will never walk toward him."

"And you'll do it?" Rila asked. "You'll talk with Catface?"

"I'll do what I can," said Hiram. "I don't rightly know what's going to happen, but I'll do my best."

TEN

Willow Bend is a small town, its business section no more than a block long. On one corner stands a small supermarket, across from it a drugstore. Straggling up the street are a hardware store, a barber shop, a shoe store, a bakery, a clothing shop, a combined real-estate and travel bureau, an electrical store and repair shop, a post office, a movie house, a bank and a beer joint.

I found a place to park the car in front of the drugstore and went around to open the door for Rila. Ben Page came hurrying across the street to intercept us.

"Asa," he said, "it's been a long time since I've seen you. You don't get down this way too often."

He held out a hand and I took it. "As often as I need," I said. I turned to Rila and said, "Miss Elliot, meet Ben Page. Ben is our mayor and the banker."

Ben thrust out his hand to Rila. "Welcome to our town," he said. "Are you staying for a while?"

"Rila is a friend," I said. "We were in the Middle East together on a dig some years ago."

"I don't know how long I'm staying," Rila said.

"You from New York?" asked Ben. "Someone told me you were from New York."

"How the hell could anyone know?" I asked. "You're the first person she has met."

"Hiram, I guess," said Ben. "He said the license plates were New York plates. He told me someone had shot Bowser with an arrow. Is that right?"

"Someone did," said Rila.

"I tell you we got to do something with these kids," said Ben. "They're up to something all the time. They

52

have no respect for nothing. They are just running wild."

"Maybe it wasn't a kid," I said.

"Who else would it be? It's just the kind of thing they'd do. They're a bunch of monsters, I tell you. Some of them let the air out of my tires the other night. Came out of the picture show and I had four flats."

"Now why would they do that?" asked Rila.

"I don't know. They just hate everyone, I guess. When you and I were kids, Asa, we never did stuff like that. We used to go fishing, remember, and hunting in the fall. And there was the time you had all of us digging in that sinkhole."

"I am still digging in it," I said.

"I know you are. Finding anything?"

"Not much," I said.

"I got to be getting on," said Ben. "I have some people coming in to see me. It was good to meet you, Miss Elliot. I hope you have a pleasant visit."

We watched after him as he went bounding down the sidewalk.

"An old pal of yours?" asked Rila. "One of the gang?"

"One of the gang," I said.

We went across the street and into the supermarket. I got a cart and started wheeling it down the aisle.

"We'll need potatoes and some butter," I said, "and soap, and I guess a lot of other things."

"Don't you make out a list?"

"I'm a disorganized housekeeper," I said. "I try to keep it in my head and I always miss an item or two."

"You know a lot of people in this town?"

"Some. Some from when I was a boy, folks who stayed on and never left. Other new ones I have met since I came back."

Slowly we loaded the cart. I forgot some items and Rila, running through a hypothetical shopping list, reminded me of others I would have forgotten. Finally, I wheeled the cart up to the checkout counter. Herb Livingston was ahead of us, putting down an armload of purchases.

"Asa," he said, the way he always talks, as if he is breathless with delight at seeing you. "I was going to phone you for a news item. I heard you had company."

"Rila," I said, "meet Herb Livingston. He is another of the old gang, and now he owns the weekly paper."

Herb beamed. "I am glad that you came to see us," he told Rila. "I hear you're from New York. New York City, I mean. We don't get many people from New York." He pulled a notebook from his jacket pocket and a short pencil from his shirt pocket. "What is your last name, if I may ask?"

"Elliot," said Rila. "Two *l*'s and one *t*."

"And you're visiting Asa. I mean that's why you're here."

"We are friends of long standing," said Rila shortly. "We worked together on an archaeological dig in Turkey back in the late fifties."

Herb made hentracks in his notebook. "And what are you doing now?"

"I'm in the import-export business."

"I see," said Herb, scribbling furiously. "And you're staying out on the farm with Asa."

"That's right," said Rila. "I came to be with Asa. I am staying with him."

When we got back to the car, Rila said to me, "I'm not sure I like your friends."

"Don't pay any attention to Herb," I said. "As a newspaperman, he is a little short on tact."

"What I can't understand is why he should be interested in me. My being here simply isn't news."

"To the Willow Bend *Record*, it is. Nothing ever happens here. Herb has to fill the paper with comings and goings. Mrs. Page holds a card party with three tables and it's a social event. Herb writes it up in detail. Tells who was there and who won the prizes."

"Asa, you don't mind? Maybe I should leave."

"Hell, no," I said. "Why should I mind? Flying in the face of convention? You can't do anything that doesn't fly in the face of convention in a place like this. And with this time-travel business, with Hiram going after Catface, it would be plain desertion if you left. You've got to see this thing through with me. I need you."

She settled into the seat as I got behind the wheel. "I hoped you would say that," she said. "I don't know about this time-travel business, but I do want to stay. Half of the time I believe travel in time is possible and the rest of the time I tell myself, Rila, stop being a fool. But I'm curious about Hiram. Nothing more than Hiram? He must have another name."

"His name," I said, "is Hiram Biglow, but most people have forgotten the Biglow part of it. He's just Hiram, that's all. He was born in Willow Bend, and at one time he had an older brother, but the brother ran away from home and, so far as I know, has not been heard of since. The family was an old family, reaching back into the time the town was founded. His father's name was Horace, an only son of a son of one of the founders of Willow Bend. The family lived in the old ancestral home, one of those Victorian piles set back from the street, with an iron fence enclosing a lawn filled with trees. I remember that I used to hang on the fence when I was a kid and wonder what it would be like to live in a place like that. My family was relatively poor at the time, and we lived in just an ordinary house, and the Biglow place seemed like a mansion to me."

"But you told me Hiram lives in a shack down by the river."

"He does and I am getting to that. Hiram's father was the town banker, in partnership with Ben Page's father . . . "

"I don't like Ben Page any better than I like that Herb person."

"You and almost everyone," I said. "He's not the sort of man who inspires a lot of confidence or admiration, although in recent years, he may have changed. There are people now who swear by him. Well, anyhow, when Hiram was ten years old or so, his father drowned in a duck-hunting accident. By this time, the older brother, who was seven or eight years older than Hiram, had lit out for parts unknown, so there was only Hiram and his mother left. The old lady lived a secluded life after that. She never left the house and she discouraged friends from calling. Hiram had always been a strange kid, backward in school and not getting along with the other kids, but no one thought too much about it. As the years went past, I suppose, his mother must have known that he wasn't exactly normal, and so she hid away with him. Pride is a dreadful thing anywhere, and in a small town, it's deadly. The two of them just sort of withdrew from life, and while people knew, of course, that they were there, they were fairly well forgotten. Which, I suppose, is what Mrs. Biglow had hoped would happen. By this time, I was long gone, of course, so what I tell you from here on is what I've heard from people after I came back.

"It turns out, finally, when the estate was settled, that Hiram's father didn't have too much interest in the bank. A few shares and his job, that was all. No one could prove it, of course, but people I talked with later were convinced that Ben's father had slickered Hiram's father out of the bank. Apparently, there was a little money left, but not much, and the old lady and Hiram managed somehow until she died. By this time, Hiram must have been twenty-five or so. When it came time to settle his mother's estate, it was found that the Biglow house was mortgaged to the bank. The bank, pleading it had carried the family as long as it could, foreclosed. By this time, Ben had taken over the bank, his father retiring, and he donated some money and got a few others in town to donate a bit more and they built this shack down by the river and gave it to Hiram and he's lived there ever since."

"The town adopting him," said Rila. "Taking care of their own. Today he'd be on relief. Or in some state institution."

"I guess you could say that," I said. "The town looks after him, sure, but not too kindly. Some people treat him okay, of course, but he has become a sort of municipal scapegoat and a lot of people laugh at him and make fun of him. They don't think that Hiram knows; so they think it's safe to make fun of him. But Hiram knows. He knows his friends and he knows who laughs at him. He may be considerably strange, of course, but he's not as stupid as a lot of people think."

"I hope he's getting some sleep," said Rila. "This is his first night of sitting up for Catface."

"He may have to spend several nights. Catface is not all that regular in his habits."

"I sit and listen to us talking like this," said Rila. "I know we are talking like this, but then I ask myself if we are really doing it. It's not sane, Asa. This whole thing. Most people wouldn't be thinking what we are thinking, saying what we are saying."

"I know what you mean," I told her, "but I have more evidence than you. I went into the Pleistocene and almost got run over by a mastodon. Bowser did bring home those bones."

"And yet we let ourselves think only so far," she said. "We accept the dinosaur bones and the Folsom point and the mastodon, but we don't allow ourselves to go beyond that. We keep ourselves from saying out loud that Catface is an alien creature that can engineer time tunnels and that he somehow escaped when an alien spaceship crashed here thousands of years ago."

"Maybe we'll come to it," I said. "We'll have to wait and see what Hiram manages."

ELEVEN

Three nights later, a loud rapping on the bedroom door brought me upright in bed, stupid with sleep, wondering what the hell was going on. Beside me, Rila stirred protestingly.

"What's going on?" I yelled. "Who's there?"

Although, if I had stopped to think of it, I'd have known who was there.

"It's me, Hiram."

"It's Hiram," I said to Rila.

The knocking kept right on. "Cut out that goddamn knocking," I yelled at Hiram. "I'm awake. I'll see you in the kitchen."

Groping around blindly, I found my slippers, scuffed into them, and tried to find a robe, but couldn't locate one. I stumbled out into the kitchen in pajama pants and slippers.

"What is it, Hiram? I hope it's important."

"It's Catface, Mr. Steele. I been talking with him. He wants to talk with you."

"I can't talk with him," I said. "There is no way I can. You're the only one who can."

"He says I don't make any sense," said Hiram. "He is glad we want to talk with him, but he says he doesn't know what I want to talk about."

"You mean he's out there now?"

"Yes, Mr. Steele. He said that he would wait while I came to get you. He says he hopes you can make some sense."

"Do you think he could wait until I got on some clothes?"

"I think so, Mr. Steele. He said that he would wait."

"You stay right here," I said. "Don't leave the house until we can go with you."

Back in the bedroom, I fumbled for my clothes and found them. Rila was sitting on the edge of the bed.

"It's Catface," I said. "He wants to talk with us."

"It'll take me just a minute," she said.

Hiram was waiting at the kitchen table when we came out.

"Where's Bowser?" Rila asked.

"Out there with Catface," Hiram told her. "Them two are good friends. I figure maybe they've been good friends all the time without us knowing it."

"Tell me," I said. "How did it happen? Was it hard to talk with Catface?"

"About the same as Bowser," Hiram said. "Easier than that robin. That robin sometimes is hard to talk with. Sometimes, he doesn't want to talk. Catface wants to talk."

"All right, then," said Rila. "Let us go and talk with him."

"How are we going to do that?" I asked.

"It's easy," Hiram said. "You tell me exactly what to say and I will say it to him. Then I'll tell you what he says. Maybe I won't understand everything he says."

"We'll do the best we can," said Rila.

"He's in that apple tree right around the corner. Bowser's watching him."

I opened the back door and waited for the others to go out.

Once around the corner, there was no trouble spotting Catface, staring out at us from the middle of the apple tree. In the light of the Moon, his face was clear. You could even see the whiskers. Bowser, sitting lopsided to favor his wounded ham, stared up into the tree at Catface.

"Tell him we are here," I said to Hiram, "and are ready to begin."

"He says he is, too," said Hiram.

"Now, wait a minute. You didn't have time to tell him what I said."

"I don't need to," Hiram said. "He knows what you

say, but he can't answer back because you can't hear what he says."

"All right, then," I said. "That makes it simpler." I said to Catface, "Hiram says that you are willing to talk with us about time travel."

"He's anxious to talk about time travel," Hiram said. "He said a whole lot more I don't understand."

"Look," I said to Catface, "let us keep this simple. One thought at a time. As simple as you can."

"He says all right," said Hiram. "He says he has missed putting time travel to work. He says he is a time engineer. Could that be right?"

"I suppose it could be."

"He says he is tired of making time roads for no one but Bowser."

"He made one for me."

"That is right, he says. But you couldn't see the road; you stumbled into it."

"Can he make roads to any place or time on this planet?"

"He says he can."

"To ancient Greece? To Troy?"

"If you tell him where these places are, he can. He says it is easy. On this world, anywhere."

"But how can we tell him?"

"He says to mark a map. He talks about lines on a map. Mr. Steele, what kind of lines are there on a map?"

"Longitude and latitude, perhaps."

"He says that is right."

"He knows how we measure time? He knows about years? He can understand a million years, a hundred years?"

"He says he does."

"There is one thing I want to ask him," Rila said. "He is an alien, someone from some other world?"

"Yes, from very far away."

"How long ago?"

"Almost fifty thousand years."

"And he has lived that long?"

"He says he does not die."

"He can make roads into time. He can travel those roads himself?"

"He says yes."

"But apparently he doesn't travel them. He's here right now. He came here fifty thousand years ago, but apparently he lived through a normal time line. He just settled in and lived in ordinary time. Otherwise, he might not be here."

"Rescue, he says."

"What does he mean, rescue?"

"If he doesn't stay in a single place and ordinary time, people who come to find him won't know where he is."

"He still hopes for rescue?"

"Now he has little hope. He must do the best he can. He makes a new life with us. That's why he's so happy."

"But he must know where his home world is. If he is able to make roads in space and time, he should be able to go home."

"He says not. He does not know where his home is from here. He does not know how to get from here to there. If someone told him, he could. But on trip here, he did not know. Someone else knew. Now that someone else is dead. He died when the ship fell."

"But Catface did not die because he is immortal?"

"He says an immortal can be killed in accident, but that is the only way. He says he was lucky. He got away before the ship hit ground."

"How did he get away?"

"Life boat, he says."

"Life boat," I said. "A sphere? A round hollow ball that came apart so he could get out?"

"He says that is right. He asks how did you know?"

"I found the life boat," I said. "It's out in the barn."

"But now he will make time roads for us?" asked Rila. "Anywhere on Earth? Any time on Earth? And keep them open as long as we may need them?"

"Catface says that is right. He can make them where you say and keep them open. Once you no longer need them, he will close them once again."

"How many? More than one?"

"Many as you need."

"When could he start doing this?"

"Right now. Say where you want to go, when you want to go."

"Tell him," Rila said, "that we aren't ready yet. It will take some time for us to get ready and we'll need to talk to him again. Perhaps several times."

"Miss, he say anytime you want. He'll hang around and wait to talk with you."

TWELVE

We sat at breakfast, with Hiram finishing his second helping of ham and eggs. Bowser dozed on his blanket in the corner.

"The one thing in question," said Rila, "is whether we can trust Catface."

"You can trust him, ma'am," said Hiram. "I had a long talk with him before I came in to get you. He's nice folks. Just like you and Mr. Steele."

"Well, that is fine," said Rila, "but we must bear in mind that he is an alien. And a most peculiar one."

"Maybe not," I said. "We don't know what aliens would be like. Compared with other aliens, he may not be peculiar."

"Oh, you know what I mean. All head, no body. Or at least he hides his body. All you can see is a face sticking out of a tree or bush."

"Ezra saw a body. That night Ranger had Catface up a tree and Ezra drew a bead on him, but didn't shoot."

"It was dark," said Rila. "Ezra couldn't see too much. Just the face when it looked at him. What I mean about not trusting him is that he may have a different ethical code, very likely has, a different way of looking at things. What might seem wrong to us might not be wrong at all to him."

"He's been around ever since people settled here. A hundred years and more. He probably had some contact with the Indians long before then. He's been watching all the time. He knows what humans are like. He's astute; he'd soak up a lot of information. He knows what to expect of humans, probably something of what they would expect of him."

"Asa, are you ready to trust him, just flat out?"

"No, I guess I do have some reservations."

Hiram got up from the table and put on his cap. "Me and Bowser are going for a walk," he said.

Bowser got up stiffly.

"Don't you want to sleep?" I asked. "You've been up all night."

"Later on, Mr. Steele."

"Remember, not a word of this to anyone."

"I'll remember," said Hiram. "I promised. I gave my word on it."

For a time after he left, we sat drinking second cups of coffee. Finally Rila said, "If it all stands up, if it really works all right, we have got it made."

"You mean we can go into time."

"Not us. Other people. People who will pay us for being sent in time. A time-traveling service. We'll sell trips in time."

"It could be dangerous."

"Sure, it could be dangerous. We'll draw up contracts absolving us of risks. The travelers will be the one who take the chances, not us."

"We'd need a lawyer."

"I know just the man. In Washington. He could help us with the government."

"You think the government might want to step in?"

"You can be sure they would. Once we get going, everyone will want to get into the act. Remember, you were afraid of the university horning in when you dug up all that stuff."

"Yes, I told you that."

"We can't afford to let anyone horn in on this. This is ours."

"I suppose we could interest some universities or museums," I said. "There are a lot of events in the past they would want to have a look at. Be willing to pay money to look at. But there would be problems. There'd have to be some rules and regulations. You couldn't go back to the siege of Troy lugging cameras. You'd have to speak the language of the day. You'd have to blend in. Wear the right kinds of clothes. Know the customs. If you intruded in any way, you could be in trouble; there would even be the chance that you would influence the very factors you set out to study. You might even change history."

"You have a point there," said Rila. "We'll have to set up a body of time-traveling ethics. Where the travelers come in contact with humans, that is. Beyond the human era, it wouldn't matter too much what you did."

"Like going back to hunt big game?"

"Asa, that's where the money is. Universities couldn't pay enough to make it worth our while. They are always strapped for funds. But big game hunters are a different matter. It used to be that a hunter could go on safari in Africa and bag a lot of different heads. Or in Asia. But that is all gone now. If you go, it's on a very limited license. They run these so-called camera safaris, but for the dyed-in-the-wool hunter, they can't be much fun. Imagine what a hunter would be willing to pay for a go at a mastodon or sabertooth."

"Or a dinosaur," I said.

"That's what I'm trying to tell you," she said. "We have to pick our shots. Not necessarily hunting exclusively. There could be a lot of other things. We could go back or send someone back to pick up some Attic pottery. You can't imagine what stuff like that would sell for. A few Athenian owls for the coin collectors. Or, more recently, some of the early stamps. We could go to South Africa and pick diamonds off the ground. That's how the early diamonds were found. Just picked up off the ground."

"But not too many of them. Only a few here and there. The Star of Africa, sure. But that was sheer luck. You could go around for years looking at the ground . . ."

"Maybe that was the way it was, Asa, because we, a few years from now, got there first. They only found what we missed."

I laughed at her. "You're money-hungry, Rila. All you talk of is money. How to merchandise time travel, how to sell it to the highest bidder. It seems to me it should be used for research. There are so many historical problems. There are geological periods about which we know so little."

"Later on," she said. "We can do all of that later on. But we have to make a financial success of it before we can afford to do the things you are talking about. You say I'm money-hungry. Maybe I am. It's been my life. I've spent my life building up a business, seeing that it paid. And this thing, before we can even get it started, will cost us money. The lawyer I have in mind doesn't come cheap. We'll have to build a fence around the property and hire guards to keep out the hordes of visitors once the news is broken. We'll have to put up an administration building and staff it. We may need public relations people."

"Rila, where are we going to get the money?"

"I can get it."

"We had that out the other day. Remember?"

"But this is different. Then I was offering to help you stay on here. This is a business venture. The two of us together. You own the land, you laid the foundation. All I do is get some money for us to begin the operation."

She stared across the table at me. "Or don't you want it that way? I'm horning in. Maybe you don't want that. If that's the case, say so. It's your land, your Catface, your Hiram. I'm just a pushy bitch."

"Maybe you're a pushy bitch," I said, "but I want you in with me. It's not something we can throw away, and I'd mess it up without you. It just shook me up, you talking about nothing but how we could merchandise it. I see your point, but to justify our position, some of the time-travel schedule should be allocated to research."

"It's strange how easily we accept the premise," she said. "Time travel is something that one automatically rejects as impossible. And yet, we sit here planning for it, basing our belief on Catface and Hiram."

"We have more than that," I said. "I did travel into time. No question about it. It couldn't be delusion. I was there for an hour or so—well, actually, I don't know how long I was in the Pleistocene. Long enough to walk from here down to the river and back. And there are Bowser's Folsom point and the fresh dinosaur bones. Intellectually, I'm still fairly sure it's impossible, but actually I know it can be done."

"Our one weak link," she said, "is Hiram. If he is not telling us the truth, if he's playing games with us . . ."

"I think I can vouch for him. I've been decent to him while many others haven't, and he worships Bowser. Almost never a day went past, even before all this, when he didn't show up here. I think, as well, that he hasn't the intellect to lie."

"But if he talks. Before we're ready to let anyone know."

"He won't intentionally. Someone may ask him questions and worm some of it out of him, or he may get to talking and a slip of the tongue will give it away. He's not all that bright."

"I suppose it is a chance we have to take. In a little while, it won't matter what he says."

She rose from the table and began picking up the dishes. "I'll have to make a few phone calls," she said. "To some people in New York and the attorney in Washington. In a day or two, I'll have to travel east for a few days. I'd like you to come along with me."

I shook my head. "I'll leave it to you. I'll stay here and hold the fort. Someone should be here."

THIRTEEN

I was washing the supper dishes when Ben Page came knocking at the kitchen door.

"I see you're alone again," said Ben.

"Rila went east for a few days. She'll be back."

"You say the two of you were on a dig together, years ago."

"That's right. Turkey. A small ruin that dated back to the Bronze Age. It wasn't much of a dig. Nothing new, nothing exciting. The sponsors were disappointed."

"I suppose you can do a lot of digging sometimes and come up with nothing."

"That is true," I said. I put away the last of the dishes, wiped my hands and sat down at the kitchen table, across from Ben. In his corner, Bowser whimpered eagerly, his feet twitching as he chased dream rabbits.

"This digging you been doing," said Ben. "Turning up much?"

"Not yet. Nothing that amounts to much."

"But it isn't just a sinkhole."

"No, not a sinkhole. I don't know what it is. Maybe a meteorite. Found some stray chunks of metal."

"Asa," said Ben accusingly, "you're not leveling with me. There is something going on."

"What makes you say that, Ben?"

"Hiram. He's acting mysterious. As if you were on to something and he was in on it. Says he can't talk about it; that he promised not to. He makes a joke about it. Says to ask Bowser."

"Hiram thinks he can talk with Bowser."

"I know. He talks with everything."

68

"Hiram's all right," I said. "But you can't depend on him. He talks a lot of nonsense."

"I don't think so, not this time. The whole thing is a little strange. You coming back and buying the farm and digging in the sinkhole. Then Rila shows up and she's an archaeologist, just like you."

"If there was anything to tell you, Ben, I would. There's nothing now, maybe never will be."

"Look," said Ben, "as mayor of this town, I have a right to ask. If you are up to something that might affect the town, I should know ahead of time. So we can get ready for it."

"Ben, I don't know what you are getting at."

"Well, for example, I own ten acres at the edge of town. Foreclosed on it some years ago, been paying taxes on it ever since. Good place for a motel. There ain't but this one flytrap of a motel here. No self-respecting person would put up in it. Money in a motel, if it's a good one and there are people who would want to use it. If something should happen that would bring a lot of people here, a motel would be a good business venture."

"What did Hiram say that made you think there might be people coming here?"

"Well, not a great deal. He acts so damn mysterious and important. He enjoys it so much I figure it must be something big. He did let one thing sort of slip without knowing it. Asa, tell me, could there be a crashed spaceship at the bottom of the sinkhole?"

"I suppose there could be," I said. "That's one thought I've had in mind. But nothing so far to support it. If there is, it would have to be an alien spaceship. One operated by intelligent people from way out in space, from another star. If you found fragments of such a ship and could show credible evidence, it would be an important find. It would be the first real evidence that there was another thinking race in the universe and that, at some time, they had visited the Earth."

Ben whistled softly. "That would bring a lot of people here, wouldn't it? People to study it. A lot of curiosity seekers. And they'd come year after year. It could be a tourist attraction that would last for years."

"I would imagine so," I said.

"It's slow going for you," said Ben. "Out there digging by yourself. How about me getting some of the boys together and coming out to help you."

"I appreciate the thought, but it wouldn't work. This kind of digging takes training. You've got to know what to look for. You have to take it easy and plot exactly where you found each item. You can't just rush in there and start throwing dirt. Get a gang in with picks and shovels and they'd destroy a lot of evidence. Little things that wouldn't mean a thing to them, but would to a trained digger."

Ben nodded gravely. "Yes, I can see how it would be. It was just a thought."

"I thank you for it," I said. "And, Ben, I'd appreciate it if you said nothing of it. It would be embarrassing to me if the word got out I was digging for a spaceship. The town would think I was crazy, and the word would filter out into academic circles and there'd be a lot of university types shooting off their faces, and some of them would be coming out to look the situation over, and most of them, I suspect, would sneer at us."

"Sure," said Ben. "Not a word from me. Not a single word from me. But do you think there could be . . ."

"I'm not sure at all. Just a hunch. Based on some evidence that may be no evidence at all. I may be doing no more than making a fool of myself. How about a beer?"

After Ben had left, I sat at the table for a long time, wondering if what I'd told him had been wise. It could backfire, I knew, but probably not with Ben. He was a grasping bastard and would probably keep his mouth shut because he'd want to be the first to know, so that he could rush in, ahead of all the others, and get his motel built—and probably other things that he had not mentioned.

I'd had to tell him something, and I'd had to throw him slightly off the track. Just a plain denial would not have satisfied him. Hiram's slip of the tongue and the way that he was acting had made Ben suspicious. And I hadn't really lied to him, I told myself. There was a spaceship out there at the bottom of the sink-hole.

I'd probably shut him up, for a time at least. And that was important, for village gossip and speculation had to be kept to a minimum at the moment. Once we started building the fence, of course, there'd be no stopping it. And Rila was right; we would need the fence.

I went to the refrigerator and got another beer.

Christ, I thought, sitting there drinking it, the entire thing was mad. Much as I might tell myself, in moments of clarity and right thinking, it was not possible for men to travel into time, I knew it was. Imprinted on my mind as nothing else in my entire life, was the memory of that big bull mastodon, with his rapid, almost gliding tread, and his trunk swinging like a pendulum between his tusks as he hurried to reach the herd. And I could not forget the terror I had felt when I realized where I was, the lostness and displacement.

Once again, I ran through the preliminary plans Rila and I had made, sitting at this very table. Thinking of the plans, I felt not only a vague unreality, but some apprehension as well. There could be so much that we had not been able to foresee, blind spots prone to wrecking the best-laid plans. What, I wondered, had we overlooked? What unsuspected circumstances would arise to plague us in the days to come?

I was bothered by how we planned to use time travel. If I had ever thought of it at all, I would not have thought of it as Rila did. I found it difficult to brush aside the conviction that time travel should be used in the furtherance of science and of understanding; that it was not something to be offered in the marketplace.

But Rila was undoubtedly right in saying that if someone else had found the secret and possessed the technique, they, for their part, would use it to their own best advantage. In her opinion, it was silly to throw away an opportunity to place travel into time on a sound economic basis; for only with such a basis could it be used consistently for research.

In his corner, the dreaming Bowser yipped wildly as he closed in on the rabbit. I finished my beer, threw the bottle in the trash can and went off to bed.

Rila was coming home tomorrow and I'd have to get up early to drive to Minneapolis and meet her at the airport.

FOURTEEN

When I first caught sight of Rila as she came up the ramp, she bore a grim, determined look, but at the sight of me, she smiled and hurried forward. I caught her in my arms and said, "It's good to have you back. The last three days have been lonely ones."

She tilted up her head for a kiss, then pressed her face against my shoulder. "It's good to see you, Asa," she whispered. "It's nice to be home again. What an awful time!"

"What's the matter, Rila?"

She pushed herself away and looked up at me. "I'm pissed off," she said. "I'm sore. I'm angry. No one would believe me."

"Who wouldn't believe you?"

"Courtney McCallahan, for one. He's the lawyer I was telling you about. We've been friends from way back. It never occurred to me that he'd disbelieve me. But he put his arms down on his desk and put his face down on them and laughed so hard he shook. When he looked up again, he had to take off his glasses so he could wipe his eyes, and he was so beat out with laughter that he could hardly talk. He gulped and strangled and said, 'Rila, I've known you for a long time, and I didn't know you had it in you. I never thought you could do a thing like this.' Like what, I asked him, and he said a joke, a practical joke, but that he forgave me because it had made his day. So I peeled off on him and said it was no joke and that we wanted him to represent us, to look out for our interests, to protect ourselves. We do need someone to look out for our interests, don't we, I asked him, and he said that if what I had told him was true, we sure did need someone. But he refused

73

to believe me. I don't think he thought it was a joke any longer; I don't know what he thought. But he still didn't believe me, no matter what I said. He took me out for dinner and he bought champagne for me, but I wouldn't forgive him for the way he acted."

"But will he represent us?"

"You can bet your life he will. He said that if I could show him proof, he wouldn't miss it for the world. Said he'd drop everything, turn all his other work over to his associates, and give us full time. He said that if he was any judge, we would need full time. But he was still chuckling about it when he took me to my hotel and said good night."

"But, Rila, proof . . . "

"Wait a minute now. That's not all of it. I went up to New York and I talked with Safari, Inc., and they were interested, of course, and they didn't really laugh at me, but they were skeptical. They plain outright thought I was lying to them—playing some sort of a con game, although it bothered them they couldn't figure out the con. Their head man is a stiff, formal old Britisher who is most correct, and he said to me, 'Miss Elliot, I don't know what this is all about, but if it should be that it is more than sheer imagination, I can assure you we'd be most interested.' And he said to me, 'If we'd not been aware of you before, I'd not listen for a moment.' "

"Aware of you before?"

"Well, not him, not this old Britisher. But his outfit. A few years back, I bought a fair amount of stuff they'd been accumulating for years and wondering what to do with. Ivory and native-carved statuary and ostrich feathers and a lot of junk like that. I took all they had and they took me for a sucker. But I was years ahead of them in knowing what the public wanted and would pay money for, and we turned a handsome profit on it. Somehow the safari outfit got wind of how well we'd done and my stock went up with them. They came around later and asked if I would be interested if they could round up some more of the junk. You see, they aren't in the retail business, so they had to find someone . . . "

"I suppose," I said, "they want proof just like your old friend Courtney."

"That's right," she said. "And the funny thing about it is that all they're interested in are dinosaurs. They fairly drooled when I asked them if they could get clients to go hunting dinosaurs. Not mastodon, not mammoth, not sabertooth cats, not cave bears, nor even titanotheres, but dinosaurs. Big ones and vicious ones. I asked them what kind of gun you'd have to use to shoot a big dinosaur and they said they didn't know, but probably the biggest that ever had been made. I asked if they had some of those guns around and they said they did—a couple of them that had never been used. They weren't even sure they were being manufactured any longer. Elephant guns, but now, with higher muzzle velocity, an elephant can be done in by a much smaller caliber. Not that there are many elephants being shot these days. So I said, by God, that I wanted to buy those two guns, and after some backing and filling, they agreed to sell them to me. By this time, I am sure, they thought I was out of my mind. They charged me a thousand apiece and swore they were losing money, throwing in a few dozen rounds of ammunition to sweeten up the bargain. I suppose they were losing money, but they were unloading items that no one else would buy. Those rifles are monsters. Must weigh twenty pounds or so. And the cartridges are banana-sized."

"Look," I said, "if you think I'm going out and knocking over a brace of carnosaurs just to offer proof, you'd better think again. I'm hell on wheels with a twenty-two, but this is something different. It takes a big man to shoot one of those old-time elephant guns."

"You're big enough," she said. "Maybe you wouldn't even have to shoot. Protection, that is all. Just in case some carnosaur should charge while I'm getting the proof on film. I bought a movie camera—color film, with sound, telescopic lens, everything one would ever need."

"But why two guns? One is all a man can carry. And you'll be packing the camera."

"I got two guns," she said, "because I'm not about to have you go out there alone. We have no idea what it will be like, but to me it sounds a little chancy. We'd be better off with two guns. I figured maybe we could persuade one of your old pals . . . "

"Rila, we've got to keep this under cover for a while. It's already beginning to leak out. Ben Page got hold of Hiram and got suspicious when Hiram began acting important . . . "

"We've got to keep it quiet," she said, "but we've got to come back alive, or all the proof in the world won't help us any."

I didn't like it, but I could see the logic of what she was saying.

"Maybe Ben would come along with us," I said. "He'd be a good man to have along. He fancies himself a mighty hunter, and he is fairly good. Each fall he goes up north for deer season, and he's hunted in Canada and Alaska. Moose, bighorns, grizzly—stuff like that. Years ago he bagged a Kodiak. And a caribou. He still talks about the caribou. For years, he wanted to go to Africa, but he never made it, and now the hunting's gone. . . . "

"Would he go with us and keep quiet about what he sees for a while?"

"I think so. I had to tell him part of it—about the possibility of a spaceship in the sinkhole—and I swore him to secrecy. He was willing to go along on the secrecy because he's got some irons of his own in the fire."

"We have to have a second man," she said. "I have no idea what it might be like in dinosaur country, but . . . "

"Neither do I," I said. "It could be pretty awful. It could be fairly safe. There'd be a lot of herbivores, all fairly peaceful, I'd imagine. But there'd be some meat-eaters. I have no idea how thick they might be, nor how pugnacious."

"I'd like to get some footage of at least a couple of the more ferocious ones. That would set up the safari outfit. I have no idea what we can squeeze out of them, but I'd guess an awful lot. After all, how much would a true, red-blooded, dyed-in-the-wool sportsman be willing to pay to be the first man to shoot a ravening, bloodthirsty dinosaur?"

We reached the escalator going down to the baggage area.

"Give me your check and I'll pick up the stuff," I said.

She opened her purse and took out her ticket envelope. "We'd better arrange for some help," she said, handing it to me. "There's more than we can carry."

"The two guns," I said.

"And the movie stuff."

"I'll get some help," I said.

"The whole trouble," she explained, "was that I couldn't tell them about some machine—a time-travel machine. If I could have told them we'd developed a machine, they'd have been more able to believe me. We place so much trust in machines; they are magic to us. If I could have outlined some ridiculous theory and spouted some equations at them, they would have been impressed. But I couldn't do that. To tell them about Catface would have only made matters worse. I simply told them that we had developed a technique for traveling in time, hoping that when I mentioned technique they would presuppose a machine. But it didn't seem to have the right effect. They asked me about a machine anyhow, and it floored them when I had to tell them there was no machine."

"With no machine," I said, "that's asking them to accept a lot on faith."

"Asa, when we go back to get our film, where shall we go?"

"I've been thinking about that," I said, "and I can't be certain. The late Jurassic, maybe, or the early Cretaceous. In either of those periods, you'd be apt to find a greater diversity of forms, though we can't be sure. The fossil record would seem to indicate those two times, but the fossil record is only what we've found. We've probably missed a lot. We make it sound as if we know much more than we do. Actually, we've found only bits and pieces; we have no clear picture. But if we went to the early Cretaceous, we'd probably miss the one dinosaur our white hunters are most interested in, old *Tyrannosaurus rex. . . .*"

"They mentioned him," said Rila.

"Rex was a latecomer," I said, "or we think he was. There may have been bigger and more vicious ones than him that never had the luck to have their fossils found. In any case, it would be nothing short of insanity to go up against him. Eighteen feet tall, a total length of fifty feet, weighing eight tons or more and filled with a senseless hunting instinct. We don't know how many of him there may be. Perhaps not many. You might have to hunt to find him. Large as he was, he probably required a territory measuring many square miles to make no more than a bare living."

"We can figure it out later," Rila said.

FIFTEEN

Late that afternoon, I phoned Ben.

"You want to get started on that motel?" I asked him.

"You've got it, then," said Ben. "It's all set. You've found what you were after."

"We're fairly close," I said. "We are on the way. Rila and I would like to talk with you. Could you drop by? It would be more private that way."

"It so happens that I've just finished for the day. I'll be right over."

I hung up and said to Rila, "I don't like this business. Ben probably will be all right; after all, he wants to get an early jump on this motel business, and he probably has some other deals in mind as well. But I have a queasy feeling. It's too early to take someone into our confidence."

"You can't keep the thing under wraps much longer," she said. "As soon as you start installing the fence, people will know something is going on. You don't put a ten-foot fence around forty acres just for the fun of it. And we need Ben, or someone else, to carry that second gun. We've already decided it's insanity to go back to face dinosaurs with only one gun. You said Ben is the man you want."

"He's the best I know. He's a hunter. He knows how to handle guns. He's big and strong and tough and he wouldn't panic in a tight situation. But this whole thing could backfire, so we'll keep our fingers crossed."

I opened up a cupboard door and took down a bottle, setting it on the kitchen table. I found three glasses; I made sure that there was ice.

"You're going to entertain him out here at the kitchen table?" Rila asked.

"Hell, he wouldn't know how to act if we sat down in the living room. It would be too formal; it would spook him. Here he'll be comfortable."

"If that's the case," she said, "I'm all for it. I like it myself. A tavern atmosphere."

Feet thumped outside on the walk, coming up to the kitchen door.

"It didn't take him long," said Rila.

"Ben's anxious," I said. "He's smelling money."

I opened the door and Ben came in. He had the sort of look a dog has on its face when it smells a rabbit.

"You have it then?" he asked.

"Ben," I said, "sit down. We have business to discuss."

Drinks poured, we sat around the table.

"Asa, what you got in mind?" asked Ben.

"First of all," I said, "I have a confession to make. I lied to you the other day. Or halfway lied. I told you only part of the truth and not the important part."

"You mean there isn't any spaceship?"

"Oh, there's a spaceship, all right."

"Then what is this all about—this half-truth business?"

"What it means is that the spaceship is only part of it, a small part of it. The important thing is that we have found how to travel into time. Into the past and maybe even into the future. We never asked about the future. We were so excited about it, that we never thought to ask."

"Ask who?" Ben had a slack-jawed look, as if someone had clobbered him with something heavy.

"Perhaps we'd better start at the beginning," said Rila, "and tell him all of it, the way it happened. These questions and answers aren't getting anywhere."

Ben emptied his glass in a gulp and reached for the bottle.

"Yeah," he said. "You go ahead and tell me."

He was believing none of it.

I said to Rila, "You tell him. I can't afford to take

the time. I've fallen a long ways behind in my drinking."

She told the story precisely and economically, without the use of an extra word, from the time I had bought the farm up to this very moment, including her interviews in Washington and New York.

During all the time that she was talking, Ben didn't say a word. He just sat there, glassy-eyed. Even for a time after she had finished, he still sat in silence. Then, finally, he stirred. "There's one thing about it," he said, "that beats me. You say Hiram can talk with this Catface thing. Does that mean he can really talk with Bowser?"

"We don't know," said Rila.

He shook his head. "What you're saying is mighty hard to swallow. There ain't no way to go back into the past."

"That's what everyone says," said Rila. "We'll have to prove it. We'll have to go back into the past, into the kind of past that no one's ever seen, and bring back movies of it. There's one thing we didn't tell you, Ben. Asa and I are going back to the time of the dinosaurs, and we want you to go with us."

"Me? You want me to go back with you? Back to the dinosaurs?"

I got up from the table and went into the living room where we'd stashed the stuff that Rila had brought on the plane. I came back with one of the two guns and laid it on the table in front of Ben.

"You know what that is?" I asked him.

He picked it up, hoisting it, weighing it. He swung around in his chair, pointed the rifle at a kitchen window and broke the breech. He squinted through the barrels.

"An elephant gun," he said. "I've heard of them, but I've never seen one. Double-barreled. Would you take a look at that bore! With a thing like that, you could knock an elephant off its feet."

He looked at me inquiringly. "Would it do the same to a dinosaur? One of the big ones?"

"No one knows," I said. "A well-placed shot should stop one. Knocking it over, I don't know. We have two of those rifles. When Rila and I go into dinosaur country, I'll carry one of them. She'll be loaded down with camera equipment. We are hoping you will carry the other gun. Back there, we won't know what to expect, but, in any case, two guns will be better than one."

Ben drew in his breath. "Dinosaurs!" he said. "You're offering me a chance to go along? With a gun like this?"

"You have it turned around," said Rila. "We aren't offering you a chance to go. We're begging you to go."

"You don't have to beg," said Ben. "You'd have to lay me out to stop me. Africa—I always wanted to go to Africa. This will be better than Africa."

"It could be dangerous. Maybe not. As Asa says, there's no way to know."

"But you're going?"

Rila said smugly, "I'll have to run the camera."

"Movies, yet," he yelled. "My God, the film boys would kill one another to get hold of that footage. A million bucks. Five million bucks. You could name your price."

"We'll take that up later on," said Rila. "Maybe the movie people would like to do their own shooting. A professional job of film making."

"And you'd sell them the rights," said Ben. "At a handsome figure."

"We'll not make it cheap," said Rila.

"And me," said Ben, "getting all excited about a little two-by-four motel. Although, it will take a chunk of capital to get this venture on its feet. How are you fixed? Any chance of buying in? Not a big slice of the action. Only a small percentage."

"We can talk about that later," said Rila. "First, let's see what kind of proof we can get when we go back to find the dinosaurs. If we don't get proof, then all bets are off. There's no future in it."

"How far back are you going?"

"We'll have to take a closer look at the possibilities," I said. "Seventy million years at least. Perhaps a good bit farther."

"We're glad you're willing to go with us," Rila said. "We need a man who can handle a gun. Someone who has done some hunting, who can rough it and who knows what to watch out for."

Ben looked at me. "You ever fire one of these things?"

I shook my head.

"If you don't handle it right," he said, "this gun could take your head off. The kick must be terrific. We'll have to practice before we go."

"There's no place here we can try them out," I said. "Too heavily populated. We couldn't take the chance. The report would be too loud, and people would begin asking questions. We can't have that. For a while, we'll have to keep this under cover."

"You have cartridges?"

"A few. Probably enough."

"And you figure one of them could stop a dinosaur?"

"It would depend on how big a dinosaur. Some of them are so big, it would take a cannon. But we don't have to worry about them if we keep out of their way. They'll give us no trouble. The ones we worry about are the meat-eaters."

Ben squinted through the barrels again. "In good shape," he said. "A little haze, probably dust. No sign of rust. Do no harm to run an oiled rag through the barrels. Ought to break them down and oil them before we use them. In a place like that, you'd want a smooth-working gun."

He slapped the barrels with an open hand. "Good steel," he said. "Never saw anything like it in my life. Must have set you back a pile."

Rila said, "I got them from the safari people at a bargain. They want to do business with us if we have anything. That is, once they are convinced we have something they can use."

"There is one thing about this trip that I want to emphasize," I said. "It is not a hunting trip. We're not going out to bag a dinosaur. Our job is to get enough good film to convince the safari people and Rila's law-yer friend. We don't start any trouble. The two of us simply stand by in case trouble comes to us. I want you to understand that, Ben."

"Oh, sure, I understand that," he said. "Later on, perhaps . . ."

"Once things have settled down," I promised, "we'll fix it up for you to do some hunting."

"That's fair enough," he said. "But once we get where we are going, we'll have to try out these guns. To see how they shoot, how we can handle them. I'd like to know what to expect of such a piece before having to fire in earnest."

"We'll do that," said Rila. "We can't fire them here."

He laid the gun back on the table. "What kind of schedule have you got?" he asked.

"Soon as we can," said Rila. "In a day or two."

"This trip is just one phase of it," he said. "The beginning, really. There are other things you have to think about. Once this deal goes public, we'll have people crowding in. You'll have to set up some sort of security. You can't have people clogging up the place and falling into time roads or whatever you may call them. You have to buy yourself some elbowroom."

"We plan to build a fence all around the forty," Rila replied. "High as we can manage. Floodlighted at night and with guards patrolling around the clock."

Ben whistled. "That will take some money. Enclosing forty acres takes a lot of fence."

"And we'll need an administration building," said Rila, "and a staff to man it. Probably only a few to start with."

"Tell you what," said Ben. "Why don't you let me set up a credit line for you down at the bank? Fifty thousand to start with, increasing if you need it. You borrow only what you need, as you need it. You write the checks and we'll honor them."

"Ben," I told him, "that's damn generous of you. Where's the flint-hearted banker?"

"Well, what I mean," he said, "is that we'll do it if this trip turns out all right. Naturally, I'd want to know what you have."

"You still have some reservations?"

"Not really reservations. When I walk out of here and go back to the car, I'll be wondering what I've let myself in for. I'll spend the night telling myself that I am a fool to listen to you, that it's impossible to travel into time. But sitting here, lapping up your booze and listening to you, I have no reservations. My hands itch to have a part in it. If it were anyone but you, Asa, I wouldn't believe a word. I remember how it was when we were boys. I was one of the gang, sure, but I was the banker's son, and a lot of the other fellows resented it. They thought my folks were better off than their folks and we really weren't, but they thought so. They never passed up a chance to shaft me. Nobody loves a small-town banker—well, I guess no one loves any kind of banker, and let us face it, my old man didn't have a record that inspired much confidence, and I suppose the same applies to me. But the point is you never shafted me, you never went along with the shafting. There were times you even fought for me. You accepted me just like anybody else."

"Hell," I said, "that's no great virtue. You were like everybody else. We were just a bunch of small-town boys and everybody was like everybody else."

"You see," Ben said to Rila. "You see why I trust this guy."

"I'm glad you do," said Rila, "and we'll be thankful for any help you give us. This is going to be a big job just for the two of us."

"Why don't you let me nose around a little on this fence deal? I can ask some questions and sort of line up some people and no one will think a great deal about it. I can sort of let it out that I'm doing it for someone who is going into the mink farming business. Nothing definite, of course, acting as if I were being cagey about it. They'd expect that sort of foxiness in me. I can get it all lined up so the fence can start moving the moment you give the word. I think I could manage to line up quite a crew of men to go to work. The thing is that the fence has to go in fast, before there's too much speculation about it. With the crops in by now, there are bound to be a bunch of farm boys who'd be glad of a chance to earn some money. I suppose you ought to have the land surveyed before you slap up the fence. No sense in taking the chance of it slopping over on someone else's land. Security guards will be a little tougher, but I think they can be gotten. The Minneapolis police department has been hit by a new city budget cutback and has let twenty or thirty of their boys go. Maybe some of them would be available. I'll talk to the sheriff over at Lancaster and see if he has any other ideas. Not telling him any more than I have to. You'll need to get some good-sized No Trespassing signs painted. I think there are some regulations about that. They have to be a certain size, and the law has something to say about the wording on them. I'll look into that."

"You think of everything," said Rila. "You're way ahead of us."

"When you're going to do a thing," said Ben, "you should do it right. A little advance planning can save a lot of trouble."

He looked at his watch. "Good God," he said. "I'll be late for supper and Myra will have my hide. There's some sort of doings she is dragging me to tonight and she wanted to eat early."

He rose and said, "We'll be in touch. You let me know when you plan on leaving. I'll have to figure out some phoney excuse for taking a few days off. A trip or something."

"Two days might be enough to do what we want to do," said Rila.

"I shouldn't have too much trouble arranging that," he said.

After he had left, Rila said, "The man's a steam-roller."

"You heard what he said early on," I told her. "He's planning to horn in."

"We'll sell him five percent," said Rila. "Has he any money?"

"The first nickel he ever made," I said, "plus the family fortune—which may not be all that great, but it is enough."

SIXTEEN

Hiram was in charge and being important about it.

"You see those stakes," he said, pointing to three red-painted stakes standing in a row, one behind the other. "Those stakes mark the time hole. You just follow them and you'll walk into it."

He handed me a bundle of similarly painted stakes. "When you get there," he said, "don't go running off without looking. Plant these stakes in front of the other end of the hole the way I lined up these three here. That way you will know where the hole is when it's time to come back."

"But you have only three stakes here," I said.

"I gave you more," said Hiram, "because you may want to mark it better. Back there where you are going, things might be running over the stakes, but there's no chance of that happening here. I made the stakes longer, too, and heavier, so you can pound them in real good."

"Hiram," Rila asked, "did you think this up all by yourself?"

"Sure I did. There was nothing to it. And don't you worry none. If you're not back in a few days, I'll send Bowser in to find you. He can lead you home. You remember, Mr. Steele, the time he led you home."

"Indeed I do," I said. "And, Hiram, thank you very much."

"You be sure you stay right here," Ben said to him. "Don't go wandering off. Keep an eye on this place. Asa left enough food in the refrigerator so you won't have to leave to eat."

"Could I maybe leave long enough to go to the bathroom?"

"Yes, of course," said Ben, "but be quick about it. And don't tell anyone what is going on. Not even if they come asking. Herb might come. He smells that something's going on and he could get itchy. If anyone comes by and asks what those stakes are, say that you don't know."

"Once we're gone," said Rila, "he could even pull up the stakes."

"No I can't," said Hiram. "What if I have to go through the hole to rescue you?"

"We won't need any rescuing," said Ben. "Even if we're a little late, don't worry. Don't send Bowser in. Don't come in yourself."

"If I have to come," said Hiram importantly, "I'll get together a posse."

"Goddamn it, no!" yelled Ben. "Don't do anything at all. You just stay here."

"All right, Mr. Page," said Hiram.

I looked at the other two and there seemed no reason that we shouldn't start. Rila was loaded down with her camera equipment, and both Ben and I were carrying backpacks as well as the big rifles. In addition, Ben had a .30-06 slung over his shoulder. He was taking it because he said we would need a meat gun.

"I never go on a hunting trip," he'd said, "that I don't shoot some meat. Living outdoors, we'll need fresh meat."

"But there are only lizards," I'd said. "Dinosaurs and lizards and other things like that."

"Who says lizards can't be eaten?" he'd demanded. "Or even dinosaur. There are a lot of people who eat lizards. I read about it somewhere. Said they taste like chicken."

So there we were, standing in a row, with me in the lead and Rila in the middle, Ben bringing up the rear.

"So let's go," I said. "One thing to remember. We may come out of the other end at night. Through millions of years, the length of the day would vary. And anyhow, Catface can't be all that accurate. At the distance back in time we're traveling, there'll be some error. He's aiming at seventy million years, but there might be an error of several years plus or minus, so you can understand . . . "

"Asa," said Ben, "cut out the lecture. Let's go."

I stepped out, and although I didn't look behind me, I knew the other two were following. I went down the line of bright red stakes, and when I passed the last one it seemed that something tripped me, but in one stride I caught my balance and was in a different place.

"Stay right where you are," I told the other two. "Keep facing in the same direction. We have to set these stakes out and there can't be any slip-up."

It wasn't until I'd said all this that I gave myself the time to see where we were. That was something I should have reminded them about before we'd left, and I was in something of a panic that somehow we'd fouled up our direction and our placement. I was remembering the terror I had felt when I had had no idea how to get out of the Pleistocene.

It wasn't night, as I had told them it might be. Rather it was broad daylight, and even if I hadn't known where we were going, I think I would have recognized the late Cretaceous.

It didn't look much different than the Willow Bend we'd left. There were more trees, of course, but they were familiar trees: maples, birches and oaks, with a scattering of evergreens. But directly in front of us grew what appeared to be a huge pineapple with a multitude of fernlike branches sprouting out of it. A cycad, and a more primitive one than I would have expected to find, but the fact remained that only in the Cretaceous, in this latitude, would one find a cycad growing among the familiar trees of home.

"All right," said Ben. "Let's start pounding in the stakes."

I half turned and handed one back to him, then unshipped my belt axe and pounded in one myself. Then I walked out a ways and pounded in another. By the time we finished, we had six stakes pounded in a line. Ben walked along the row, pounding each succeeding stake a little deeper than the preceding one.

"There," he said, "we'll know what direction to go. The taller stakes are nearer home."

"A cycad," Rila said to me. "They've always fascinated me. I bought a bunch of fossil ones several years ago."

"A what?" asked Ben.

"A cycad. That crazy pineapple with a topknot."

"A pineapple. Yeah, I see it. Is it really a pineapple?"

"No, it's not," said Rila.

Ben and I shucked out of our packs and eased them to the ground. Rila hung onto her camera junk.

"Now, look here," said Ben. "You been fooling me. Where are all them dinosaurs?"

"They're around," said Rila. "For instance, look over there on that ridge. There's a herd of them."

Ben squinted at the ridge. "But those are small," he said. "No bigger than sheep."

"Dinosaurs come in all sizes," said Rila. "From chicken size on up. Those are herbivores. Too far away to identify."

She and Ben must have sharper eyes than I do. I could just barely make them out. If some of them had not moved now and then in their grazing, I'd not have seen them at all.

The sun stood straight overhead. The air was warm, but not too warm, and a little breeze was blowing from the west. It reminded me of a day in early June before the summer heat clamped down.

First I had seen the homelike trees, then the cycad. Now I began to notice other things as well. The ground was covered, although not entirely, by dwarf laurel, sassafras and other little shrubs. Grass was growing in scattered patches—rough, tough grass and not too much of it—nothing like the grass of the Pleistocene that tried to cover every square inch of soil. I was surprised at the grass. There shouldn't have been any. According to the textbooks, grass hadn't shown up until much later, several millions of years later. But here it was to show us how wrong we could be. Here and there, at a distance, between the groves of homelike trees, grew small patches of palmetto. We stood, I knew, at the transition point between the early development of the deciduous trees and the dying out of the older, more primitive flora; the two here intermingled. Because the ground cover was not as extensive as it would be some millions of years into the future, when true grasses had developed and taken over, the ground was rough, pocked and runneled by small channels where the soil had washed away in sudden summer showers—if, in fact, this world had anything but summer. It was the kind of ground that could not be trusted. Every minute of the time that we were here, we'd have to watch our step. The shrubs would impede walking, and the channeled ground would offer unsure footing.

Ben bent and hoisted his packsack to his shoulder. "We'd better look around for a place to camp," he said. "Near water, if we can. Somewhere around here we should find a spring. Back home, there used to be a lot of springs. Remember, Asa, when we were boys. But now, with the trees cut down and a lot of the land turned to pasture, most of them have dried up."

I nodded. "We should find one without too much trouble. I'm trying to get the geography straightened out. The river is still over there, to the west and south, but its course has changed. Look, it runs straight now and hasn't got a bend. It runs straight through the place where Willow Bend will stand."

"I see," said Ben. "Everything looks a little fuzzy, but I guess the hills and swales seem pretty much the same. We'll get it straightened out."

"This is ancient land," said Rila. "There has been nothing to change it much between now and Willow Bend. No epicontinental seas. No glacial action. The Kansas Sea lies a good many miles to the west of us. Except for possible lakes, we have no big bodies of water in the area. For that reason, we probably won't find sauropods."

I hoisted my pack and shrugged into it. Rila shifted her camera equipment to a more comfortable position. With Ben in the lead and myself taking up the rear, we moved out. In a patch of shrubbery over to our right, something squeaked and ran, rustling through the underbrush. Perhaps, I thought, a small mammal. There would be a lot of them here, mouse to rabbit size. There probably were rabbits, certainly opossum. Maybe even squirrels. Hiding out against the more vicious beasts that roamed, watching to satisfy an ever-present hunger, these little scurriers would emerge from hiding ten million years or so from now to take over a world left empty by the massive extinction of the reptiles.

Ben led us toward the river, circling to the west. The walking was hard. You had to feel your way. There was a tendency to watch underfoot, to see where you were walking. But if you did that, you couldn't keep close watch, and here was a place where you knew instinctively you had to keep close watch of everything around you.

The gun was growing heavier and more awkward by the minute. I couldn't find a comfortable way to carry it, and I wondered what the hell I'd do if some slavering carnivore should hove in sight and come thundering toward us. The pack was bad enough, but the gun was worse.

A turtle—a huge turtle—poked a head as big as a barrel out of a small grove of birches a few hundred feet away. The turtle poked its head out, paused, blinking at us, then kept coming. At the sight of it emerging from the birches, we froze. Ben brought up his gun halfway to the shoulder.

It looked like a turtle, faintly, but it was not a turtle. It didn't have a shell; it had armor plate. And it kept on coming, blinking at us all the time, a nictitating membrane flickering over and off its eyes. It waddled when it walked, and its short legs held it only a short distance off the ground.

To my right I could hear Rila's camera whirring, but I didn't look at her. I kept looking at the beast.

"It's all right," I said, hoping I was right. "It's an ankylosaur. It's not a predator."

By now it was free of the birches—all fifteen feet of it. Its dragging tail had a massive bony club at the end of it.

The camera kept on with its whirring and now old

armor-plate had stopped. It grunted at us and lifted that great club of a tail and beat it on the ground.

"I'll be damned," said Ben. "It's warning us off."

"It's not scared," I said. "Not of anything at all. Let one of the carnosaurs have a go at it, and it would give the carnosaur that tail right in the teeth."

Deliberately the ankylosaur swung about, away from us, and sedately trundled off. Rila lowered her camera. "Let's find that camping site," said Ben.

A half-hour later we found it, a spring gushing out of a hillside, hidden by a patch of oaks and maples, mighty trees that made me think of an artist's conception of the ancient English forests drawn to illustrate an old edition of Tennyson.

"It's perfect," said Ben. "We have protection. None of the big stuff can get at us easily, here among the trees."

"Maybe we're overestimating the ferocity of the carnosaurs," I told him. "Maybe they don't go for you on sight. We'll seem strange to them, not like their usual prey. They might shy off from us. And another thing—there may not be many of them about."

"Even so," insisted Ben, "we won't take any chances. We all stick together. No one goes wandering off. And we don't take a thing for granted. When we get the camp set up, we'll test-fire the guns."

We quickly got the camp set up (a simple camp, with two small tents pitched underneath the trees), a fire pit dug, dead wood chopped, brought in and stacked, and our kits unpacked.

"You and I will take turns standing guard tonight," Ben said to me. "We don't want something blundering in on us."

With the camp all tidy, Ben and I test-fired the guns.

"The thing to do," said Ben, "is to hang in there easy. Don't get tense, don't stiffen up. Hold the butt to your shoulder, but don't hug it too tight. There has to be a little play, but you have to have control of it so the butt doesn't bounce off your shoulder and clip you on the chin. And lean into it. Not too far, but lean into it."

Ben had no trouble. He'd fired big-caliber before,

but none as big as the ones we carried. With me, it was a bit different. I'd never fired anything bigger than a .22, but I remembered what Ben had told me, and it didn't go too badly. The first shot almost took my shoulder off and drove me back a step or two, but it didn't knock me over. The second shot was better. The third seemed quite natural. The fourth and last shot, I didn't even notice the recoil. The big lone birch tree we had used as a target was chewed up by the impact of the bullets.

"That's good," said Ben approvingly. "You can't let it hurt you too much. If you let it wallop you too hard, if you don't stand up to it, you become afraid of it and you flinch each time you fire it. When that happens, you might just as well throw it at whatever's coming at you. Flinching, you can't hit the broad side of a barn at thirty paces."

"Asa," Rila said softly, off to one side.

I turned and saw that she was sitting cross-legged on the ground, her elbows resting on her knees to hold the binoculars steady. "Come take a look," she said. "There's a lot of stuff out there. Small groups and loners, but they blend into the background and are hard to see. Look over there, just to the left of the little group of four trees on the ridge running back from the river."

She handed me the binoculars, but they were so heavy that standing, I couldn't hold them steady. I had to sit down and use my knees to support my elbows, as she had been doing.

It took a while to pinpoint what she wanted me to see, but finally I caught the thing in the field and fiddled with the adjustment wheels to bring it more sharply into focus. It was in a squatting position, resting, reared back with its knees flexed so that its great tail gave it support. The huge body was almost upright and the ugly head kept swinging from side to side as if keeping watch of the countryside.

"What do you think?" asked Rila. "A tyrannosaur?"

"I don't know," I said. "I can't be sure."

The trouble, of course, was that no one could be sure. All we had ever seen of any of the dinosaurs were their bones, plus, in a few instances, fossil mummies with part of the skin intact. Our visual impressions of them came from artists' conceptions, which were fine, so far as they went, but couldn't even pretend to be sure of many details.

"Not rex," I said. "The forelegs are too big. Maybe a trionychid. Maybe another kind of tyrannosaur we've never found a fossil of; we can't be sure we've found the fossils of all the different kinds of tyrannosaurs. But whatever he is, he's a big brute. Sitting up there resting, taking it easy, looking around for something that's worth his while to gobble up."

I kept on watching the brute. Except for his swinging head, he did not stir.

"The forelegs are too well developed," said Rila. "That's what puzzled me. If we were a few million years farther back, I'd be tempted to say it's an allosaur. But up here there aren't supposed to be any allosaurs. They died out long ago."

"Maybe not," I told her. "We're acting as if we knew the entire history of the dinosaurs from the fossils we have found. If we find one dinosaur in an old stratum and find him in none after that, we're inclined to say he became extinct. What could happen is that we simply failed to look in the right place to find him in the younger strata. Allosaurs could have existed up to the very end."

I handed the glasses to Ben, pointing out the clump of trees. "Over to the left of them," I said.

"Asa," said Rila, "I want some film of him. He's the first big thing I've seen."

"Use the telephoto lens," I said. "That will catch him."

"I have," she answered, "but it comes up awfully fuzzy. At least, what I can see does. I suppose on the film as well. To convince the safari people, to get them all fired up, I have to have something sharp and close."

"We can try to get closer," I said. "He's a long way from here, but we can have a try."

"The beggar's moving off," said Ben. "Going up the ridge. He is moving fast. Maybe he spotted something he's after."

"Damn it," said Rila bitterly. "It was you guys and your test-firing. It made him uneasy."

"He didn't look uneasy to me," I said. "He was just sitting there. From this distance, the firing would not have been very loud."

"But I've got to get some big stuff," said Rila.

"We'll find it," I said, trying to comfort her.

"There is a lot of little stuff out there," she said. "Ostrich dinosaurs and small herds of little fellows, turkey size or so. A few ankylosaurs. A few small horned varieties. All sorts of lizards. Some big turtles down by the river, but who cares for big turtles? Some flying reptiles. Pterosaurs, I suppose. Some birds. But nothing spectacular."

"It would be senseless to go chasing after that big fellow," Ben said. "He was traveling fast. Like he knew where he was going. By the time we get out there, he'll be clear out of the country, the rate that he was going. We can take a small stroll, if that is what you want. Maybe we can stir up something. But we shouldn't go too far. It's getting well into the afternoon and we should be back here well before night sets in."

"We'll likely be safer after dark than at any other time," I told him. "I doubt that any of the reptiles would move around too much once the sun has set. They get lethargic then, or are supposed to. They're cold-blooded. Their temperature tolerance is narrow. They take shelter at noon when the sun gets hot, and don't move around much when the temperature falls at night."

"You are probably right," said Ben. "Undoubtedly, you are. You know about such things. But me, I'll feel more comfortable at night in camp with a good fire going."

"We can't be absolutely sure about dinosaurs not moving around at night," said Rila. "For one thing, we can't be sure that even with the sun gone the temperature will fall a great deal. And another thing, there is some evidence that dinosaurs may not be cold-blooded. There is a fairly persuasive opinion among some paleontologists that they were, in fact, warm-blooded."

She was right, of course—there was some evidence of warm bloodedness. I had read some of the argument and had not been impressed with it. I didn't say so, though. Apparently Rila did accept it and this was no place to get into an academic argument.

Somewhere to the north, something began to bellow. We stood and listened to it. It didn't get any nearer, nor did it recede; the bellowing just kept on. Everything else fell silent, and in between the bellows, there was nothing to be heard. We had not been aware of the background noise before, but now we noticed the absence of other sounds, of the grunting, feeble honking, the multitude of different squeaks.

"Wonder if that's our pal from over on the ridge?" asked Ben.

"It could be," said Rila, "It could be something else."

"I didn't know dinosaurs made sounds."

"No one knew. The general belief, I think, has been that they were silent creatures. Now we know they're noisy."

"If we climb the hill," said Ben, "once we get to the top, we may be able to spot this bellower."

We climbed the hill, but we didn't find the bellower. The bellowing quit before we reached the hilltop. A search with the glasses failed to pick up anything big enough to have been making all that noise.

We didn't find the bellower, but we stirred up a lot of life. Small bands of ostrich dinosaurs that looked for all the world like six-foot naked birds went racing away from us. A grunting bunch of little horned monsters, two feet at the shoulder, waddled away from a patch of ground they had torn up with their horns in search of roots and bulbs. Snakes slithered out from beneath our feet. We raised a flock of grotesque, awkward birds, the size of grouse or maybe a little bigger, that fluttered protestingly. They were funny-looking things. Their feathers seemed to be put on wrong, and they were not good at flying. A little distance off, we saw a few iguanodons standing six feet high or so.

They should have been much bigger; more than likely, according to the fossil record, they shouldn't have been there at all. They were flabby, evil-looking beasts, and when they opened their mouths, they showed fine sets of teeth. There was no question they were meat-eaters. Those teeth were never made to deal with vegetation. We edged up close to them, Ben and I on the alert, rifles ready. I was braced for a charge, but they weren't sore at anyone. They regarded us sleepily and suspiciously for a time, then they wheeled about and went lumbering off.

During the afternoon, Rila's camera kept up an almost ceaseless whirring. She used up a lot of film, having to stop every now and then to reload. But except for iguanodons, she wasn't getting anything big.

As we turned to go home, Ben pointed at the sky. "Look there," he said.

He was pointing at a flock of birds far off. There must have been a hundred of them, looking like black gnats in the sky, flying east.

I focused the glasses on them and, although they remained fairly small, there was no mistaking them.

"Pterosaurs," I said. "There must be big water out there somewhere."

The sun was only an hour or so above the horizon when we turned back for camp. Halfway there, we ran head-on into a group of six ostrich dinosaurs. They hesitated at the sight of us, began to turn away. Ben thrust his elephant gun at me. "Hang onto this for a minute," he said.

He lifted the shoulder strap of the .30-06, and as he swung around, the ostriches were off, running fast with their powerful, swinging stride. Ben's rifle came up and he swung it, following them. It coughed with a flat vicious sound, and one of the fleeing dinosaurs spun head over heels. It landed on its back and its slender legs stuck up in the air, kicking.

"Supper," Ben said, grinning. He slung the strap of the smaller rifle over his shoulder and reached out for the one I was holding for him.

"Did you get it?" he asked Rila.

"I got it," she said grimly. "It's on film. The first dinosaur kill."

Ben grinned even more broadly. "What do you know about that!" he said.

We walked to the kill. Ben leaned the big gun against it and took a knife out of the belt sheath.

"You grab hold of the leg," he told me, "and pull." Still hanging onto my gun with one hand, I grasped the leg with the other and pulled. Ben's knife made quick, expert slices, cutting around the ham.

"All right," he said. He grasped the leg with both hands and twisted savagely. It came free, but some muscles still held. He slashed twice more and the quarter was severed from the body.

"I'll carry it," I said. "You have the extra gun."

He grunted. "We could take the other leg, but this should be enough. No use trying to get meat ahead. It will only spoil."

"How do you know this will be good to eat?" I asked.

"It won't poison us," he said. "If we don't like it, we can throw it out and fry up some bacon."

"We won't have to throw it out," said Rila. "It will make good eating."

"How can you be so sure of that?" I asked.

"We eat chicken, don't we?"

"I may be stupid," said Ben, "but what have chickens got to do with it?"

"Chickens are close to dinosaurs. The closest thing we have today. Direct descendants, if you stretch a point or two."

Stretch a point or two, indeed, I told myself, but I kept my mouth shut. She was not, of course, entirely wrong. I had kept quiet about the warm-bloodedness, I told myself, and for the sake of harmony, I might as well keep quiet about this one, too.

We didn't throw it out. It tasted good. It faintly resembled veal, but it wasn't veal, either. It had a sweet, succulent taste all its own. We ate a lot of it.

We built up the fire after the cooking was done and sat beside it. Ben broke out a bottle of whiskey and poured into our coffee cups. "A small drink," he said.

"A hunter's drink. Just enough for us to feel a little warm and happy. Something to warm the gut."

He handed us the cups and put the bottle away.

We sat there sipping at it, and the world was good. We were snug beside the fire and we had film and everything was all right. We didn't do much talking. With the tramping we had done, we were too tired to talk.

In the underbrush around us, we heard rustlings and squeakings.

"It's the mammals," said Rila. "Poor little scurriers, they hide out all day."

"Don't feel pity for them," said Ben. "They'll make out all right. They'll still be here when the dinosaurs and all the rest of them are gone."

"That's one way to look at it," she said.

"We ought to be getting some sleep. I'll take the first watch," he said to me. "I'll wake you at . . . " He looked at his watch. "Hell, it says four o'clock. It would. Our time is no good here. Anyhow, I'll wake you in four hours or so."

"There are three of us," said Rila.

"You get your sleep," he said. "Asa and I can take care of it."

We had set up the tents, but it was good weather and we didn't use them. We spread out our bedrolls and lay down. It took me a long time to go to sleep, although I tried to. We had a hard day coming up. Ben sat by the fire for a while, then picked up the heavy gun and walked toward the edge of the grove.

All around us in the grove, the little rustlings and squeakings continued. There must be, I thought, a lot more little skittering mammals in this world than anyone had suspected.

"Asa," Rila said, "are you asleep?"

"You go to sleep," I said. "It will be a rough day tomorrow."

She didn't say any more and I lay there, drifting, encouraging myself to drift, and, finally, I must have gone to sleep, because the next I knew Ben was shaking me by the shoulder. I threw back the blanket and got up.

"Everything all right?" I asked.

"Nothing's happening," he said. "It'll be dawn before too long."

"You stood more than your share of the watch."

"I couldn't sleep, anyway," he said. "Too excited. But I'm tired. Maybe I can now. If you don't mind, I'll use your bedroll. No sense in unrolling mine."

He kicked off his boots and got into the bedroll, pulled the blanket over him. I walked over to the fire, which was burning briskly. Ben apparently had put a few sticks of wood on it just before he'd wakened me.

Some of the squeaking and rustling had died down and everything was quiet. It was still dark, but the feel of the air said that dawn was coming. Off somewhere out beyond the grove something began cheeping. I figured it was a bird—or birds, rather, for there seemed to be a lot of cheeping, more than one thing cheeping.

I tucked the rifle under my arm and walked out to the edge of the grove. The surrounding countryside was half lighted by a pale sickle Moon.

Nothing seemed to be moving and then, down in the narrow flatness of the river valley, something did move. I couldn't make out what it was. The movement had stopped, but suddenly it moved again. In a moment, I told myself, when my eyes became adapted to the darkness, I would make out what it was.

Ten minutes or so later, it seemed to me that I could make out a number of dark lumps in the valley. I tried to concentrate to make out what they were. They remained dark lumps, but now there seemed to be fleeting reflections as well, the momentary reflection of the thin moonlight off something that was moving. All this time, the cheeping kept on, and it seemed to me that it came from the valley, that there was more and more of it, and that it was getting louder. It was a tricky sort of sound and hard to place. But I could almost have sworn that it was the lumps that were cheeping.

I squatted down and watched, but I couldn't see much—just those lumps that seemed at times to be moving, although if they were moving, they weren't getting anywhere.

I don't know how long I squatted there, but it was a long time. Something held me there, watching whatever was moving in the valley. The eastern sky began to lighten, and behind me, in the grove, a bird twittered sleepily. I turned my head to look at the grove, and when I looked back at the valley again, it seemed to me that I could see those black lumps more distinctly than I had before. They were bigger than I had thought they were at first, and they were just ambling about, not all of them at once, but one or two of them moving and stopping, then another one or two moving. They looked to me like cattle grazing, and thinking this, I knew that whatever might be down there were doing exactly that—grazing. A herd of grazing dinosaurs.

Whether it was thinking in this direction or because the light of the still hidden sun had imperceptibly intensified, I was able quite suddenly to make out what they were: triceratops, a herd of triceratops. Now that I knew what they were, I could make out the flaring frills and the whiteness of the two horns that sprouted and thrust forward just above the eyes.

I rose slowly and cautiously—perhaps more cautiously than was necessary, for at my distance, there was little chance of spooking them—and went back to camp.

I knelt and shook Rila's shoulder and she murmured sleepily, "What now?"

"Wake up," I said. "Easy. No noise. We've a herd of triceratops."

She came up out of the blanket, still only half awake.

"Triceratops," she said. "Horns and everything?"

"A herd of them. Down in the valley. Like a herd of buffalo. I don't know how many."

Ben rose up, sitting on his bedroll, scrubbing at his eyes with doubled fists. "What the hell is going on?" he asked.

"Triceratops," said Rila. "Asa spotted them."

"Those are the ones with the horns growing out of their face?"

"That is right," I said.

"Big brutes," said Ben. "They have a skeleton of one in the Science Museum at St. Paul. I saw it several years ago."

He stumbled to his feet and picked up the gun. "Well, let's go get them," he said.

"It's too dark yet," I said. "We have to wait for light. Let us have some breakfast first."

"I don't know," said Rila. "I don't want to miss them. A herd of them? You said a herd of them, didn't you? Regular triceratops, not some of those little horned fellows we found yesterday?"

"Big," I said. "I couldn't make out how big, but they are good-sized. If you two want to go out and keep an eye on them, I'll cook some eggs and bacon. When it's done, I'll bring it out to you."

"Be careful," warned Rila. "Don't make any noise. Don't go banging pots."

The two of them left and I dug out the eggs and bacon, got the coffee started and settled down to cooking. When I took their plates and the coffee pot out to them, it was beginning to get light. The triceratops were still there, down in the river valley.

"Did you ever in your life," asked Rila, "see anything so beautiful?"

For a fact, the herd was quite a sight. For a couple of miles up and down the river, the valley was simply covered by them. They were busy cropping at the grass and low-growing ground cover. There were some young ones, not much bigger than hogs, and others slightly larger that I took to be yearlings, but there were a lot of big ones. From where we sat, the big ones appeared to be five feet tall or more, and including their tails, perhaps twenty feet in length. The massive frills made their heads appear enormous. They kept up their contented cheeping.

"How do we get at them?" I asked.

"We walk toward them," said Ben. "Walking slow. Making no sudden motions and no sound. If some of them look up at us, we stop. When they look away again, we move. It will take a lot of patience. Rila in the middle, with one of us on either side. If they should take a notion to come at us, Rila drops back, the two of us stand firm."

We finished eating and left the plates and coffee pot there, not bothering to take them back to camp. Then we began our stalk, if it could be called a stalk.

"It doesn't make sense," I said, "standing up like this in plain sight."

Ben disagreed with me. "If we hunkered down and tried to sneak up on them, we'd panic them. This way they can look us over and probably we don't look too dangerous."

It was a slow business. We moved only a few steps at a time, stopping whenever some of the brutes lifted their heads from grazing to have a look at us. But it seemed that Ben was right. They didn't appear to be too concerned with us.

We stopped a couple of times to let Rila expose some film, panning the camera up and down the valley. We got to within fifty yards or so of them before they took any serious notice of us. A couple of the big bulls stopped their grazing and swung around to face us, heads held high, their wicked horns aimed straight at us. They snapped their sharp, recurved beaks at us. We stopped. To my left, I could hear the camera running, but I kept my eyes on the bulls, rifle lifted to ready. One motion would put it on my shoulder. Funny thing about it—it had proved a heavy thing to pack, but now it seemed to have no weight at all.

The cheeping stopped. All the cheeping stopped. Those farther back in the herd lifted their heads and stared at us. The entire herd, somehow, had been put on alert.

Ben spoke softly. "Start backing off. Slow. One step at a time. Be sure of your footing. Don't stumble."

We started backing off.

One of the big bulls rushed forward a few steps. I brought my gun to my shoulder. But after those few quick steps, he stopped. He shook his head at us savagely. We kept on backing off.

Another bull made a rush, stopped as had the other one.

"It's bluff," said Ben. "But let's not push them. Keep on backing off."

The camera kept on purring.

The two bulls stayed watching us. When we were a hundred yards away, or maybe slightly more, they swung about and trotted back to the herd. The rest of the herd resumed its grazing.

Ben let out his breath in relief. "That was close," he said. "We walked a bit too close."

Rila lowered the camera. "But it made good film," she said. "This is what we need."

"You got enough?" I asked.

"I think I have," she said.

"Then let's get back," I said.

"Keep on backing for a while," said Ben. "Don't turn your backs just yet."

We backed up for a while longer, then turned around and walked toward the camp.

Behind us, the cheeping grew in volume as the herd settled down to grazing. All was well again. The pestiferous intruders had been driven off and the triceratops could get back to business.

I said to Ben, "Just how did you know we could walk up to them that way? How could you know what dinosaurs would do?"

"I didn't," he said. "I took a chance. I figured they wouldn't be much different than the animals of our time."

"But in our time," I said, "you don't walk up to a moose or mountain goat."

"No, of course you don't," he said. "Maybe you never could walk up on a moose or mountain goat. Now the animals know what we are and won't let us get too close. But in the old days, before they'd met many men, you could walk up to herd animals. In Africa, the early ivory hunters walked up on elephants. In the old American West, before the hide-hunting days, a man could walk up on a herd of buffalo. There was a sort of invisible line that you couldn't cross. Most of the old hunters could calculate the location of the line."

"And we went beyond the line?"

Ben shook his head. "I don't think we did. We reached it and they let us know. If we'd stepped across it, they would have charged."

Rila made a warning sound. We stopped in our tracks.

"The cheeping," Rila said. "They have stopped the cheeping."

We swung around and saw what had stopped the cheeping.

Coming down the slope, a quarter-mile or so from us, heading for the herd, was a monstrosity that made me catch my breath: no other than old rex himself. There was no mistaking him. He didn't look exactly as our twentieth-century artists had depicted him, but he was close enough that there was no mistaking him.

The pitifully shrunken, ridiculous little forelegs dangled on his chest. The huge, muscular hind legs, ending in wide clawed feet, moved with elaborate deliberation, eating up the ground, driving the ponderous, vicious creature forward with a grim sense of unstoppable power. It was the head, however, that provided the real horror. Close to twenty feet above the ground, it was mostly jaws, the six-inch fangs gleaming in the early sunlight. Below the lower jaw hung an elaborate dewlap that no artist could have been aware of—a dewlap that displayed an awful, iridescent beauty. It shone in the sunlight with colors that seemed to ripple across its surface—purple, yellow, blue, red and green—ever-changing colors that reminded me momentarily of the stained glass windows I had seen at one time in an ancient church, and, in that moment, I was annoyed that I could not remember where I'd seen the church.

Rila's camera was making its purring noise and I took a step or two forward so I'd be between her and this great monstrosity. Out of the corner of my eye, I saw that Ben also was walking forward.

"A tyrannosaur," Rila was saying to herself, speaking in a prayerful whisper. "A real honest-to-God old tyrannosaur."

Down in the valley, the triceratops had stopped their feeding. Ringed in the forefront of the herd was a line of big bulls, almost shoulder to shoulder, facing the oncoming carnivore, forming a fence of flaring bony frills and outthrust horns.

The tyrannosaur was angling toward us and by this time was considerably less than the quarter of a mile away he had been when we first had sighted him. He halted and stood for a moment, hesitant. It must be apparent to him, I thought, that he'd find no easy picking in this herd of triceratops. While the big bulls stood considerably less than half his height, their horns would reach well up into his gut. While he just possibly might be able to mangle one or two of them with his powerful jaws, they'd have him disemboweled before he could reach any of the others.

He stood poised on those powerful hind legs, the massive tail sticking out behind him, barely clearing the ground, swinging his heavy head from side to side, as if he might be seeking a safer angle of attack.

Then he must have caught sight of us, for suddenly he pivoted around on one of his legs, thrusting himself around to face us with a powerful stroke of the second leg. He started for us even as he pivoted, and with every step he made, he was twelve feet closer. I had the gun on my shoulder and was surprised to find that there wasn't even a quiver in the barrels. When you have to get a job done, you often do it better than you think you can. I had it sighted just about the place where those tiny forelegs sprouted from the body, and I dropped the gun a little so it was aimed about the point where I thought the heart should be. The gun hammered at my shoulder, but I didn't really hear it go off, and my finger slipped off the first trigger and found the second one. But there was no need to fire again. Out in front of me, the tyrannosaur was rearing back and falling over. At the edge of my vision, I caught sight of Ben and saw that a small trickle of smoke was issuing from one of the barrels of his gun. The two of us, I knew, had fired almost simultaneously, and two of those big bullets were more than the huge dinosaur could take.

"Look out!" yelled Rila, and even as she yelled, I heard a crashing to my left.

I swung in that direction and saw another tyrannosaur bearing down upon us. He was far too close for comfort and was coming fast. Ben's gun roared and, for a moment, the beast was thrown off its stride, sliding down the slope, but it recovered and came on. And now something inside of me said, it is up to you. Ben's gun was empty and I had just the one cartridge left. The tyrannosaur's head was coming down and the jaws began to open wide and there was no chance at a decent body shot. I don't know how I did it. There was no time to think. What I did, I'm sure, was simple reflex, a natural and instinctive protective action. I aimed the gun right in the middle of that gaping mouth and pulled the trigger and out in front of and above me, the dinosaur's head exploded and his body went tumbling to one side. I distinctly heard the thump and felt the vibrations in my feet when eight tons of flesh hit the ground not more than thirty feet away.

Ben, who had thrown himself aside to escape the charge, was scrambling to his feet, clicking cartridges into the barrels. Behind me, the camera was running.

"Well," said Ben, "we know something now. The damn things hunt in pairs."

The second dinosaur was dead, its head torn from its body. It still twitched and kicked, striking out viciously with one clawed hind leg. The first one was trying to get to its feet, but tipping over and falling back each time it did. Ben walked down the slope toward it, fired another bullet into its chest, and it slumped into a mound of flesh.

Rila walked slowly down the hill taking close-ups of the two dead beasts from several angles, then shut off the camera and lowered it. I opened my gun and reloaded, then tucked it under my arm.

Ben came up the hill toward me. "I don't mind telling you," he said, "that I'm a bit shook up. That second one damn near ran me down. You got him in the head. You blew his fool head off."

"It was the only thing I could do," I said. I didn't mean to sound smug about it, but I couldn't explain to him that some primitive sense of self-preservation had taken over for me—that it was not I who had blown off the dinosaur's head, but some instinct that took over. I couldn't explain it even to myself.

"The other one, however, still has a head," said Ben. "We ought to chop it off and haul it back. Just as proof."

"We have the proof," I said. "Rila has the proof."

"I suppose so," said Ben, "but it's a shame. If you ever wanted to part with it, that head, mounted, would bring a lot of money."

"It probably weighs several hundred pounds," I pointed out.

"The two of us . . ."

"No," I said. "We have a couple of miles or more to go to find the stakes. We'd better start getting out of here."

"I don't see why."

I gestured at the two dead dinosaurs. "Fifteen tons of meat," I said. "All the scavengers will start flocking in. Every stinking meat-eater from miles around. By nightfall, their skeletons will be picked clean. I want to be out of here before they start arriving."

"It would give us some good film."

I said to Rila, "You have enough film? You are satisfied?"

She nodded. "I never missed a lick—the killing of those two beasts. If that doesn't convince Safari, Inc., nothing ever will."

"All right," I said, in a tone of voice that told them I meant it, "we're heading out for home."

"You're chicken," Ben told me.

"So, I'm chicken. We have what we came for. We're leaving while we can."

"I really think," said Rila, "we should leave. I'm scared down to my toenails."

SEVENTEEN

We had returned from the Cretaceous early Monday morning. It was Friday. A great deal had been going on in those four days. A start had been made on building the fence around the forty—high steel posts set in concrete, heavy wire fencing installed upon them and welded into place. Trenches were being dug along the interior perimeter of the fence to lay electric cable for the floodlights. Foundations had been poured for the administration building and lumber was being delivered. Ben's motel was going up. Rila had left the day before for New York with the film that she had taken. Courtney McCallahan, the Washington attorney, was flying into New York to sit in with Safari, Inc., on the showing of the films. The films were to be developed in Safari's laboratory, making it unnecessary to take them outside the organization.

I had worked my tail off to get things going, with a lot of help from Ben. He had made a lot of the necessary contacts, had twisted arms and pleaded, had scrounged up gangs of workmen to turn loose on the projects. A lot of the men were no more than common laborers—farm boys, mostly—but Ben had found some competent foremen to place in charge as well, and things seemed to be going well.

"The idea," he had said, "is to get started and get the fence and administration building finished as soon as possible, before too many people begin asking questions. Once we get the fence up, they can ask all the questions that they want and, behind the fence, we can thumb our noses at them."

"But, Ben," I had protested, "you have things to do yourself. You have your motel to be built and the bank to run. You have no direct interest in this deal."

"You're borrowing a lot of money from me and the bank is earning interest," he'd said. "You gave me an edge on starting the motel and I've been doing a lot of other things besides. I've bought up every acre around here that is loose. I picked up that farm to the east of you just the other day. Old Jake Kolb stuck me for more than he thought that it was worth, figured I was a sucker, buying it. What he doesn't know is that it'll be worth ten times more than I paid for it once your business here gets started. And you took me on that hunting trip after dinosaurs. I wouldn't have missed that for the world. I would have paid you to take me on it. And I figure that before I'm through with it, you'll let me in for a small percentage of this deal of yours."

"Let us get the business started first," I'd said. "The whole thing may fall into a heap."

"Hell," he'd said, "I don't see how it can. This is the biggest thing that ever happened. Everyone, the whole world, will go mad over it. You'll have more business than you can handle. You just hang loose. You keep an eye on things. If you need help, reach for the phone. I tell you, boy, the two of us have it made."

I was sitting in the kitchen talking with Hiram. The two of us were having a beer. It was the first sitting time I'd had since it all had started. I sat there, drinking my beer, feeling guilty at not doing anything, racking my brain to figure out if there was something that I should be doing.

"Catface," said Hiram, "is excited about what is going on. He asked about the fence and I tried to explain it to him. I told him once it was finished, he could make a lot of time holes and he was pleased at that. He is anxious to get started."

"But he could make time holes anytime he wanted. He could have been doing it all along. There was not a thing to stop him."

"It seems, Mr. Steele, that he can't make time holes for just the fun of it. They have to be used or they aren't any good. He made a few for Bowser, but there wasn't much satisfaction in that."

"No, I don't suppose there would be. Although Bowser had a lot of fun with them. He used one of them to bring home the dinosaur bones."

I went to the refrigerator to get another beer.

"You want one?" I asked Hiram.

"No, thank you, Mr. Steele. I don't really like the stuff. I just drink it to be sociable."

"I asked you to talk with Catface about how big the time holes can be made. The Safari people will probably want to take in some trucks."

"He says it ain't no problem. He says the holes are big enough to take anything at all."

"Did he close the one we used? I'd hate to have some of those dinosaurs stumbling through."

"He closed it," Hiram said, "right after you got back. It's been closed since then."

"Well, that is fine," I said and I went on drinking beer. It was good just to be sitting there.

Footsteps sounded on the steps outside and there was a knocking at the door.

"Come on in," I yelled.

It was Herb Livingston.

"Grab a chair," I said. "I'll get a beer for you."

Hiram got up. "Me and Bowser will go and look around outside."

"That's all right," I said, "but don't move off the place. I may need you later on."

Bowser got up from his corner and followed Hiram out. Herb pulled the tab on the beer can and tossed it in the wastebasket.

"Asa," he said, "you're holding out on me."

"Not you alone," I said. "I'm holding out on everyone."

"Something's going on," Herb said. "And I want to know about it. The Willow Bend *Record* may not be the world's greatest newspaper, but it's the only one we have here, and for fifteen years, I have told the people what is happening."

"Now hold up, Herb," I said. "I'm not going to tell you and you can yell at me and pound the table and I still won't tell you."

"Why not?" he demanded. "We were boys together.

We've known one another for years. You and me and
Ben and Larry and the rest of them. Ben knows. You
have told Ben something."

"Ask Ben, then."

"He won't tell me anything, either. He says any
information has to come from you. He gave out to
start with, about this business of the fence, that he
was putting it up for someone who was going into mink
farming. But I know you aren't going into mink farming. So the reason is something else. Someone else had
the idea you found a crashed spaceship in that old
sinkhole. One that crashed a thousand years ago. Is
that what this is all about?"

"You're fishing now," I said, "and it won't do you
any good. I have a project underway, that's true, but
any publicity right now could raise hell with it. When
the time comes, I'll tell you."

"When you need the publicity, you mean."

"I suppose that's it."

"Look, Asa, I don't want the big city papers scoop-
ing me on this. I don't want them to write the story
before I have a crack at it. I don't want to be scooped
in my own backyard."

"Hell, you're scooped all the time," I said. "On all
the important stories. What else can you expect with
a weekly paper? News doesn't happen on a weekly
basis. Your strength isn't the big stories. They don't
come often enough. People read the *Record* because
you write about the little things, what people do and
the small events that happen here. Look at it this way.
If I'm able to pull off what I'm trying to do, it will put
Willow Bend on the map. It will help everyone. It will
help the businesses here, it will provide more advertising dollars for you. You'll be better off because it
happened. Do you want to muff my chance and yours
by rushing into print when that rushing into print
might kill the deal?"

"But I've got to write a story of some sort. I just
can't not write anything."

"All right, then, write your story. Write about the
fence, about Ben's motel, about all the rest of it. Spec-
ulate, if you want to, on what is going on. I can't stop

you. I wouldn't want to. You have every right. Say you talked with me and I would give you nothing. I am sorry, Herb. That's the best that I can do."

"I suppose," said Herb, "you have the right not to tell me. But I had to ask. I had to lean on you a little. You understand, don't you?"

"Sure, I understand. How about another beer?"

"No, thanks. Haven't got the time. We go to press tonight. I have to write this story."

After Herb had left, I sat there for a while, feeling sorry about the way I'd had to treat him. But I couldn't give him the story. I understood how he felt, how any newspaperman might feel. The hell of it was that he would get scooped. Before he went to press again next week, the story probably would be out. But there was, I told myself, no way I could help that.

I got up and threw the empty beer can into the wastebasket, then went outdoors. It was getting into the late afternoon, but the crews were still at work and I was surprised to see how well the fence was progressing. I looked around to see if there was any sign of Catface. I would not have been surprised to have found him staring at me from one of the apple trees. In the last few days, there had been a lot of evidence of him. Instead of hiding from us, as had been his habit, he had begun sort of mingling with us. But at the moment there was no sign of him, nor of Hiram and Bowser. I walked down the fence line until I reached where the men were working. I stood around for a while watching them, then returned to the house.

A sheriff's car was parked out in front and a man in uniform was sitting in one of the lawn chairs. When I came up to him, he rose and held out his hand to me.

"I'm Sheriff Amos Redman," he said. "You must be Asa Steele. Ben told me I'd probably find you here."

"Glad you dropped by," I said. "What do you have in mind?"

"Ben told me a few days ago, you might need some guards to patrol the fence. Would you mind telling me what is happening?"

"I'll tell you one thing, sheriff, it's legal."

He chuckled faintly at the bad joke. "I never thought it would be anything else," he said. "Seems to me you were a Willow Bend boy some years ago. How long have you been back?"

"A little less than a year," I said.

"It appears that you plan to stay."

"I hope so."

"About the guards," he said. "I talked with the police association in Minneapolis and they think they can fix you up. Some of the men there have lost their jobs because of an economy cut and should be available to you."

"I'm glad," I said. "We will need trained personnel."

"You having any trouble?" the sheriff asked.

"Trouble? Oh, you mean sightseers."

"That's what I mean. There've been some funny stories going about. One of them is about a crashed spaceship." He looked at me closely to see how I would take it.

"Yes, sheriff," I said. "I think there might be a spaceship. Out there in the woods, under tons of overlay."

"Well, I'll be damned," he said. "If there is such a thing, you'll be swamped by crowds. I understand why you might need a fence. I'll tell my deputies to swing around here once in a while and keep an eye on you. If you need any help, you know how to reach me."

"Thanks," I said. "And I think you'll understand. I'd just as soon no credence be given, quite yet, to that spaceship story."

"Certainly," he said importantly. "Just between the two of us."

The phone rang when I was coming in the door. It was Rila.

"Where have you been?" she asked. "I've been trying to get you."

"Just out for a walk. I hadn't expected to hear from you this soon. Is everything all right?"

"Asa, it's better than all right. We ran the films this afternoon. They are wonderful. Especially that

part with you and Ben polishing off those tyrannosaurs. Everyone was sitting on the edge of his chair.
It was so exciting. That cheeping done by the triceratops was weird, primitive. God, I don't know what.
Out of this world. Sent a funny feeling up your spine.
Safari is champing at the bit, but we won't talk with
them."

"Won't talk with them! For Christ's sake, Rila, that
was the whole idea. That's why we risked our
necks . . . "

"Courtney has some wild idea. He shut me up, said
we would talk later. We are coming back tomorrow."

"We?"

"Courtney and I. He wants to talk with us. He
flew back to Washington this afternoon, but will come
back to New York in the morning and pick me up."

"Pick you up?"

"Yes, he flies his own plane. I guess I never mentioned that."

"That's right. You never did."

"We'll be landing at Lancaster. It's a small plane.
The field there is big enough. I'll let you know when."

"I'll pick you up."

"Probably sometime before noon. I'll let you
know."

EIGHTEEN

Courtney McCallahan was a somewhat younger and bigger man than I had expected. It's strange how one will picture someone mentally before ever meeting him. I suppose it was his name that did it; I had pictured McCallahan as a little gnome of a man, suave, round faced, snow white hair, with an unhurried grace. In actuality, he was a big man and no longer young, but younger than I had pictured him. His hair was turning and had reached the iron gray stage; his face was cragged, like a block of rough wood that someone had chopped into a face with a dull hatchet. His hands were like hams. Instinctively, I liked him.

"How is the fence coming along?" he asked.

"It's going up," I told him. "We'll build right through the weekend. No Saturday or Sunday off."

"Double-time, I suppose."

"I don't know about that," I said. "I left that up to Ben."

"This Ben is a good man?"

"He's been my friend," I said, "for the greater part of my life."

"If you'll allow me," he said, "I thought you and Ben were magnificent in that tyrannosaur bit. Took a lot of guts to stand up to those creatures. I'm afraid I might have flunked it."

"We had big guns," I said, "and, besides, there was no place to run."

We got into the car, with Rila next to me. She put both hands on my arm and squeezed hard.

"The same to you," I said.

"I forgot to tell you about the films," she said. "And you forgot to ask. They're safe. In the vault of a New York bank."

"As soon as this matter becomes public," said Courtney, "we'll have distributors bidding for them, and bidding high."

"I'm not sure," I said, "that we'll want to sell them."

"We'll sell anything," said Rila, "if the price is right."

I backed out of the parking space. There were only a few other cars. Courtney's plane and another were the only ones on the strip. Over in the ramshackle hangar, on the other side of the field, I knew, were a few others, locally owned.

A mile or two down the road, at the edge of town, we came to a small shopping center—a supermarket, a hardware store, a small department store, a branch bank, a men's clothing store, and a few other shops.

"Let's pull in here and park," said Courtney. "Away from other cars."

"Sure, if you want to," I said, "but why?"

"Please humor me," he said.

I pulled in and found a place to park at the near edge of the parking area. There were no other cars nearby. I shut off the motor and sat back in the seat.

"This is a conspiracy," said Courtney. "I shudder at the possibility of eavesdropping."

"So go ahead," I said. I looked at Rila and saw that she was as puzzled as I was.

Courtney squirmed into a comfortable position. "I've spent a lot of sleepless nights," he said, "considering your position, and in many respects it seems to me you could be vulnerable. Oh, so far as I can determine, this project of yours is entirely legal. Unique, of course, but legal. But the thing that worries me is that Internal Revenue can clobber you but good. If everything goes as well as I expect it will, you'll be making a lot of money, and when someone makes a lot of money, it's always been my position that as much of it be kept as is possible within the framework of the law."

"Courtney," said Rila, "I don't quite understand . . ."

"Do you have any idea the bite IRS can take," he asked, "out of a million dollars?"

"I have a rough idea," I said, "but only a rough idea."

"The trouble is," he said, "that you won't have the opportunity of the business pattern, such as is found in large corporations, to set up the sort of tax shelters and loop holes that will afford some protection. We could set you up as a corporation, of course, but it would take a lot of time and would have a number of built-in disadvantages. There is one possibility, however. It looks good to me and I want to see what you think about it. If you did not conduct your business in the United States there'd be no problem. Income tax does not apply to businesses outside the country."

"But we have to stay at Willow Bend," said Rila. "That's where our business is."

"Not so fast," said Courtney. "Let's give it a little thought. Let us say you used your time-travel capability to provide you a residence a thousand years into the past, or a million years, or wherever was best to go. I suppose that any time prior to the emergence of the United States would do, but it might be better to pick a time prior to any European knowledge of North America. If you could find some desert island, of course, unclaimed by any world power, that would do as well, but I don't know where one is or even if one exists. If it does, you'd still be a long ways from Willow Bend, but if you resided in time, as I suggest, you'd be just a short walk from the farm in Willow Bend."

"I don't know," I said. "We'd still be living on land that, in time, would be a part of the nation."

"Yes, I know," said Courtney, "and IRS might try to make something of that. They might bring suit, but if they do, I think we could prove that national sovereignty does not extend through time."

"But the farm in Willow Bend is really where we'd conduct our business," Rila said.

"Not if you lived someplace else. We'd be very sure you conducted no business in Willow Bend. Nor provided any services there. You could get Hiram and this Catface thing to move into time with you?"

"I don't know," I said.

"But Willow Bend would still be there," said Rila.

"Only as your American agency," said Courtney. "You'd have to have someone to serve as your agent. I had your friend Ben in mind. The time road or tunnel or whatever you want to call it would simply be an entry port to your place of residence, where you'd conduct your business and provide your services. The time roads used to supply your services would be set up from your place of residence. You'd pay your agent a commission—perhaps one percent of all the business that he sent you. That seems the safest way. In effect, he'd then be the agent for a foreign firm. I think it might be best, as well, to sell the farm to him. That way, IRS couldn't seize it as your property for nonpayment of taxes. Ben would be paying his taxes, of course, and that way, they'd not be able to grab the farm, which is your port of entry. Also, it would lend weight to his being in business for himself."

"But they still might try to seize it," I said.

"Certainly, they might try. Faced with the facts, I don't think they would. Especially if Ben paid a fair price for it before you went into the time business. That's the crux of the matter. To have even a prayer of escaping the IRS, you can't do any business in the United States. That's why I refused yesterday to talk business with Safari. If they want to talk business, they have to come to your place of residence."

"But I talked to Safari originally," said Rila, "and we showed them the film."

"That fact could make matters a little sticky," said Courtney, "but I think I can handle that. I think I could demonstrate to the satisfaction of the courts that no business actually was done. As to what happened yesterday, I could show that we refused to negotiate."

"But there'll be contracts," said Rila.

"Drawn and executed in New York or in other cities where the party of the second part is headquartered, between an American firm and a non-American company. That is customary. It would stand in law. No trouble there. But you'd have to have an address. Where do you think you might like to set up residence?"

"In one of the more recent interglacial periods," I said. "Probably the Sangamon. The climate would be good, the environment more homelike."

"Dangerous?"

"Mastodons," I said. "Sabertooths. Some bears. Dire wolves. But we could manage. They probably sound worse than they are."

"We could call our new home Mastodonia," said Rila.

"Perfect," Courtney said. "That name carries with it the implications of another time and place."

"But would we have to stay there all the time?" asked Rila. "I don't think I would like that."

"Not all the time," said Courtney, "but enough of the time so you could honestly call it home. You could visit Willow Bend frequently, travel otherwise as you wished. But all your business would have to be conducted from Mastodonia. I had even toyed with the idea that you could proclaim yourself a nation and apply to the State Department, and to other countries, of course, for recognition. But with only two or three residents, that might be hard to do. I'm not sure it would be of any advantage, either. If doing so eventually became advisable, could you get some of your Willow Bend neighbors to move there?"

"Maybe," I said. "I'm not sure."

"There'd be advantages. Free land for the taking. No taxes. Lots of elbow room. Good hunting and fishing."

"I still don't know," I said.

"Well, we can talk about that later on."

"How about money and banking?" asked Rila. "How do we handle all that money you say we're going to get? Certainly not in American banks, where the IRS can get their hands on it."

"That's easy," said Courtney. "Open an account in Switzerland. Probably Zurich. Your clients can make payment to your Swiss account. They could, of course, pay you some of it in cash so you'd have funds to pay Ben his commissions and to take care of other expenses. But if you are going to do that, you should open an account right away so your record will seem a little cleaner. If you opened an account before you start transacting any time-travel business, we'd be able to pull the rug out from under anyone who tried to charge concealment of funds. The initial payment into the account should be fairly substantial so that no one can say it was only a token deposit."

"I sold my share of the import-export business to my partner in New York the other day," said Rila. "His first payment, to be made in a day or two, is a hundred thousand. But we wouldn't have to wait for it. I could assign the first check to Ben's bank and then he could loan us the hundred thousand. We're into him for quite an amount right now, but I think he'd do it."

"Fine," said Courtney. "A hundred thousand would be just fine. Before you move into Mastodonia, but giving your address for the account as Mastodonia. I take it you approve of my suggestions."

"It seems just a little devious to me," I said.

"Of course, the whole thing is devious. But, by and large, it's legal. We could be challenged, of course, and probably will be, but we have solid grounds for argument."

"Half of the business world is devious," said Rila.

"Even if we should go to court and lose on some points," said Courtney, "you'd be no worse off than you are now and probably better. We'd have enough room to strike deals, if necessary. But I'd not go into it with any idea of a deal. I'd go to court to win. We've only talked about the court matter. A non-American resident would have other advantages. No governmental regulations or interference, no reports to be filled out, no statements to be filed."

"All things considered I think what you suggest is the right thing to do," Rila said. "To tell you the truth, I've been worried about the tax situation."

"You know about such things," I said. "I don't."

"So, almost immediately," said Courtney, "you'll move into Mastodonia and set up residence. I would think, perhaps, that a mobile home . . . "

"I'll take care of that," said Rila, "while Asa is off to Zurich." She said to me, "I seem to remember you can speak French."

"Some," I said. "Enough to get by fairly well. But you should be the one . . ."

"I don't speak French," she said. "Only Spanish and a little German—a very little German. That's why you are going to Zurich. I'll stay here and see that matters are taken care of from this end."

"You seem to have everything in hand," Courtney said. "So I'll leave the rest up to you. Phone me on any little question. Don't wait for the big one; phone on the little ones as well. I suppose you'll want to make that Zurich account a joint one. If that's the case, Rila, be sure Asa has a notarized copy of your signature before he leaves. And don't make Ben your agent until you're settled in Mastodonia."

"One thing," I said. "If we exasperate the government sufficiently, could they declare us *personae non gratae,* prevent us from moving back and forth between Mastodonia and Willow Bend, perhaps close the time road into Mastodonia?"

Courtney said, "I suppose they could try, but we'd give them a hell of a fight. Take the matter to the United Nations if we had to. I don't think they'll try."

"I guess that's it," I said. "The decision's been made. Strange we could settle such a deal in so short a time."

"The plan makes sense," said Rila. "You don't argue with good, sound reasoning."

"If that's the case," said Courtney, "you can take me back to the airstrip."

"You mean you're not even coming out to the farm?" asked Rila. "I thought you wanted to meet Ben."

"Some other time," he said. "I've told you all I wanted to, where no one else could hear. These are going to be busy days and there's no time to waste."

He rubbed his hands together delightedly. "This is going to be more damn fun," he said, "than I have had in years."

NINETEEN

On the return flight from Zurich, we had a layover in London. I bought a paper and there it was—a great screaming headline: MYSTERY AMERICANS TRAVEL IN TIME!

I bought other papers. The sober *Times* treated the story sedately, all the others thundered in bold, black type.

A lot of the facts were jumbled, but the stories essentially were correct. Rila and I were represented as a mystery pair. She was not to be located; rumor had it that she was living in a place called Mastodonia. No one knew exactly where Mastodonia might be, but some speculation came close to the truth. The popular speculation was that I had gone abroad, although no one knew exactly where. But that did not stop the newsmen from making what seemed to me rather fantastic guesses. Ben had been interviewed. He had acknowledged he was our American agent, but gave them little else. Herbert Livingston, Ben's public relations officer, was quoted as saying, rather curtly, that the announcement was premature and that he would have nothing further to say until a more appropriate time. I wondered, as I read the story, just how in hell Herb suddenly had become our PR man. The story was based on what was described as an authoritative source without any attempt to pinpoint the source. But Safari, Inc., which somehow had been tied into the story, admitted that a film did exist of a dinosaur hunt staged in an era some seventy million years in the past. One movie company executive was even quoted as being at least marginally interested. The Safari people openly admitted their interest. Courtney was not mentioned and from this omission, I was fairly certain where the leak to the press had originated.

Four noted physicists, one of them a Nobelist, had been interviewed, each of them saying with varying degrees of smugness that time travel was impossible. Each of the stories assumed that a time machine was involved—which was understandable since only five people, perhaps six, now that Herb was involved, knew that one was not. There was considerable agonizing among the so-called science writers of the various newspapers as to what kind of form the machine would take and what principles would be involved. Only one of the stories I read failed to mention H. G. Wells.

My first sight of the first paper with its blaring headline left me all tensed up, but before too long, having read some of the other stories, I had become mush inside. As long as only a few people had known about our time-travel capability, it had been possible for me to accept the idea as a sort of silly, almost boyish, secret. But the situation was different when our secret was shared by the entire world. I found myself looking around and behind me to see if anyone might recognize me, but that was rather foolish since none of the London papers had pictures of either Rila or me. But it would not take long, I knew, until our pictures would be splashed across the tabloids. In those early stories, there was no identification of who either of us might be, but before the day was over, the newsmen would run down exactly who we were and would then find photos of us.

I found myself wild with the wish to be in Willow Bend again, where I felt I would be relatively safe from the outside world. I regarded with something close to terror the prospect of those hours of travel still ahead. Foolishly, I suppose, I found a shop in the airport where I could buy a pair of dark glasses. I felt silly wearing them, for I never had before, even in the field. But they were something to hide behind, at least symbolically, and I put them on.

At first, I was going to leave the papers I had bought, having no wish even marginally to advertise the fact

I might have some interest in the story. Then thinking of the kick Rila and Ben would get out of the stories, I bundled all the papers together and carried them underneath an arm.

My seat partner, a stuffy, middle-aged American I pegged as being a banker—although perhaps he was not—had a paper stuck in his jacket pocket, but seemed to have no wish to talk with me, for which I was extremely thankful. But after the steward brought us our evening meal, he loosened up and paid me the courtesy of acknowledging my presence.

"You read this rot," he asked, "about someone traveling in time?"

"I noticed it," I said.

"You know, that can't be done," he said. "I wonder how the papers fell for stuff like that. Newspapermen, you know, aren't stupid people. They should have known better."

"Sensationalism," I said. "They'll do anything to sell their papers."

He didn't answer me and I thought the conversation was at an end, but a few minutes later he said, not as if he were talking to me exactly, but more as if he were addressing the world in general: "Dangerous business, you know. Messing around in time could cause a lot of trouble. It could change history, even, and we can't be doing that. Hard enough as it is without someone messing everything up."

The rest of the way he said nothing further. He turned out to be a good seat partner.

I settled down to some steady worrying, which did me no good at all, but I couldn't help myself. I wondered if the fence was up, if the floodlights were installed and working, if we had plenty of guards to patrol the fence. Courtney McCallahan, if he, in fact, had been the one who had tipped off the reporters, would certainly have checked to see that everything was ready at Willow Bend before giving out the story.

The hours spun out and finally I fell asleep and did not wake until we were coming down at Kennedy.

I half expected, illogically, of course, that I might find newspapermen waiting for me at Kennedy, but apparently no one had any idea I'd be on the plane. I grabbed a New York *Times* as fast as I could and there were our pictures, Rila's and mine, on the front page. Both were photos that had been taken some years ago, but I suppose we could have been recognized by them.

I debated whether I should phone Rila or Ben or maybe even Courtney in Washington, then decided not to. If there were no newsmen waiting in New York, there'd probably be none at Minneapolis. Rila and Ben knew what plane I would be on and one of them would be at the airport waiting for me.

Neither one of them was. Waiting for me instead was Elrod Anderson, manager of Willow Bend's one supermarket. I would have passed right by him, for I didn't know him that well, but he grabbed me by the arm and told me who he was. Then I recognized him.

"Ben couldn't get away and neither could Rila," he said. "There are newspapermen hip deep in Willow Bend and if either Ben or Rila had driven off, they would have followed them. Ben phoned me and asked me to pick you up. He said this way you may have a chance of sneaking in without anyone knowing who you are. I brought along some clothes you can change into and some false whiskers."

"I don't know if I'll go for the whiskers," I said.

"I thought maybe you wouldn't," said Elrod, "but I brought them anyhow. They're real good. Look like the real thing. There is a big crowd gathering and more coming all the time. I don't know what they expect to see. Some of them are already disappointed because there really isn't much to see. A few of them came in campers, as if they were planning to stay for a while. Ben is renting out space for the campers on that farm he bought just east of you, and he has a big parking lot there, too, for the other cars. I don't mean Ben is doing the work himself. He is hiring people to do it. Old Limpy Jones is in charge of the parking lot and Limpy hasn't worked for almost thirty years. Best man at ducking a job I ever saw. But Limpy is working now. Likes all the excitement, he says. Probably raking something off the top of the money he takes in. But he won't get away with that. Ben will catch him, sure as shooting. Ben is about the sharpest operator I have ever seen."

"I suppose the fence is finished," I said.

"Yup," said Elrod, "a couple of days ago. And the building is up, too. It has a big sign across the front that says *Ben Page, Agent for Time Associates*. What is that all about? I thought it was you that figured out how to go skating around in time. How come Ben has such a big hand in it?"

"Ben is our agent," I said. "For the United States, maybe even North America."

"But you are there, too. Or, at least, in a little while you will be. And this woman of yours, Rila, she is there. Why ain't you two handling it?"

"Fact is we don't live there any more," I said.

"The hell you don't. Where do you live?"

"In Mastodonia."

"By God," he said, "I did hear something about that. Where at is this Mastodonia?"

"It's back in time. About one hundred fifty thousand years back in time. Mastodons live there. That's how come the name."

"Is it a nice place?"

"It should be," I said. "I've never seen it."

"You're living there. How come you've never seen it?"

"Rila and Hiram set it up and moved there after I left for Europe."

"What has Hiram got to do with all this?" Elrod asked. "He's a trifling sort of fellow and never seemed too bright."

"He has an awful lot to do with it," I said.

The morning sun was shining brightly out in the parking lot. It was a beautiful day. Not a cloud in sight.

Elrod settled behind the wheel and backed out of his space.

"Ben told me to drop you off at the parking lot at home," he said. "Said for you to get into the crowd of tourists and wander up to the gate. The sheriff has some deputies guarding it and sort of keeping order.

Tell them who you are. They'll be expecting you and will let you in. I have an old pair of work pants and a denim jacket and an old felt hat. You can put them on before you get there. If you don't waste any time, no one will recognize you. They'll think you're just another country boy come to see what is going on. I think you should wear them whiskers, too."

Five miles or so out of town, we pulled into a township road and parked while I got into the clothes. But I didn't put on the whiskers. I couldn't bring myself to do so.

TWENTY

Rila and Ben were waiting for me, with Herb Livingston hovering in the background. In the front room of the new office building, which smelled of fresh sawdust, half a dozen people sat at desks, not doing much of anything.

Rila rushed forward and I caught her in my arms and held her tight. I'd never been so glad to see anyone. What I had seen outside had been frightening—parked cars lining the road, others ranked in Ben's parking lot, hot dog, hamburger and souvenir stands, men selling balloons. And people everywhere, mostly standing in groups and gawking, but with a strange sense of excitement. The whole thing was a cross between a county fair and a carnival.

"I worried about you," said Rila. "And look at the get-up you have on. Where are your other clothes?"

"In Elrod's car," I said. "He supplied these."

Ben shook hands gravely. "There've been changes since you left," he said.

Herb came up to shake hands. "How's the PR business?" I asked. "I read about you in the London papers."

"Well, hell," said Ben, "we needed someone real fast to handle those news jockeys out there when they came swarming in and Herb seemed to be the man. He's getting along all right."

"They're yelling for a press conference," said Herb, "but I haven't had the guts to go out and face them. We didn't want to do anything until you got back. I been handing out little press releases. Not really telling them anything, but giving them some small things for

130

new stories. What shall I tell them about you being back?"

"Tell them," said Ben, "that he returned and immediately left for Mastodonia. That's something we should always emphasize. He and Rila aren't here; they live in Mastodonia."

"Just wait until you see Mastodonia," said Rila. "It's beautiful. So wild and beautiful. We drove in a mobile home the day before yesterday and are all settled in there. We have a couple of four-wheel drives, as well."

"Hiram?" I asked.

"Hiram and Bowser are there."

"And Catface?"

"Catface moved along with them. There's a cluster of wild crab-apple trees just down the ridge and he's taken up residence in them. Hiram says he likes the place. Says he wonders why he stuck around here so long and never went time-traveling on his own."

"Let's get back into my office," said Ben. "I got some comfortable chairs there and a bottle to break open. We ought to have a drink on this."

We settled down in the chairs, which were comfortable, and Ben poured the drinks.

"You have a good trip?" Herb asked me.

"I guess it was," I said. "My French turned out to be a little rusty, but I managed. I had no trouble in Zurich. I'm not used to such things, but everything went all right."

"Those Swiss," said Ben, "will always take your money."

"What I've been wanting to ask," I said, "is who tipped off the press. The news break came a whole lot sooner than I had thought it would."

"Courtney did," said Rila. "Really not Courtney himself, but someone he knows who is an expert at leaking news. Really, it was Safari. They put pressure on Courtney. They are anxious to find what the prospects are in the dinosaur-hunting business. They want to know before they talk with us. It makes sense that sportsmen would jump at a chance to bag a dinosaur, but Safari wants to be dead certain sure. They want to get some prospective clients lined up before they start negotiating for our license."

"It's too early yet to know, I suppose."

"We haven't heard from Courtney in a day or two. They'll be in touch with him."

"There has been a feeler or two here already," said Ben. "A man was in this morning to see if we could put him into Inca territory before the conquistadors arrived. He wanted to study the ancient Incan culture, he said, but it quickly became apparent that what he was interested in was Incan treasure. I told him to get lost. A mining engineer came in with the idea that maybe we'd be willing to send him back to the Black Hills of South Dakota prior to the gold strike there. He was quite above board about his intentions. He wanted to skim the cream of the gold locations. Said he had no money, but he'd go shares with us. I liked the man and put him on hold. Said all I could do was pass on the word to you. Then there was a committee from some church organization. They wanted to talk about going back to the days of Jesus. I couldn't make out what they really wanted. They were inclined to be a bit close-mouthed. Maybe later on, you should talk with them."

I shook my head. "I don't know about that. That is the kind of sticky business I had hoped we could avoid. When anyone travels into any sort of historical situation, a lot of care must be taken or you'll wind up with a mess on your hands."

"But you must have known," said Herb, "that the problem would come up. Everyone, if they could afford it, would want to go back to see the Crucifixion."

"But that's the point," said Rila. "Almost no one could afford to at the rates we'll ask. Tourism should be discouraged even if people are willing to pay. Tourists would be trouble."

"I think," said Ben, "we should take business as it comes. Weed out the phonies, like our Inca character, but take a hard look at all legitimate proposals."

We talked then, idly, easily about other matters, paying attention to our drinks. Ben's motel was up and a few of the units were ready for occupancy. The building was larger than he originally had intended and he was considering constructing a second one. The parking lot was making money. A lot of people in the village were offering rooms for rent. We were having trouble getting enough guards to patrol the fence and guard the gate; for the moment, the sheriff had assigned deputies to the gate until we could find men to replace them. Herb had turned the operation of his paper over to his former assistant and was planning to print daily free advertising sheets of four to six pages, to start with, to be handed out to the flood of visitors who were anticipated, the first surge of them already in evidence. Some village people were upset by the public influx, which they thought would change the easy life the town had known before, but various church organizations, particularly the women's groups, were planning chicken suppers, strawberry ice cream festivals and other fund-raising schemes.

We finished the drinks and Rila said to me, "And, now, Mastodonia. I'm dying to show it to you."

TWENTY-ONE

It was spring in Mastodonia and everything was beautiful. The mobile home stood on top of a little ridge no more than a half-mile or so from where the time road brought us through. Just down the slope from the home, a grove of wild crab-apple trees was ablaze with pink blossoms, and the long valley that lay below the ridge was dotted with clumps and groves of crab apples and other flowering trees. The open places were a sea of spring flowers, and the entire area was swarming with songbirds.

Two four-wheel drives were parked to one side of the mobile home. From the front entrance, an awning extended outward, and just beyond the awning was a large lawn table, a gaily striped umbrella sprouting from the center of it.

Overall, our new home had a distinctly festive look.

"We bought a big one," said Rila. "Sleeps six, has a nice living area and the kitchen has everything you'd want."

"You like it?" I asked.

"Like it? Asa, can't you see? It's the kind of hideaway that everyone dreams about—the cabin by the lake, the mountain hunting lodge. Except that this is even better. You can practically feel the freedom. There's no one here. You understand? Absolutely no one here. The first men to reach North America won't cross from Asia for a thousand centuries. There are people in the world, of course, but not on this continent. Here you are as alone as anyone can manage."

"You done any exploring?"

"No, not by myself. I think I'd be afraid alone. I was waiting for you. And how about you? Don't you like it here?"

"Yes, of course," I said. That was the truth; I did like Mastodonia. But the concept of aloneness, of personal independence, I knew, was something to which one would have to become accustomed. You'd have to let it grow upon you.

Ahead of us, someone shouted and it took a moment to locate the place where the shout had come from. Then I saw them, the two of them, Hiram and Bowser, rounding the slope just above the grove of blooming crab-apple trees. They were running, Hiram with an awkward, loping gallop, Bowser bouncing joyously, every now and then letting out a welcoming bark as he bounced along.

Forgetting any dignity—and in this world there was no need for dignity—we ran to meet them. Bowser, running ahead, leaped up to lick my face, gamboling around in doggish raptures. Hiram came up panting.

"We've been watching for you, Mr. Steele," he said, gasping for breath. "We just took a little walk and missed you. We went down the hill to see one of the elephants."

"Elephants? You mean mastodons."

"I guess that's right," Hiram said. "I guess that's the name for them creatures. I tried to remember the name, but I forgot. But anyhow, we saw a real nice mastodon. It let us get up real close. I think it likes us."

"Look, Hiram," I said, "you don't go up real close to a mastodon. It's probably peaceful enough, but if you get too close to it, you can never know what it might do. That goes for big pussycats, as well—especially those that have long teeth sticking out of their mouths."

"But this mastodon is nice, Mr. Steele. It moves so slow and it looks so sad. We call it Stiffy because it moves so slow. It just shuffles along."

"For Christ's sake," I said, "an old beat-up bull that has been run out of the herd is nothing to fool around with. It probably has a nasty temper."

"That's right, Hiram," Rila agreed. "You steer clear of that animal. Or any animal you find here. Don't go making friends with them."

"Not even with a woodchuck, Miss Rila?"

"Well, I guess a woodchuck would be safe enough," she said.

The four of us went up to the mobile home.

"I have a room all my own," Hiram said to me. "Miss Rila said it is my room and no one else's. She said Bowser could sleep in it with me."

"Come on in," said Rila, "and see what we have here. Then you can go out in the yard . . ."

"The yard?"

"The place with the lawn table; I call that the yard. Once you look around inside, go out in the yard and look around. I'll make lunch. Will sandwiches be all right?"

"They'll be fine."

"We'll eat outside," said Rila. "I just want to sit and look at this country. I can't seem to get enough of it."

I looked through our new home. It was the first time I'd ever been inside one of them, although I had known a number of people who had lived in them and seemed well satisfied. I particularly liked the living area—seemingly plenty of space, comfortable furniture, large windows, thick carpeting on the floor, a bookcase filled with books Rila had taken from my small library, a gun rack beside the door. The whole thing was a lot more luxurious, I had to admit, than the house back on the farm.

Going outside, I walked down the ridge, with Hiram striding along beside me and Bowser bouncing ahead.

The ridge was not particularly high, but high enough to give a good view of the surrounding countryside. There below us to the right flowed the stream, the small river which had flowed in the Cretaceous and still flowed in the twentieth century through Willow Bend. Through millions of years, the land had changed but little. It seemed to me that the ridge was somewhat higher than it had been in the Cretaceous, perhaps higher than it would be in the twentieth century, but I could not be certain.

The river valley was fairly open, broken only by the scattered clumps of flowering shrubs and smaller trees, but the ridges other than the one we stood on were heavily timbered. I kept an eye out for game herds, but there seemed to be none. Except for a couple of large birds, probably eagles, flying high in the sky, there was no other sign of life.

"There he is," Hiram called, excited. "There is Stiffy. Do you see him, Mr. Steele?"

I looked in the direction of Hiram's pointing finger and made out the mastodon in the valley just below the ridge. He was standing at the edge of a clump of small trees, stripping leaves off them with his trunk and stuffing them into his mouth. Even from the distance at which we stood, he had a faintly moth-eaten appearance. He seemed to be alone; at least no other mastodons were in sight.

When Rila called to us, we went back down the ridge. Plates piled high with sandwiches and cakes were set on the lawn table. There were dishes of pickles and a jar of olives and a large carafe of coffee. For Bowser there was a large plate of roast, cut up in small pieces that would be easy for him to chew.

"I put down the umbrella," said Rila, "so the sun can shine on us. The sun seems so nice here."

I looked at my watch. It said five o'clock, but the sun said noon. Rila laughed at me. "Just forget the watch," she said. "There are no watches here. I left mine on the bedside table the first day that I was here. By now, it's probably run down."

I nodded, pleased with the idea. It was good enough for me. There were not many places where a man could cut free of the tyranny of timepieces.

We ate in the sunshine, unhurriedly, and lazed away the afternoon watching the shadow from the western hills creep across the river and the valley.

I nodded at the river. "There should be good fishing there."

"Tomorrow," Rila said. "Tomorrow we'll go fishing. Take one of the cars and go exploring. There is so much to see."

Late in the afternoon, we heard far-off trumpeting that could have been mastodons. In the middle of the night, I was wakened by a sound. Lying tensed in bed, I waited for it to come again, a vicious but muted squalling from a northern ridge. A cat, no doubt of that. A sabertooth, perhaps, or some other cat. I told myself that I was hung up on sabertooths, fascinated with them, curious about them. I had to get the idea of them out of my head; there must be cats of many other kinds in this world of the Sangamon. The crying in and of itself was a chilling sound, but I felt little actual fear of it. I was safe. Beside me Rila slept, undisturbed by the squalling from the north.

After breakfast, we packed a lunch, put two 7 mm. rifles and some fishing gear in the car and set out to explore, Rila and I in the front seat, Hiram and Bowser in the back. Several miles down the valley, we came upon and circled a herd of about a dozen mastodon. They lifted their heads to look at us, flapping their ears, seeking our scent with upraised trunks, but made no move toward us. At noon, we parked beside the river and I went fishing for not more than five minutes, coming back with three good-sized trout, which we cooked over a driftwood fire. While we ate, a half-dozen wolves trotted out on a bald bluff that rose across the river and watched us. They seemed to me larger than the usual wolf and I wondered if they might be dire wolves. We flushed deer, which went bounding off ahead of us. We sighted a tawny cat on a rocky hillside, but it was cougarlike and was no sabertooth.

We returned home well before sundown, tired out and delighted. It was the best vacation that I had ever had.

Over the next two days we made other trips, setting off in different directions. We saw a number of mastodons, one small herd of giant bison, much larger than the buffalo of the historic western plains, with great spreading horns. We found a marsh where ducks and geese rose in clouds at our approach, and a bit beyond the marsh came upon our greatest discovery, a colony of beavers that were as large as bears. They were working on a dam that had created the marsh that was home for the ducks and geese. We watched them from afar, in fascination.

"One beaver, one fur coat," Rila observed.

I lost all track of time. I forgot everything. I envisioned endless days of wondrous exploring, gorgeous loafing stretching out ahead of us.

But the idyll came to an end when we returned on the third day. Ben was waiting for us, sitting at the lawn table. He had glasses and a bottle waiting for us.

"Here, drink up," he said. "We're going into business. Courtney is flying in the Safari bunch tomorrow. They're ready to talk. Courtney says they're eager. Pretending not to be, but eager."

TWENTY-TWO

I woke the following morning feeling vaguely apprehensive, not knowing why I should feel that way. It was just one of those feelings that you sometimes get, without any reason. So I crawled out of bed, careful not to wake Rila. But I failed to accomplish that, for as I was sneaking out the door, she asked, "What's the matter, Asa?"

"Probably nothing at all," I said. "Just going out to have a look."

"Not in your pajamas," she said. "Get back here and put on some clothes. The Safari people are coming today and they may arrive early. Their clocks are running some five hours earlier than ours."

So I got dressed, with the horrible feeling that I was wasting time. Then I went out as quickly as I could without seeming to be in too much of a hurry. But once I had opened the door and had a look, I ducked back in again and grabbed one of the 7 mm. rifles from the rack beside the door. Just down the ridge, not more than five hundred feet away, stood this old mastodon that Hiram had named Stiffy. There was no mistaking him, for he had that moth-eaten look about him, more apparent now than the other day, when he'd been much farther off.

He was standing in a sort of woebegone manner, with his trunk hanging listlessly between his two great tusks, and in spite of the fact that he stood nine feet tall or so, he was not particularly prepossessing. Standing in front of him, not more than fifty feet separating them, stood Hiram. Standing beside Hiram, wagging his tail with all the good nature in the world, was Bowser. Hiram was talking to this great beast, who was waggling in reply the one ear that I could see—not the great flapping ear one would find in an African elephant, but still an ear that had some size to it.

I stood petrified, grasping the rifle in my hands. I didn't dare to yell at Hiram nor to call Bowser back. All I could do was stand and hold the rifle ready. In the back of my mind, I was remembering that many years in the future, in the nineteenth century, old Karamojo Bell had killed hundreds of African elephants for their ivory with a gun no bigger than the one I had in hand. Even so, I hoped I wouldn't have to try it, for most of Karamojo's shots had been to the brain, and I was not absolutely sure where to aim to hit the brain.

Stiffy was just standing there and then he made a move. I thought he was going to come at Hiram and I brought the rifle up. But he really wasn't going anywhere; he didn't move forward at all. He just lifted up first one foot, then another, in a ragged sort of sequence; then he put them down again, as if they hurt and he was trying, one after the other, to get his weight off them. This business of lifting up his feet and then putting them down again rather tenderly imparted a slight rocking motion to his body, and it was the silliest thing I ever saw—this stupid elephant standing in front of Hiram and rocking gently back and forth.

I took a quick step forward, then thought better of it before I took a second step. So far, everything seemed to be all right, although perhaps a trifle touchy, and I didn't want to do anything that would change it.

Out in front of me, Hiram took a short step forward and then another. I wanted to yell at him, but held it back somehow, for I knew I had better not. If anything happened, I had the rifle and I could put three or four slugs into old Stiffy so fast you couldn't count them. I kept hoping, though, that I wouldn't have to. Hiram was still inching forward, step by careful step, but Bowser didn't move. I swear to Christ that Bowser had more sense than Hiram had. Once this thing was over, I told myself, I was going to kick hell right out of Hiram. I had told him and told him to leave that mastodon alone, and here he had sneaked out in the morning before I was out of bed and was cuddling up to it. But that, I knew, was the way that Hiram was. Back home, he had talked with woodchucks and robins, and had a grizzly bear come along, he would have talked with it. Take him back to the Cretaceous and he'd get chummy with the dinosaurs.

By now, Hiram was a lot closer and was holding out his hand to the beast, which had quit its rocking. Bowser stayed where he was, but no longer wagged his tail. Apparently, he was as worried about all this as I was. I held my breath and watched, wondering if, maybe, after all, I should have yelled at Hiram to get back. But it was too late. If the mastodon made a single lunge, that would be the end of Hiram.

The mastodon put out its trunk, sort of leaning forward on its toes, and Hiram stopped dead still. The mastodon sniffed at Hiram, running the tip of its trunk up and down his body, from his head down to his feet. It made a gentle snuffling sound as it smelled him. Then Hiram put out his hand and stroked the inquisitive trunk, rubbing back and forth and making scratching motions. That great silly beast made a sort of moaning sound as if it liked the scratching, so Hiram took another step and then another one until he was standing underneath Stiffy's head, which bent forward. Hiram ran his hands up and down the trunk and reached one hand high to scratch underneath the ridiculously small lower lip of his mighty friend. Stiffy groaned with pleasure. That goddamn mastodon was as crazy as Hiram could ever hope to be.

I heaved a sigh of relief, hoping that it was not premature. It didn't seem to be. Stiffy kept on standing there and Hiram kept on scratching him. Bowser, with some disgust, turned around and trotted back to sit beside me.

"Hiram," I said, as quietly as I could. "Hiram, listen to me."

"You don't need to worry, Mr. Steele," said Hiram. "Stiffy is my friend."

I'd heard that ever since I'd returned to Willow

Bend and renewed my acquaintance with Hiram. Everything was Hiram's friend; he had no enemies.

"You better be sure of that," I said. "He's a wild animal and he is awful big."

"He's talking to me," said Hiram. "We talk with each other. I know that we are friends."

"Then tell him to get out of here. Tell him to keep his distance, to stay off this ridge. First thing you know, he'll be butting at our home and tipping it over. Tell him that if that ever happens, I'll take a two-by-four to him."

"I'll take him down to the valley," said Hiram, "and tell him that he has to stay there. I'll tell him that I'll come and visit him."

"You do that," I said, "and then get back here as fast as you can. There'll be things for you to do."

He put out his hands and pushed on Stiffy's shoulder and Stiffy set himself in motion, shuffling around, taking mincing steps, heading down the slope, Hiram walking beside him.

"Asa," Rila called from the door, "what is going on?"

"Stiffy wandered up here," I said, "and Hiram's taking him back where he belongs."

"But Stiffy is a mastodon."

"Yeah, I know," I said. "He's also Hiram's friend."

"You better get in here and shave," she said. "And, for goodness sakes, comb your hair. We have company."

I looked down the ridge. Five figures were walking in line, one behind the other. Ben was leading. He wore boots, khaki pants, and a hunting coat, and carried a rifle. The others were dressed in business suits and either were carrying briefcases or had portfolios tucked beneath their arms. One of them was Courtney. The other three, I figured, must be the Safari people. It struck me as hilarious—these staid business types carrying their badges of office through this howling wilderness.

"Asa," said Rila sharply.

"It's too late," I said. "They'll be on us in a moment. This is the new frontier. They'll have to take me as I am."

I ran a palm across my chin and the whiskers rasped. I had a fairly heavy and untidy growth.

Ben came up to us and said good morning. The others ranged themselves in line expectantly. Courtney stepped forward and said, "Rila, you know these gentlemen."

"Yes, of course," said Rila. "But none of you have met my partner, Asa Steele. You'll pardon his appearance. There was some mastodon trouble this morning and . . ."

The military-looking old gentleman at the end of the line said, "You'll excuse me, madam, but am I seeing right? It appears to me there's a man and mastodon going down the ridge together. The man has hold of the mastodon's trunk, as if he were leading it."

"That's only Hiram," Rila said. "He has a way with animals. He claims to talk with them."

"So Hiram's already at it," said Ben. "It didn't take him long."

"He's had a few days here," I said. "That is all he needs."

"Never saw anything like it," said the old military gent. "Can't believe my eyes. Quite impossible."

"Asa," said Rila, "our disbelieving friend is Major Hennessey. Major, my partner, Asa Steele."

"Pleased, I'm sure," said Hennessey. "I must say, you have quite a setup here."

"We like it," I said. "Later on, we'll take you on a tour, if you have the time."

"Unbelievable," said Hennessey. "Absolutely unbelievable."

"Mr. Stuart," said Rila. "Mr. Stuart is chief counsel of Safari, Inc., and Mr. Boyle. If I remember correctly, Mr. Boyle, you are general manager . . ."

"In charge of travel arrangements," said Boyle. "I'm looking forward to safaris after dinosaurs. It should be quite challenging."

In more ways than you are thinking, I told myself. Just by the sight of him, I didn't like the little punk.

"Since we all know one another," said Stuart, "why not get down to business. I would like it if we could stay out here. It's very stimulating."

Hennessey thumped his chest. "Smell that air," he said. "Absolutely clean. No pollution here. I've not breathed air like this for years."

"Please find chairs," said Rila. "I'll bring out some coffee."

"You need not bother, really," said Boyle. "We have had our breakfast. Mr. Page gave us coffee, also, just before we left."

"I want some," said Rila tartly, "and I suppose Asa does as well. I'd hoped that you would join us."

"Why, of course," said the major. "We would be most happy to. And thank you very much."

They found chairs around the table and set their briefcases down beside them, all except Stuart, who put his on the table and began taking papers out of it.

"You'll have to keep a close watch on Hiram," Ben said to me. "Maybe a mastodon's all right, but there are other animals . . . "

"I've talked with him about it," I said. "I'll talk to him again."

Rila brought out a tray with cups and I went into the house to bring out the coffee. Sitting on the work-table was a sliced coffee cake and I brought that out as well.

By the time I got back, everyone was seated around the table and seemed about ready to get down to talking. The table was full so I took a chair and sat off to one side.

The major said to me, "So this is Mastodonia. Pleasant, I must say. Would you tell me how you managed to pick such a delightful place?"

"Hunch, mostly," I said. "From what we guessed about this time. Not us, of course, but the geologists. This is the Sangamon, the interglacial period that lies between the Illinoisian and the Wisconsin glacial periods. We picked it because we felt it would be the most familiar of the various periods that we might have chosen and because the climate should be ideal.

We can't be sure of that yet since we haven't been here long enough."

"Amazing," said the major.

"Mr. McCallahan," Stuart said, "are you ready to begin?"

"Certainly," said Courtney. "What do you have in mind?"

"You understand," said Stuart, "what we want. We'd like to arrange the rights for our safaris to be introduced into the Cretaceous."

"Not the rights," said Courtney. "We won't give you rights. We keep those for ourselves. For a consideration, we'll grant you a limited license."

"What the hell do you mean, Courtney? Limited?"

"I've been thinking in terms of a year," said Courtney. "Renewable, of course."

"But such an arrangement would not be worth our while. We'd have to commit a lot of capital. We'd have to set up a staff . . . "

"A year," said Courtney. "To start with."

"You'd give us all counsel and consideration . . . "

"That's how you have it written out?" asked Courtney, gesturing at the papers Stuart had spread out in front of him.

"That's the way we'd thought of it. We're new to this business of the Cretaceous and . . . "

"All we give you," said Courtney, "is the license. Once you have that, the rest is up to you. That doesn't mean that we won't give whatever counsel and assistance we can offer, but as a matter of good will, not by contract."

"Let's quit this haggling," said the major. "We want to send in safaris. Not one safari, but a lot of them. A lot of them early on before the novelty wears off. If I know sportsmen, and I do, it would be important for any one of them to be among the first to bring out a dinosaur. And we don't want to pile one safari on the other. We want to keep the hunting areas as clear as we can manage. We'll need more than one time road."

Courtney looked at me, questioning.

"It would be possible," I told him. "As many as

they want, each separated by, say, ten thousand years. We could cut it finer and make the interval less than that."

"You realize, of course," Courtney said to Hennessey, "that each time road will cost you."

"We'd be willing," said Stuart, "to pay you as much as a million dollars for three time roads."

Courtney shook his head. "A million for the license for one year. Let's say a half-million for each time road after the first."

"But, my God, man, we'd be losing money!"

"I don't think you would," said Courtney. "Are you willing to tell me what you'd charge for a two-week safari?"

"We haven't gotten around to discussing that," said Stuart.

"The hell you haven't. You've had a couple of weeks to consider it. With all the publicity, you must have a waiting list."

"You're talking economic nonsense," said Stuart.

"Don't talk to me like that," Courtney replied. "You're on your last legs and you know it. Up in the twentieth century, the hunting's gone. What have you got left—a few limited big-game trips, camera safaris? Here you have a chance to get back in business. An unlimited chance. Hundreds of years of hunting. New and fascinating game animals. If some of your clients would rather have a go at titanotheres or mammoth or a dozen other kinds of big and dangerous game, all you have to do is say the word; we'll take you there. And we're the only ones who can take you there."

"I'm not so sure," said Stuart. "If Miss Elliot and Mr. Steele can develop a time machine . . . "

"That's something I tried to tell you," said Rila. "You wouldn't listen or you didn't believe. You just glossed over it. There is no machine."

"No machine? What, then?"

"That," said Courtney smoothly, "is a trade secret that we're not divulging."

"They've got us, Stuart," said Major Hennessey. "There's no ducking it. They are right. No one else can get us there. Miss Elliot did say no machine. From the very start, she said it. So why don't we sharpen up our pencils and get down to figuring. Perhaps our friends would be willing to take a cut of our net. Twenty percent, perhaps."

"If you want to go that route," said Courtney, "fifty percent of your gross. No less. We'd rather operate on a license fee. It would be a cleaner deal."

I had been sitting there, listening to all of this, and my head was spinning just a little. You can talk about a million dollars and it doesn't mean too much; it's just a lot of figures. But when it's your own million bucks, that's a different thing.

I walked down the ridge. I'm not sure the others even knew I had left. Bowser crawled out from under the house and trailed after me. There was no sign of Hiram and I was worried about him. I had told him to come right back, and still there was no sign of him. Stiffy was ambling slowly across the valley, heading for the river, perhaps to get a drink, but Hiram wasn't with him. I stood on the ridge and looked everywhere. There was no sign of him.

I heard a sound behind me. It was Ben. His boots made a hissing sound as he walked through the foot-high grass. He came and stood beside me and together we stared off across the valley. Far down it there were a lot of moving dots—perhaps mastodons or bison.

"Ben," I asked, "how much is a million dollars?"

"It's an awful lot of cash," said Ben.

"I can't get it straight in my mind," I said, "that back there they are talking about a million and perhaps more than that."

"Neither can I," said Ben.

"But you're a banker, Ben."

"I'm still a country boy," said Ben. "So are you. That's why we can't understand."

"Country boy," I said, "we've come a long way since we roamed these hills together."

"In just the last few weeks," said Ben. "You're worried, Asa. What is troubling you?"

"Hiram," I told him. "He was supposed to come straight back once he led Stiffy out of here."

"Stiffy?"

"Stiffy is the mastodon."

"He'll be back," said Ben. "He's just found a wood-chuck."

"Don't you realize," I asked him, "that if anything were to happen to Hiram, we'd be out of business?"

"Sure, I know," said Ben, "but there'll nothing happen to him. He'll get along all right. He's half wild animal himself."

We stood and looked a while longer and saw nothing of Hiram.

Finally Ben said, "I'm going back and see how they're coming."

"You go along," I said. "I'm going to find Hiram."

An hour later I found him, coming out of the crab-apple grove below the house.

"Where the hell have you been?" I asked.

"I was having a good long talk with Catface, Mr. Steele. With all the exploring we been doing for the last few days, I've been neglecting him. I was afraid he would get lonesome."

"And had he gotten lonesome?"

"No," said Hiram. "No, he said he hadn't. But he's anxious to get to work. He wants to lay out some time roads. He wonders why it's taking us so long."

"Hiram," I said, "I want to talk with you. Maybe you don't realize it, but you're the one important person in this entire setup; you're the only one who can talk with Catface."

"Bowser can talk with Catface."

"All right. Maybe he can. But that does me no good. I can't talk to Bowser."

I laid out the situation for him. I explained most carefully. I practically drew him diagrams.

He promised to do better.

TWENTY-THREE

When Hiram and I got back to the house, Rila and Courtney were sitting at the table. The others were gone; so was one of the cars.

"Ben took the others for a drive," said Rila. "We wondered what happened to you."

"I was tracking Hiram down," I said.

"I stayed here," said Courtney, "because there are a couple of things I want to talk about with you two."

"The IRS?" I asked.

"No, not the IRS. They won't start stirring around until they get wind of the deal with Safari."

"How did the negotiations turn out?" I asked. "I suppose the deal was made."

"It didn't take too long," said Courtney. "They're hurting and we had them across the barrel."

"A million for the license," said Rila, "and a quarter-million for each time road. They want four time roads. That's two million, Asa."

"For one year," said Courtney. "They don't know it yet, but next year the price goes up. By that time, we'll have them hooked."

"And this is just a start," said Rila.

"That's what I wanted to talk with you about," said Courtney. "Ben told you about the church group?"

"Yes," I said. "Interested in the time of Jesus."

"A couple of them came to see me the other day," he said. "Ben had told them to talk with me. Damned if I can figure them. I don't know what they want. They're interested, but they wouldn't open up. I don't know if we should waste time on them."

"I don't like it," I said. "The whole thing could get sticky. To start with, we should stay away from anything controversial. Pay some attention to our image. Not create an issue the country, or the world, can choose up sides on."

"I think the same," said Rila. "There is not apt to be too much money in it, anyhow, and it could be a headache."

"I feel pretty much the same," said Courtney. "They'll be back to see me. I'll try to cool them off. There's someone else who has me worried. Senator Abel Freemore. He's from Nebraska or Kansas, I can never remember which. He's been trying to set up an appointment with me and my secretary has been fending him off. But you can fend off a United States senator for only so long. One of these days, I'll have to find out what he wants."

"You have no idea?" Rila asked.

"None at all. He's a big agricultural man, of course. Hellbent for the poor downtrodden farmer. But that's not all—he's three kinds of bleeding heart. Whatever he has in mind, I'm afraid it's nothing good."

"Anything else?" I asked.

"Not really. It's too early. Everyone is sitting back. Intrigued, of course, but still filled with a natural skepticism. Waiting to see what's going to happen. When the first safari brings out a dinosaur, then is when everything will break. But until then, mostly all that we will get are opportunists and con artists. There's that mining engineer who wants to go out into the Black Hills country and skim off the easy gold. No money, but he's willing to give us half of what he finds—more likely, half of what we force him to admit to. I sort of like him. He's an engaging sort of buccaneer. Utterly without principle and figures everyone else is the same. What was that idea you had, Rila, of going to South Africa and picking up all the easy diamonds off the ground?"

Rila said, "Yes, I admit to the idea. It probably wouldn't work. Maybe there never were a lot of diamonds waiting to be picked up. But it had a nice sound to it."

"This safari business," said Courtney, "is apt to be

one of the most straightforward, least complicated deals that we can make. An easy one to handle. No tricky angles. What bothers me is that none of your scientific or intellectual types have crawled out of the woodwork. Wanting to study the techniques and motives of the prehistoric cave painters or to observe the Neanderthalers at work and play or to sit in on Marathon or Waterloo."

"They have to be convinced first," said Rila. "They are sitting in the smug composure of their academic retreats, telling one another that it can't be done."

"There is another outfit that has been sniffing around," said Courtney. "I almost forgot them. Genealogists—those people who, for a price, will trace back the family tree. Seems now they have the idea of providing a more personal, and, of course, a more expensive service. Not just tracing back the record, but actually going back to talk with and, possibly, to sneak pictures of someone's ancient forebears. Great-great-great-uncle Jake being hung for horse thievery—things like that. They're being fairly cagey in their approach to us, but they'll be around again.

"There will be others. Or I think there'll be. With a thing like this, you can never be sure. Can't foresee how time travel will strike the general public and those you might suspect would be interested in using it. It would seem to me that as time went on, we ought to be hearing from the petrochemical people and the coal and iron interests. There are a lot of natural resources back in time."

"I've thought of that," said Rila. "It worries me. What I don't understand is this: The natural resources are back there, sure, and there is nothing to stop us from grubbing them out. There is no question they're there for the taking. But if we take them, then what happens in the nineteenth and twentieth centuries? Will those essential minerals still be there to take, and the answer seems they will be because we have, indeed, taken them. If you're worried about paradoxes, there's a classic one for you to mumble over."

"Rila," said Courtney, "I just don't know. I suspect

we're just not thinking right, that our thinking on things like that will have to be readjusted. At the moment, there are other things to do; I'm not going to worry about it."

TWENTY-FOUR

So began a period of waiting. Safari had said it might be ten days or two weeks before the first of their parties arrived. We went on a few trips into the surrounding country. We saw a number of mastodons and bisons. We found another colony of giant beavers. We sighted a number of bears and a few cats, but none of the cats was a sabertooth. I began to wonder if the sabertooths might be thinning out or be already extinct, although that seemed unlikely. Once Rila thought she glimpsed a glyptodont, one of the prehistoric giant armadillos, but when we arrived at the place where she had thought she'd seen it, we were unable to find any trace of it. We kept a lookout for horses, but saw none. There were a lot of wolves and foxes.

We selected a spot for a garden—Rila said we should put the virgin soil to use—but we never got around to doing anything about it. One thing we did do was lay in a telephone line from Ben's office so that someone wouldn't have to come trotting into Mastodonia each time they wanted to talk with us. We got the line in, but it wouldn't work; a signal would not pass through whatever it was that separated Mastodonia from the twentieth century. I had Ben get me a number of steel rods. I painted their tops red and hammered them into line to serve as guides into the time roads that Catface would be setting up into the Cretaceous. Hiram's wooden stakes had been all right, but the steel rods were more permanent; they could not be broken off as could the wooden stakes. I laid out lines for four time roads, and still had plenty of rods remaining to mark the other ends once we had the time roads.

Between Catface and Stiffy, Hiram was kept busy. Whenever he wasn't visiting one of them, he was with the other. Bowser usually was with him. I did some worrying about this loose-footedness of Hiram's, envisioning all the different kinds of trouble he could get into, but nothing happened and I told myself that it was foolish of me to worry so much, but I somehow couldn't stop it.

Early one afternoon, I was sitting at the lawn table having a can of beer. Rila had gone into the house to make a salad she had planned for dinner. The place was peaceful, as it always seemed to be. On the slope below me, I saw Hiram coming up the hill. I watched him idly, looking for Bowser. Then I saw the dog, a little way from Hiram, nosing at the grass as if he might have picked up something interesting.

Suddenly, Hiram let out a frightened bellow and bent forward, seeming to stumble. He went down on his knees, then got up again, thrashing around as if his foot was trapped in something. Bowser was running toward him, ears laid back. I jumped up and started running down the hill, yelling for Rila, but not looking back to see if she had heard.

Hiram began screaming, one ragged scream and then another, never letting up. He was sitting down and bending forward, holding his left leg with both his hands. Off to one side of him, Bowser pounced on something in the grass, then jerked his head up and shook it savagely. He had something in his jaws and was shaking it. One look at it told me what it was.

I reached Hiram and grabbed him by the shoulders, forcing him back.

"Let go of that leg," I yelled. "Lay back."

Hiram quit his senseless screaming, but he bawled at me, "It bit me, Mr. Steele. It bit me!"

"Lie back," I said. "Be quiet."

He did lie back the way I told him, but he wasn't quiet. He was doing a lot of moaning.

I pulled my jackknife out of my pocket and ripped his left pant leg open. When I pulled it back, I saw the darkening bruise and the two punctures, with a bright drop of blood glistening on each of them. I used the knife to rip the pant leg lengthwise, then hauled the pants up so much of the thigh was exposed.

"Asa," said Rila behind me. "Asa. Asa. Asa."

"Find a stick," I told her. "Any kind of stick. We'll have to put on a tourniquet."

I unfastened my belt and stripped it from the loops, then wound it around his leg above the wound. Rila crouched on the other side of him, facing me. She thrust a stick at me, a dry branch. I looped it through the belt and twisted.

"Here, hold this," I said. "Keep it tight."

"I know," she said. "It was a rattler. Bowser killed it."

I nodded. The wound had told me that much. No other North American snake in these latitudes could inflict such a wound.

Hiram had quieted down somewhat, but was still moaning.

"Hang on," I told him. "This will hurt."

I gave him no chance to protest. In telling him, I was only being fair, giving him fair warning.

I sliced a deep gash in his leg, connecting the two puncture marks. Hiram howled and tried to sit up. Rila, using her free hand, pushed him back.

I bent my mouth to the cut and sucked, tasting the warm saltiness of blood. I sucked and spat, sucked and spat. I hoped to God there were no broken tissues in my mouth. But it was no good thinking of that now. Even had I known there were, I would have done the same thing.

"He's fainted," Rila said.

I sucked and spat, sucked and spat. Bowser came up to us, sat down ponderously, watching us.

Hiram moaned. "He's coming to," said Rila.

I rested for a moment, then went back to the sucking. Finally, I quit. I'd pumped out at least some of the venom; I was sure of that. I sat back on my heels and reached for the stick. I loosened the tourniquet for a few seconds, then tightened it again.

"Get one of the cars turned around and headed for

Willow Bend," I told Rila. "We've got to get help for him. I'll carry him up."

"Can you handle the tourniquet and still carry him?"

"I think so." I said to Hiram, "Put your arms around my neck. Tight as you can. And hang on hard. I have only one arm to carry you."

He locked his arms around me and I managed to get him lifted and started staggering up the slope. He was heavier than I'd thought he'd be. Ahead of me, Rila was running for one of the cars. She had it turned around and waiting for me when I got there. I hoisted Hiram into the back, got in beside him. "Come on, Bowser," I said. Bowser leaped aboard. The car was already moving.

People came tumbling out of the rear door of the office building when Rila pulled up and leaned on the horn. I lifted Hiram from the car. Herb was the first to reach us. "Snake bite," I told him. "Rattler. Get an ambulance."

"Here, let me have him," said Ben. "There's a bottle of whiskey in my lower left desk drawer. I don't suppose you gave him any."

"I'm not sure . . . "

"Goddamn it, I am. If it doesn't help, it won't hurt. I've always been told it helps."

I went for the whiskey and brought it back to the front office, where Hiram was stretched out on a sofa. Herb turned from the phone. "The ambulance is on its way," he said. "There'll be a paramedic with it. He'll take over. I talked with a doctor. He said no whiskey."

I put the bottle on a desk. "How are you, Hiram?" I asked.

"It hurts," said Hiram. "I hurt all over. I hurt terrible."

"We'll get you to a hospital," I said. "They'll take care of you there. I'll go with you."

Herb grabbed me by the arm and pulled me to one side. "I don't want you to go," he said.

"But I have to. Hiram is my friend. He'll want me."

"Not with those newsmen out there. They'll follow the ambulance. In the hospital, you'll be fair game to them."

"The hell with them. Hiram is my friend."

"Be reasonable, Asa," Herb pleaded. "I've built you and Rila up as mysteries. Recluses. Publicity shy. Exclusive people. We need that image. For a while longer, at least."

"We don't need an image. Hiram needs help."

"How can you help him? Hold his hand? Wait while the doctors work on him?"

"That's part of it," I said. "Just being there."

Ben joined us. "Herb's right," he said. "I'll go along with Hiram."

"There has to be one of us. Myself or Rila. It should be me."

"Rila," said Herb. "She'll be upset, hysterical."

"Rila hysterical?"

"The newsmen won't press her as hard as they would you," said Ben. "If she says she won't talk, she'll have to say it fewer times than you would. She could build up her exclusiveness, while you . . ."

"You're bastards!" I shouted. "Both of you are bastards!"

It did me no good. In the end, Ben and Rila rode the ambulance and I stayed. I felt horrible. I felt I'd lost control, that I was no longer my own man, and I felt a terrible rage and fear. But I stayed behind. On this end of the operation, Ben and Herb were calling the shots.

"This will give us a fresh headline," said Herb.

I told him what he could do with his fresh headline. I called him a ghoul. I rescued the bottle we hadn't used for Hiram and went into Ben's office, where I worked on the bottle morosely. The drinking didn't help. I didn't even get a buzz on.

I phoned Courtney and told him what had happened. For a long time after I had finished, there was a silence on his end of the line. Then he asked, "He's going to be all right, isn't he?"

"I don't know," I said. "I'm waiting to hear."

"Hiram is the one who talks to Catface, isn't he?"

"That's right."

"Look, Asa, in a few days, Safari will be there to

go into the Cretaceous. Is there anything that can be done? The time roads, I suppose, aren't open yet."

"I'll try to talk with Catface," I said. "He can hear what I say, but I can't hear what he says. He can't answer back."

"But you'll try?"

"I'll try," I told him.

"I'll be seeing you in a few days. That senator I was telling you about—he wants to talk with you. Not with me, with you. I'll bring him out."

I didn't ask him if he had any idea what the senator wanted. I didn't give a damn.

"If Hiram doesn't make it," I said, "there's no use bringing anyone. If that happens, we're dead. You know that, don't you?"

"I understand," he said.

He sounded sad about it.

Herb brought me some sandwiches and coffee. There had been no word from Rila or Ben. We talked for a while and then I went out the back door. Bowser was waiting for me and we walked across the lawn to the house. We sat on the back steps, Bowser close beside me. He knew there was something wrong and was trying to comfort me.

The barn still stood, the lopsided door hanging crookedly on its hinges. The chicken house was the same as ever and the hens were still there, clucking and scratching about the yard. The rosebush stood at the corner of the chicken house—the rosebush where I had seen Catface looking out at me when I had gone out to get the fox and, instead, had walked into the Pleistocene.

That much was familiar, but little else was. The strangeness of the rest of it seemed to make the barn, the chicken house, the rosebush unfamiliar, too. The fence stood high and spidery and inside the fence humped the strangeness of the floodlights. Guards walked along the fence and outside of it were clustered knots of people. They were still coming to stand and gawk at us. I wondered why they continued to come. Certainly, there was nothing to be seen.

I stroked Bowser's head, talking to him. "You

remember what it was like, Bowser, don't you? How you'd go to dig out a woodchuck and I had to bring you home. How we'd go in the evening to shut the chicken house. How Hiram would come to visit you almost every day. That front lawn robin."

I wondered if the robin was still there, but didn't go to look. I was afraid I wouldn't find him.

I got up from the steps and went into the house, holding the door so Bowser could go in with me. I sat down in a chair at the kitchen table. I had intended to walk through the rest of the house, but I didn't. The house was too quiet and empty. The kitchen was too, but I stayed. It had a bit of home still left in it. It had been my favorite room, a sort of living room, and I'd spent a lot of time there.

The sun went down and dusk crept in. Outside, the floodlights went on. Bowser and I went out and sat on the steps again. In daylight, the place had looked strange and foreign. With the coming of night and the flaring of floodlights, it was a bad dream.

Rila found us sitting on the steps. "Hiram will be all right," she said, "but he'll have to stay in the hospital for quite a while."

TWENTY-FIVE

The next morning, I went looking for Catface. I didn't find him. I walked through the crab-apple patch below the mobile home, crisscrossing it in several directions, calling him softly, looking everywhere for him. He did not appear. After several hours of this, I wandered to other groves of trees and looked.

Back at the house, Rila said to me, "I should have gone to help you, but I was afraid I might scare him off. He's known you for a long time. I'm a newcomer."

We sat at the lawn table, despondent. "What if we don't find him?" Rila asked. "Maybe he knows what has happened to Hiram and is hiding, unwilling to show himself until Hiram's here."

"If we don't find him, we don't find him," I said.

"But Safari . . ."

"Safari will have to wait," I said. "Even if we find him, I don't know if he will work with me."

"Is it possible he went back to Willow Bend?" she asked. "To the orchard on the farm. That was his favorite hangout, wasn't it? Maybe if he knows about Hiram, he'd feel closer to him there."

In the Willow Bend orchard, I found him almost immediately. He was in one of the trees close to the house. He looked out of it at me with those great cat eyes. He even grinned at me.

"Catface," I said, "Hiram has been hurt, but he'll be all right. He'll be back in a few more days. Catface, can you blink? Can you shut your eyes?"

He shut his eyes and opened them again, then closed them and opened them again.

"All right," I said, "I want to talk with you. You can hear me, but I can't hear you. Maybe we can work out a way. I'll ask you questions. If your answer is yes, close your eyes once. If your answer is no, close them twice. Do you understand?"

He closed his eyes once, then opened them.

"That is fine," I said. "You understand what I told you about Hiram?"

He closed his eyes once.

"You understand that he'll be back in a few days?"

Catface signaled yes.

"And you're willing to talk with me this way? Work with me this way, by closing your eyes?"

Yes, indicated Catface.

"It's not a very satisfactory way to talk, is it?"

Catface blinked twice.

"All right, then, in Mastodonia—you know where Mastodonia is, don't you?"

Yes, indicated Catface.

"Back in Mastodonia, we need four time roads laid out. I have set out four lines of stakes, painted red, with a red flag at the end of each line, the red flag marking the point where we want to go into time. Do you understand?"

Catface signaled that he did.

"You have seen the stakes and flags?"

Catface said he had.

"Then, Catface, listen closely now. The first time road should go back seventy million years. And the next one ten thousand years less than that—ten thousand years less than seventy million years."

Catface didn't wait for me to ask him if he understood; he signaled yes.

"The third one," I said, "ten thousand years less than the second and the fourth one, ten thousand years less than the third."

Yes, said Catface.

We went through it all again to be sure he understood.

"Will you do it now?" I asked.

He said he would and then he disappeared. I stood there, staring stupidly at where he'd been. I suspected that he had taken me at my word, that he was now back in Mastodonia setting up the roads. At least, I hoped he was.

I found Ben in his office with his feet cocked up on the desk.

"You know, Asa," he said, "this is the best job I ever had. I like it."

"But you also have a bank to run."

"I'll tell you something I shouldn't tell anyone; the bank runs itself. Of course, I'm still in charge, but now I do barely any work. Only some of the tough decisions and a few papers that I have to sign."

"In that case, how about getting off your big fat butt and going into the Cretaceous with me?"

"The Cretaceous? You mean you did it, Asa?"

"I think so. I'm not sure. We ought to check it out. I'd like company. I'm too chicken to do it alone."

"You still have the elephant guns at your place?"

I nodded. "No hunting, though. Not this time. We just check out the roads."

Rila went along with us. We debated taking a car, but decided to go on foot. I was quite prepared, as we walked down the first line of stakes, to have nothing happen. But it did. We walked straight into the Cretaceous. It was raining there, a steady downpour. We set the stakes we carried and walked out a ways, far enough to pick up a clue as to where we were—a bunch of silly ostrich dinosaurs that went skittering away at our approach.

The other three roads were there as well. It was not raining at the ends of any of them. So far as I could see, all the places looked fairly much alike. There'd not be much change in forty thousand years—not at first glance, that is. If we'd spent some time, I suppose we could have detected a number of changes. But we spent almost no time at all. We pounded in the stakes and left. In the fourth time road, however, Ben knocked over a small ankylosaur, six or seven feet long, probably a yearling. The big bullet from his gun almost took its head off.

"Dinosaur steaks tonight," said Ben.

It took the three of us to haul it back to Mastodonia. There we used an axe to cut through the armor. Once we had a cut down the length of the body, it was possible to peel off the armor, but it wasn't easy. Ben cut off the clublike tail as a trophy. I hauled the broiler out from under the mobile home and got a fire going.

While Ben was broiling thick slabs of meat, I went down the hill to the crab-apple grove and found Catface. "I just want to say thank you," I told him. "The roads are magnificent." He blinked his eyes at me, four or five times, grinning all the while.

"Is there anything I can do for you?" I asked.

He blinked his eyes twice, saying no.

The ostrich dinosaur that we had eaten on our exploratory trip into the Cretaceous had been tasty, but I figured the anky steak might be a disappointment. Ankylosaurs are such crazy-looking beasts. There was no disappointment, however. I wolfed down the steaks, faintly ashamed of how much I ate.

Later on, we cut up the rest of the carcass, putting a few cuts in our refrigerator and wrapping up the rest of it for Ben to take back home.

"We'll have a dinosaur cookout tomorrow night," he said. "Maybe I'll invite those news jockeys in to have a taste of it. It'll give them something to write about."

We hauled the rest of the carcass down the hill and buried it. Left where it was, it would have stunk up the place in a few days. Two days later, walking down that way, I found that something, probably wolves or foxes, had dug out the remains and performed a remarkable scavenging job. There were only a few pieces of armor plate scattered about.

With Ben gone, Rila and I took it easy, sleeping late, doing a lot of sitting at the lawn table, looking out over our domain. I took a shotgun and set out with Bowser to hunt for rattlesnakes. We found none. Stiffy came up the hill to visit us. He kept shuffling in closer, putting out his trunk to sniff in our direction, flapping his ears at us. I knew something had to be done; otherwise, he'd be right in our laps. While Rila held a rifle covering me, I walked up to him, going slowly, shaking in my boots. He smelled me over and I scratched his trunk. He rumbled and groaned in ecstasy. I moved in closer, reached up to scratch his lower lip. He liked that; he did his best to tell me that he liked me. I led him down into the valley and told him to stay there,

to keep the hell away from us. He grunted companion-
ably. I was afraid he'd try to follow me back home, but
he didn't.

That evening as we sat watching dusk come across
the land, Rila said to me, "Something is bothering
you, Asa."

"Hiram upset me," I said.

"But he's going to be all right. Just a few more days
and he'll be back here with us."

"It made me realize how shaky we are," I said.
"The time business is based on Hiram and Catface.
Let something happen to either one of them . . ."

"But you did all right with Catface. You got the
time roads open. Even if everything went sour right
now, we'd have them, and it is this deal with Safari
that will be the backbone of our business. There'll be
other things, of course, as time goes on, but it's the
big-game hunting . . ."

"Rila, would you be satisfied with that?"

"Well, no, I suppose not satisfied, but it would be
more than we had before."

"I wonder," I said.

"You wonder what?"

"Please try to understand," I said. "Bear with me a
moment. The other day, the day you took Hiram to
the hospital, I was at the farm. Me and Bowser. We
walked around a bit and sat on the back steps the way
we used to. We even went into the house, but I didn't
go farther than the kitchen. I sat at the kitchen table
and thought how it once had been. I felt lost. No matter what I did, no matter where I went, I was lost.
Things had changed so much."

"You didn't like the changes?"

"I'm not sure. I should, I know. There's money now
and there never was before. We can travel in time now
and no one ever did that. I suppose it was Hiram and
the realization of how thin we run. . . ."

She took one of my hands in hers. "I know," she
said. "I know."

"You mean you, too?"

She shook her head. "No, Asa. No, not me. I'm the
pushy bitch, remember. But you, I know how you

might feel. I feel just slightly guilty. I pushed you into it."

"I was easy to push," I said. "Don't blame yourself. There is nothing against which to assess any blame. The thing is, I loved that farm. When I saw it the other day, I knew I'd lost it."

"Let's go for a walk," she said.

We walked hand in hand down the ridge and all around us was the peace of Mastodonia. Off in the hills, a whippoorwill struck up his chugging cry and we stopped, enchanted. It was the first time here that we'd heard a whippoorwill. Never for a moment had I expected to hear one; I had illogically assumed there'd be no whippoorwills. But hearing the cry, I knew it as the sound of home, bringing back to me memories of years plunged deep in summer with the scent of freshly mown hay blowing from a new-cut field and the tinkling of cow bells as the herd filed out to pasture once the milking had been done. As I listened, I felt a strange contentment flooding over me.

We went back to the mobile home and called Bowser in. He went stalking into Hiram's room. For a time we heard him pawing at the blanket on the floor, making his bed before he lay down to sleep. In the kitchen, I fixed up a pitcher of manhattans and took them into the living room. We sat drinking, relaxed and civilized.

"Do you remember that day when I appeared?" asked Rila. "After twenty years, suddenly here I was."

I nodded. I did remember. I think that I remembered every minute of it.

"I asked myself all the time I was driving to Willow Bend," she said, "if the time might ever come when I might regret coming here. From time to time since then, I've asked myself the question. Asa, I want to tell you now I have never regretted it. I don't ask the question any more. I don't mean the time travel and the fun and money. I mean you. I've never regretted coming back to you."

I put down my glass and went to where she was sitting on the davenport. I sat down beside her and took her in my arms. We sat for a long time, like a pair of silly kids who suddenly have discovered they love one another. I was thankful she had told me, and I thought maybe I should tell her so, but there were no words that I could put together to tell her how I felt, I told her, instead, what was in my heart. "I love you, Rila. I think I always have, from the first day that I saw you."

The next day, shortly after noon, Courtney came driving in, with a car that Ben had loaned him. With him was Senator Abel Freemore.

"I deliver him into your hands," said Courtney. "The old so-and-so won't talk with me. He has to talk with you. He must go to the horse's mouth. Also, the IRS has come to life; they've been in to see me. But I don't think the senator's business with you has anything to do with them."

"Not at all," said the senator. "Like all sensible men, I keep my distance from them."

He was a little wisp of a man with a farmer's face. His hair was white and skimpy; his hands and face were weather-beaten. He stood small beside the car and looked around.

"So this is Mastodonia," he said. "Courtney has been telling me of it. When are you going to start subdividing it?"

"We aren't going to," said Rila sharply. "We don't own it."

"I should tell you," said Courtney, speaking to us, "that Safari will be coming in tomorrow. Ben phoned several days ago to say the roads are open. I'm glad you managed it."

"No sweat," I said.

"I'd like to stick around and witness the first safari going in. So would the senator. Do you have the room to put us up for the night?"

"We have two rooms," said Rila. "You are welcome. One of you will have to let Bowser sleep in the same room with you."

"Would there be a chance of going in with them?" asked the senator. "Just for a look around. A quick look around, then I'd come right back."

"That would be up to the Safari people," I said. "You can talk with whoever is in charge."

The senator looked at Courtney. "How about you?" he asked. "If they allow us, would you go along?"

"I don't know," said Courtney. "I saw the film. There are bloodthirsty brutes back there. I'd have to think on it."

The senator stalked around for a while, looking things over, then gravitated toward the table. Rila had brought out coffee. The senator, sitting down, held out a cup. "Thank you, my dear," he said to Rila when she poured. "I'm an old farm boy. I prize a cup of coffee."

The rest of us joined him around the table and Rila filled cups for us.

"I suppose," said Freemore, "that I might as well get said the things I want to say. It's not a proposition. Nothing very weighty. Nothing to do with the Senate or the government. Just some questions that keep bouncing in my mind."

The senator spilled a few drops of coffee on the table, then wiped it off with the palm of his hand, taking his time about it.

"I fear," he said, "you may think me a foolish old man, jumping in fright at shadows. But there is a problem that has caused me many sleepless nights. There are two problems, actually. Now, how should I put this in the best possible light, in the least foolish way?"

He paused as if to ponder. He had no need to ponder, I was sure. It was just an oratorical trick. Through the years, he had declaimed too often on the Senate floor.

"Simply put," he said, "we do have two overriding problems: the state of agriculture in the world and the great masses of poverty-stricken people, many of them in our own country. The disadvantaged, the unemployed, the bottom of the social heap.

"So far, we have been able to grow enough food to feed all the people of the Earth. When people starve, it is a matter of poor distribution, not a problem of supply. But I fear the day may not be too distant when the supply, as well, will fail. Meteorologists tell us, and very convincingly, I must say, that at least the northern hemisphere and perhaps the entire world as well is entering upon a colder, drier cycle. We've had it good, they tell us, for sixty years or more—the most favorable weather the world has known for hundreds of years. Now we are beginning to experience droughts. Vast areas of our productive croplands are getting little rain and the climate is growing colder. If this cold trend continues, the growing season will be shortened. All this spells less food. If food production is cut even marginally, say ten percent or so for several years, there are areas that could face mass starvation. During our years of unparalleled growing weather, the world has made great social and economic advances, but the population has also grown, with no prospect that the growth can be slowed, so that in only a few favored areas has the economic boom operated to alleviate human misery.

"You can see, no doubt, what I am driving at. Your mind is leaping ahead of my words. With the advent of time travel, a concept I was, at first, reluctant to accept, we now have the capability of opening up vast new agricultural areas that would more than compensate for the drop in food productivity that will come about if the climate deteriorates as much as our meteorologists seem to think it will.

"That is one of the problems. You remember I said there were two problems. The other problem is that there exist vast segments of our population who face no future other than lifelong privation. You find great masses of these unfortunates in the ghettos of the larger cities and other pockets of them scattered throughout rural areas, and still others, single examples of bad fortune, almost everywhere. It has seemed to me that some of these people could be sent by time travel to certain virgin areas of the past where they would have a chance to help themselves. So far as my thinking has gone, I see them as a new generation of pioneers transported to a new land where, with some land to call their own, with the natural resources undestroyed, they might be able to fashion for themselves a better life. I am painfully aware that many of these people would not make good pioneers. Their poverty and dependence, their bitterness toward society, their self-pity may have robbed them of any possibility of standing on their feet. Perhaps, no matter where you put them, they'd be no better off than they are now . . ."

"But at least," I said, "you'd be getting them out of our hair."

The senator glanced sharply at me. "Young man," he said, "that was unfair and perhaps unworthy of you."

Courtney said, "You make it all sound easy, but it wouldn't be. It would cost a lot of money. You couldn't just tuck these people out of the way somewhere in another time and say to them, now you're on your own. Government and society would still have to bear some responsibility. You'd have to see to it that they had a decent start. And I would suspect a lot of them would not want to go, many of them would refuse to go. There'd be some advantages, of course. You'd reduce the welfare load and I wonder if that is not what you're counting on for support when you get around to announcing your plan. But in all conscience, you can't reduce welfare costs simply by throwing people into a howling wilderness and telling them you've washed your hands of them."

The senator nodded. "Courtney, you're making me sound like an ogre. You can't believe I failed to have these factors you have mentioned very much in mind. The program, if there were to be such a program, would have to be carefully worked out. The initial cost probably would exceed any savings in welfare by several times over. The humanitarian aspects of the move would have to be of equal weight with the economic aspect. I have talked with no one yet—no one, except you three. Before I move, I need some answers from you. It seems to me that by certain astute moves, you people have this time-travel business sewn up neatly. You are offering it as a service. You have made a business of it. I have the strong personal feeling that it should be viewed as a public utility, subject to rules and regulations. But, by operating it from your so-called Mastodonia, you appear to have effectively removed any such possibility. I have no idea if the concept of Mastodonia would stand up in court . . . "

"We are convinced it would," said Courtney. "My feeling is, it will never be contested."

"You're bluffing now," said the senator. "You are making lawyer talk. I have a feeling that it will. But that matters neither here nor there. What I seek from you is some indication of how sympathetically you would view such a program and how much co-operation we could expect from you."

"We can't give you an answer," said Courtney in his best grave, gray lawyer tone. "We would have to see some concrete proposals and have a chance to study them. You realize that you would be asking us to commit to your purposes vast time areas, thus forcing us to give up our option of granting licenses for their use by others."

"I realize that," said Freemore. "When one comes down to it, that is the nub of the situation. Could you possibly view going along with my proposed program as a public contribution, a gift to society? Needless to say, if you demanded the kind of fees I suppose you could ask of others, the program would be doomed. It would never get off the ground. My proposal would cost enough without piling license fees to Time Associates atop the budget."

"If you are asking us to search our consciences," said Courtney, "that we are quite willing to do. But at this juncture, we're not prepared to give you a commitment."

The senator turned to me. "If such a program were decided upon," he said, "where in the past would be the best place to site it? Right here? Right in Mastodonia?"

Rila beat me to it. "Not Mastodonia," she said. "We're homesteading it. We will not give up this place."

TWENTY-SIX

The first safari group arrived shortly after noon. It was made up of two heavy trucks, three four-wheel drives and a crew of perhaps twenty-five men. The equipment had been flown into Minneapolis on a cargo plane, with some of the crew riding along. A company plane had flown in those not on the cargo flight, including the three clients. From Minneapolis, the safari had driven to Willow Bend. At the front gate, they had been besieged by newspapermen and camera crews.

"The press conference, if that is what it could be called, delayed us a full hour and was exasperating," said Percy Aspinwall, the man in charge. "However, I couldn't cut it short and had to be as gracious as possible. The folks back in New York want maximum publicity."

"What you went through today," I told him, "will be nothing to what will happen when you come out, especially if you bring out a few good heads."

"Steele, I'm glad of this chance to talk with you," he said. "I'd hoped we could get together for a while. You can tell me something of what to expect when we go in. You are one of the three people who have been in the Cretaceous."

"I was there scarcely more than a day," I told him. "We saw a lot of fauna. The place crawls with strange animals, and not all look the way our paleontologists have said they did. You saw the film Rila made?"

"Yes. Good job. In ways, a little terrifying."

"Then you've seen most of what we saw. You're carrying big rifles?"

"Six hundreds. The same as you."

"One thing," I said. "Don't wait too long to allow your clients to make the kill. If there's something coming at you and you can't be sure, clobber it. What kind of clients do you have?"

"Steady people," said Aspinwall. "Getting a bit older than I'd like, but all of them have hunted before. In Africa, before the game fields there went sour. They have field experience, they won't get rattled, they'll perform. Jonathon Fridley and his wife, Jessica. She brought down one of the biggest tuskers I have ever seen. Fridley is chairman of a steel company. The third one is Horace Bridges. President of a chemical conglomerate. Solid people. All three of them."

"Then you shouldn't have too much of a problem."

"No. If I have to get in on a kill, they'll understand."

"Senator Freemore wants to go along. Has he talked with you?"

"He collared me almost immediately. I told him no way. I can't take the responsibility. I'd like to accommodate him, but I can't stick my neck out. He didn't like it. He got a little nasty. But I can't take along hitch-hikers. However, if you'd like to go . . ."

"No, thanks," I said. "There'll be other safaris coming along. I should stay here. Besides, I've been there."

"They're getting the rigs lined up," he said. "I have to leave. Nice talking with you."

I stuck out my hand. "Aspinwall," I said, "good luck."

I stood and watched them go, the vehicles moving along, one behind another, each one in turn blanking out as they hit the time road. Rila drove Courtney and the senator back to Willow Bend. The senator was pouting. I went down to the crab-apple grove looking for Catface; found him roosting in a tree at the west end of the grove. I told him one of his time roads was being used and that in the next few days, the others would be put to use. I asked if that pleased him and he said it did. It was a little awkward talking with him. The only way I could do it was to ask him questions that he answered yes or no by blinking. So after a time, I quit trying to carry on a conversation and just stood there, looking at him and feeling friendly toward him. He looked back at me, half grinning in what I suppose was a friendly fashion.

I tried to figure out exactly what he was and somehow or other, I began building an impression that he was not an actual creature—that he did not actually have a body, that he was not made of flesh and bone, although if that was true, I was unable to figure out exactly what he was.

I found out something else. Up until now, I had regarded him simply as an alien, an inexplicable being that could not be understood. But now I began to think of him as a personality, as another person, as someone I knew and thought of, just possibly, as a friend. I wondered about those fifty thousand years that he'd been here and I tried to imagine what they may have been like for him. I tried to imagine how it would have been for me (if I could have existed for fifty thousand years, which was impossible, of course) and then I knew that this was a wrong way of thinking, that I could not equate myself with Catface, since we were two entirely different life forms. I brought to mind the things that he had done, the contacts that he'd made in the last few years—playing a senseless game of hunter and hunted with Ezra and Ranger, making time roads for Bowser to use (I wondered how many trips Bowser may have made into the past), talking occasionally with Hiram, or trying to talk with him, for Hiram had not understood what Catface had been saying and, in consequence, had not liked him. But all that was only now, in the last few years. Other people, apparently, had seen him (or he had shown himself to them) and they had been frightened. In ages past, I wondered, had he at times been in contact with the Indians and earlier than that, with the proto-Indians? Might he not have been considered a god or spirit by some of these wandering tribesmen? Could he have been known to the mammoth, the mastodon and the ancient bison?

I had quit standing and had sat down at the foot

of a tree. Catface had slithered lower down his tree so that we were opposite one another, face to face.

I heard Rila drive back up the ridge, coming home from Willow Bend. I got up and said to Catface, "I'll visit you again in a day or two and we can talk some more."

Rila brought word that Ben had been in contact with the religious group again and they'd be coming to Willow Bend the next day. Ben would bring them in to talk with us. He still had no hint as to what it was they wanted.

Word from the hospital, she said, was that Hiram could not be released for a while. Ben had driven to Lancaster to see him a few days before and said he'd not found him looking well. He had asked after Bowser and the two of us and Catface; he'd asked how Stiffy was getting along. But other than that, he had done little talking.

Ben brought in the committee for the religious group the next day. There were three of them, but only one of them did the talking; the other two just sat there, wagging their heads and agreeing with the spokesman, whose name was Hotchkiss. The day was cloudy and chilly, with an occasional mist falling, so we talked with them in the living room.

Hotchkiss wasn't a man who believed in wasting time. He was a big man with a doomsday face— sharp and angular, like the muzzle of a wolf. A smile would have been inappropriate on such a face. I doubt if he ever smiled.

He got swiftly down to business. The usual pleasantries were held to a minimum. He did not express any wonder or doubt about time travel. Apparently, he had accepted it. He did not ask us if it really worked; he asked for no guarantees.

"What we are interested in," he told us, "is acquiring the rights, or license, or whatever you may call it, to that period of time covered by the life of Jesus. Exclusive rights, you understand. We and no one else."

"I told you," said Ben, "when I first talked with you, that we are willing to consider any legitimate proposal, but that we would not be able to give you an answer until we have given the proposal some study. You are asking for exclusive rights to a fair-sized chunk of time and we have to know, before we do anything at all, if conflicts might exist."

"What kind of conflicts?" Hotchkiss asked.

Ben was patient with him. "Time segments," he said, "can be put to many uses. It would help us to know what use you expect to make of the time and the geographical limits that you have in mind. It would cost you a great deal to reserve the entire world for a specific number of years."

"We have a fund," said Hotchkiss, "that should be sufficient. If necessary we could raise more."

"There's still another factor," said Rila. "Any group that plans to conduct investigations into historic time must be aware of possible dangers. Going into historic time carries the obligation of doing so in a manner that would not upset history. No one living in that time must ever suspect that someone from the future has come into his time. Investigators must dress like the people there, must know the customs and the language, something of the history . . . "

"You can rest easy on that matter," Hotchkiss told her. "We'll do no investigating."

"But if you don't want to investigate, if you don't want to go back and see . . . "

"That is precisely the point," said Hotchkiss. "We do not want to go back, but we want no one else to go. That is why we must have exclusive rights."

"I don't understand," I said. "This is an area, it seems to me, that any theologian would give his good right arm to study. There is scarcely anything known . . . "

"Right there," said Hotchkiss, "you have hit upon our reason. There always has been a question of the historicity of Jesus. Nothing is known about Him. There are only one or two literary mentions of Him and these may be later interpolations. We don't know the date or the place of His birth. It is generally accepted He was born in Bethlehem, but even on this, there is some question. The same situation holds true in every other phase of His life. Some students have even questioned the existence of such a man. But through the centuries, the myths that have been brought forward regarding Him have been accepted, have become the soul, the structure, the texture of the Christian faith. We want it left that way. To go probing back would operate to destroy the faith that has been built up through the ages. It would result in unseemly controversy. What do you think would happen if it were found that Jesus was not born in Bethlehem? What would that do to the Christmas story? What if no evidence were found of the Magi?"

He stopped and looked from one to the other of us. "You do understand?" he asked.

"We can understand your viewpoint," I said. "I would have to think about it for a while."

"Before you decided if what we're asking for is right or not?"

"Something like that," I said. "What you're asking us to do is slam the door in the face of everyone."

"I would not have you think," said Hotchkiss, "that we are men of little faith. The truth is that our faith is so all-encompassing that we can and do accept Christianity even knowing that little is known of Our Lord and that that little may be wrong. What we fear is that if the story as it now is known should be torn to shreds by investigations, Christianity itself would be torn to shreds. You hold in your hands an awesome power. We're willing to pay you well for not employing it."

Rila asked, "Exactly who are you? You talk of we. Who are we?"

"We're a committee," said Hotchkiss, "very hastily put together, our members including those who very early recognized the danger when we read of the discovery of time travel. We have received support and promise of support from a number of church organizations. We are busily contacting others from which we anticipate support."

"You mean money support?"

"Yes, madam, money support. It will take money, I assume, to buy the rights we seek."

"A lot of it," said Rila.

"If we're willing to sell at all," I said.

"Promise me this," said Hotchkiss. "At least let us know when you get other offers, for you will get other offers, I am sure. Give us a chance to meet the terms the others offer."

"I'm not sure we can do that," said Ben. "I'm fairly sure we can't. But we'll consider your proposal."

Standing outside the mobile home, watching the delegation go down the path to Willow Bend with Ben, I sensed trouble in them. Their attitude, their viewpoint, went against my grain, but I could not analyze or define the repugnance that I felt. As a matter of fact, I told myself, I should hold some sympathy for them, for without realizing it until now, I knew that I held some reservations about entering into certain areas of mankind's history. Much of what was buried in the past should be allowed its burial in the past.

"Asa, what do you think?" asked Rila.

"I don't like the sound of it," I said. "I don't know why. It just goes against the grain."

"I feel much the same," she said. "They talk about paying well. I can't imagine they have too much. Mention a million and they'd fall down dead."

"We'll see," I said. "I dislike having anything to do with them. I feel just a little dirty at the thought of it. I suppose we'll have to see what Ben and Courtney think."

Two more safaris arrived and went into the Cretaceous. The fourth arrived a few days later.

Stiffy came shambling up the hill to visit us. Rila fed him some lettuce and a few carrots she found in the refrigerator. He chomped down the carrots, but after sampling it, rejected the lettuce. I guided him back to the valley, with him grunting and mumbling at me all the way.

I went to see Catface again. Not finding him in Mastodonia, I ran him to earth in the orchard on the farm. We did little talking, for talking was difficult, but we did sit together, feeling friendly toward one another, and that seemed to satisfy Catface. Strangely, it satisfied me as well. Contact with him somehow made me feel good. I got the funny feeling that Catface was trying to talk with me. I don't know what made me think this, but I did get the impression that he was trying to communicate.

I remembered how, as a boy, I used to go swimming in Trout Creek—which was a funny name for it, for it had no trout. Maybe in the pioneer days, when white men first came to the area, there might have been some trout. The creek flowed into the river just above Willow Bend, and it wasn't much of a stream—in some places, just a trickle—but there was one place, just before it joined the river, where there was a pool. When my pals and I were small, before we got big enough for our parents to let us go swimming in the river, we used the pool as a swimming hole. It wasn't more than three feet deep and there was no current; a boy would have had to make a determined effort to drown in it. We used to have a lot of fun there in the lazy summer days, but the thing that I remembered best about it was that when I had got tired of horsing around in the deeper water, I would lie at the shallow edge of the pool, with my head resting on the gravel shore, the rest of me extending out into the water, but barely covered by it. It was good to lie there, for at times you could forget you had a body. The water was just deep enough to buoy up your body so that you became unaware of it. There were a lot of minnows in the pool, little fellows two or three inches long, and if you lay there long enough and were quiet enough, they would come up to you and nibble at your toes, just sort of lipping you with their tiny mouths. I suppose they found dried flakes of skin and maybe tiny scabs—most of us had scabs on our feet because we went barefoot and always had some cuts and bruises—and I suppose these little minnows found the flakes of dried skin and the tiny bloody scabs a very welcome fare. But anyhow, I'd lie there and feel them at my feet, and especially at my toes, bumping against me very gently and lipping at my flesh. Inside of me, there'd be a quiet and bubbling laughter, a bubbling happiness that I could be so intimate with minnows.

That was the way with Catface. I could feel his thoughts bumping in my brain, lipping at my brain cells, exactly as those minnows in that time of long ago had bumped against my toes. It was a sort of eerie feeling, but it was not disquieting and I felt, much as I had with the minnows, a sense of bubbling laughter that Catface and I could be so close together. Later on, I told myself that it must have been my imagination, but at the time, I seemed to feel those bumping thoughts quite clearly.

Once I left the orchard, I went to the office to see Ben. When I came in, he was just hanging up the phone. He turned to me with a broad smile on his face.

"That was Courtney," he said. "There's a movie outfit on the Coast that is getting serious. They want to make a film showing the history of the Earth, going back to the Precambrian and jumping up the ages."

"That's quite a project," I said. "Do they realize how long it might take?"

"It seems they do," said Ben. "They seem to be sold on the idea. They want to do a decent job. They're prepared to take the time."

"Do they realize that in the earlier periods they'd have to carry oxygen? There can't have been much free oxygen in the atmosphere until the Silurian, some four hundred million years ago. Perhaps even later."

"Yes, I think they do. They mentioned it to Courtney. It seems they've done their homework."

"Does Courtney feel their interest is genuine? I would suppose that a movie outfit would have the tendency, at first, to make a cheap, run-of-the-mill movie using one of the prehistoric periods as a background. Not something as ambitious as this. It would cost billions. They'd have to have a scientific staff, people who could interpret what they put on film."

Ben said, "You're right about the cost. Courtney seems to think that we will be able to collect a good slice of the budget."

This was good news, of course, and I was glad to hear it, for we had really made only one deal—the one with Safari, Inc.

"Did you talk with Courtney about the Jesus Committee?" I asked.

"Yeah, I did. He doesn't think too much of them. Doubts if they can pull together the cash. They claim wide church support, but it is doubtful if they can come up with anything."

"They're fanatics," I said, "and fanatics don't wear well. It seems to me we should write them off."

Four days later, safari number three, the first group to return, came out several days ahead of the scheduled time. They had had a good hunt: a half-dozen huge triceratops, three tyrannosaur heads, a gaggle of other trophies. They would have stayed out the allotted two weeks, but the hunter-client had become ill and wanted to return.

"Sheer funk," the white hunter told me. "It's hairy back there. He shot well, but it got to him. Christ, it got to me. Look up and see a monster with a mouthful of teeth coming at you out of nowhere and your guts just turn to water. He's perked up now that we are out. He'll be the great hunter, fearless, intrepid, nerves of iron, when we go through the gates and the newsmen start closing in."

He grinned. "We'll not stop him. Let him play the role to the hilt. It is good for business."

Rila and I stood and watched the safari outfit go rolling down the ridge and disappear into Willow Bend.

"That does it," Rila said. "Once the pictures of those trophies are shown on television and appear in newspapers, there'll be no doubt, any longer, that traveling in time is possible. We no longer have to prove it."

The next morning, before we were up, Herb was pounding at the door. I went out in robe and slippers.

"What the hell?" I asked.

Herb waved a copy of the Minneapolis *Tribune* at me.

I grabbed the paper from him. There, on page one, was the picture of our client-hunter, posing beside the propped-up head of a tyrannosaur. A six-column headline trumpeted the story about the return of the first safari. In the space underneath the few inches of type under the bigger headline, before the two-column type plunged down the page, was another headline that said:

CHURCH GROUP CHARGES
TIME TRAVEL DISCRIMINATION

The first paragraph of this second story said:

New York, N.Y.

Dr. Elmer Hotchkiss, head of an independent church committee that is committed to the prevention of any study of the times and life of Jesus Christ, declared today that Time Associates has refused to sell it the rights to the time block covering that period of history. . . .

I lowered the paper and said, "But, Herb, you know that's not accurate. We did not refuse . . . "

Herb was practically jigging with excitement. "But don't you see?" he shouted. "Here's a controversy, an issue. Before the day is over, church groups and theologians all over the world will be choosing up sides. Asa, we couldn't buy publicity like this."

Rila came out the door. "What's going on?" she asked.

I handed her the paper.

I had a gone feeling in my guts.

TWENTY-SEVEN

Hiram was still in the hospital and, once again, I hunted up Catface and found him in the orchard. I told myself I only wanted to keep contact with him to keep him from getting lonely. Hiram had talked with him almost every day, and since Hiram wasn't here, I thought that someone should make a point of seeing him. But in the back of my mind were those little minnows that had been nibbling at my brain, and I couldn't help but wonder if, when I saw him again, the minnows would resume their nibbling. I had a queasy feeling about it, but was nevertheless somewhat mystified. Maybe, I told myself, this was Catface's way of talking, although if it was, I was certainly badly in need of an interpreter. I wondered if the nibbling had been what Hiram had felt and, through some strange quirk in his mind, had been able to understand the language. Maybe this was the ability that enabled Hiram to talk with Bowser and the robin, if he did actually talk with either one of them.

Once I found Catface, I didn't have to wait long to have my question answered; almost immediately the minnows were in there, nibbling away at me.

"Catface," I asked him, "are you trying to talk with me?"

He blinked his eyes for yes.

"Tell me, do you think that you can do it?"

He blinked three times, very rapidly, which amazed me somewhat as to meaning, but, after a bit of thought, I decided that it meant he didn't know.

"I hope you can," I said. "I'd like to talk with you."

He blinked his eyes for yes, which I imagine meant that he would, too.

But we weren't able to talk. It seemed to me that while the minnows were more persistent than they had been before, we were getting nowhere. For a time, I tried to open my mind to the minnows, but that didn't seem to help. Perhaps nothing I could do, I told myself, could help. Whatever was to be done, if anything was to be done, was strictly up to Catface. I had the feeling that he must have thought he had a chance, or he never would have tried. But once I thought that over, I detected a lot of wishful thinking in it.

When the session came to an end, it didn't seem to me we were at all ahead of what the situation had been when it had first started.

"I'll be back tomorrow," I told Catface. "You can try again."

I didn't tell Rila about it because I was afraid she might laugh at my simple-mindedness. To me, of course, in a sort of sneaking way, it was no simple-mindedness. If Catface could fix it so we could talk together, I sure as hell was willing to give him a chance to do it.

I had told him I'd be back the next day, but I wasn't. In the morning, another of the safaris, number two, returned. They brought back only one tyrannosaur, plus several triceratops, but also three crested hadrosaurs and a *Polacanthus,* an armored dinosaur with a ridiculously small, tapering head and big horn-like spikes sticking out of its back the entire length of its body. *Polacanthus* was distinctly out of place. It shouldn't have been in our part of the Cretaceous; it was supposed to have died out in the early Cretaceous and should not have been in North America at all. But, there it was, in all its grotesque ugliness.

The safari had brought back the entire body. Despite being dressed out, its body cavity scraped and cleaned as well as possible, the carcass was beginning to get a little high.

"Be sure to call this one to the attention of the paleontologists," I told the hunter-client. "It will drive them up the wall."

He grinned a toothy and satisfied grin at me. He

was a little squirt and I wondered how a man of his size could stand up to a dinosaur gun. I tried to remember who he was and it seemed to me I had been told that he was some aristocratic bird from somewhere in England, one of the few who had somehow managed to keep a tight grip on the family fortune in the face of the British economy.

"What's so special about this one?" he asked. "There were quite a few of them. I picked out the biggest one. How would you, sir, go about mounting such a specimen? It's a sort of unwieldy creature."

I told him what was so special about it, and he liked the idea of confounding the paleontologists.

"Some of these learned types," he told me, "put on too many airs."

The safari had barely disappeared into Willow Bend when number four came back. It had four tyrannosaurs, two triceratops and a bunch of other stuff. It was lacking one truck, however, and two men were on stretchers.

The white hunter took off his hat and wiped his brow. "It was those damn things with horns," he said. "The ones with parrot beaks. Triceratops, is that what you call them? Something scared them and they came at us, a dozen or more of the big bulls. They hit the truck broadside and made kindling out of it. We were lucky no one was killed. We had a hell's own time rescuing the men who were in the truck. We had to stand off the bulls. I don't know how many we put down. They were milling all around us and had their dander up. Maybe we should have gone back and picked up some of the heads. But when we finally fought our way free, we sort of voted against it."

"It was rough," I said.

"Rough, sure. But when you go into new country, before you know what to expect, it can get rough. I learned one thing: Never press in too close to a herd of triceratops. They're short-tempered, ugly brutes."

After the day's second safari was gone, Rila said to me, "I'm worried about number one. They are overdue."

"Only by a day," I said. "They all set two weeks

as the time they would be out, but a couple of days one way or the other doesn't matter."

"The one that just left got into trouble."

"They made a mistake. That is all. Remember how Ben stopped us when we walked up too close to the triceratops? He said there was an invisible line that you don't cross over. These folks walked over that line. They'll know better next time."

I saw Stiffy shuffling up the hill. "We've got to get him out of here," I said.

"Yes, but be nice about it," Rila said. "He's such a lovable old guy."

She went into the house and got a couple of bunches of carrots. Stiffy shuffled up and accepted the carrots very gracefully, grunting and mumbling at us. After a while, I led him off the ridge, back into the valley. "We'll have to take it easy on the handouts," I warned Rila. "If we don't, we'll have him up here all the time."

"You know, Asa," she said, paying no attention to what I had said, "I've decided where we'll build the house. Down there by that patch of crab apples. We can pipe water from the spring and the ridge will protect us from the northwest wind."

It was the first time I had heard about the house, but I didn't make a point of that. It was a good idea, actually. We couldn't go on living in a mobile home.

"I suppose you've decided what kind of house you want," I said.

"Well, not entirely. Not the floor plan. No detailed plan. Just in general. One story, low against the ground. Fieldstone, I suppose. That's a little old-fashioned, but it seems the kind of house that would fit in here. Expensive, too, but we should be able to afford it."

"Water from the spring," I said, "but what about the heating? After the telephone line that didn't work, I'm fairly sure we can't pipe in gas."

"I've thought about that. Build it tight and solid, well insulated, then use wood. A lot of fireplaces. We could get in men to cut and haul the wood. There's a lot of it in these hills. Off somewhere where we couldn't see the cutting. We wouldn't cut it nearby.

It would be a shame to spoil the woods we can see."

We talked about the house through supper. The more I thought about the idea, the better I liked it. I was glad Rila had thought of it.

"I believe I'll go over to Lancaster tomorrow and talk to a contractor," she said. "Ben should know a good one."

"The newsmen outside the gate will gobble you up," I said. "Herb still wants you to remain a mystery woman."

"Look, Asa, if need be, I can handle them. I handled them at the hospital that night we took Hiram in. At worst, I could hunker down in the back of the car, cover myself with a blanket or something. Ben would drive me out. Why don't you come along? We could go to the hospital and see Hiram."

"No," I said. "One of us should stay here. I promised Catface I'd see him today and didn't get around to it. I'll hunt him up tomorrow."

"What's this with you and Catface?" she demanded.

"He gets lonesome," I said.

The next morning, Catface was in the crab-apple patch, not in the old home orchard.

I squatted down and said to him, half joking, "Well, let's get on with it."

He took me at my word. Immediately, the minnows began bumping at my mind, lipping it, sucking away at it, but this time there seemed to be more of them and smaller—small, tiny slivers of minnows that could drive and wriggle themselves deeper and deeper into my mind. I could feel them wriggling deeply into the crevices of it.

A strange, dreamy lassitude was creeping over me and I fought against it. I was being plunged into a soft grayness that entangled me as the gossamer of a finely knit spiderweb might entrap an insect that had blundered into it.

I tried to break the web, to stagger to my feet, but found, with a queer not-caring, that I had no idea where I was. Found, as well, that I really had no concern as to where I might be. I knew, vaguely, that this was Mastodonia and that Catface was with me and that Rila had gone to Lancaster to see a contractor about building a fieldstone house and that we'd have to get men to bring in a winter's supply of wood for us, but this was all background material, all of it segregated from what was happening. I knew that, for a moment, I need not be concerned with it.

Then I saw it—the city, if it was a city. It seemed that I was sitting atop a high hill, beneath a lordly tree. The weather was fair and warm and the sky was the softest blue that I had ever seen.

Spread out in front of me was the city, and when I looked to either side, I saw that it was everywhere, that it went all around me and spread to the far-off horizon in all directions. The hill stood alone in the midst of the city, a fair hill, its slopes covered by a dark green grass and lovely flowers, blowing in a gentle breeze, and atop it, this one lordly tree beneath which I sat.

I had no idea of how I'd gotten there; I did not even wonder how I'd gotten there. It seemed quite natural that I should be there and it seemed as well that I should recognize the place, but, for the life of me, I couldn't. I had wondered on first seeing it if it was a city and now I knew it was, but I knew as well that it was something else as well, that it had a significance and that a knowledge of this significance was simply something I had forgotten, but would recall any minute now.

It was like no city I had ever seen before. There were parks and esplanades and wide, gracious streets and these all seemed familiar, although they were very splendid. But the buildings were not the kind of buildings one would have expected anywhere. They had no mass and even little form; rather, they were spiderwebby, lacy, filmy, foamy, insubstantial. Yet, when I looked more carefully at them, I could see that they were not as insubstantial as I had thought, that once I'd looked at them for a time, I began seeing them better, that when I first had looked at them, I had not seen them in their entirety, had been seeing only a part of them and that behind this facade of first seeing, the structures took on a more substantial

form. But there was still something about it all that
bothered me, and in time I realized it was the pattern of the city. The buildings did not stand in the
massive rectangles dictated by street patterns, as was
the case with cities on the Earth. That was it, I
thought: This was not an Earth city, although why this
surprised me I don't know, for I must have known
from the very beginning that it was no city of the
Earth—that it was Catface's city.

"It is headquarters," said Catface. "Galactic headquarters. I thought that to understand it, you should
see it."

"Thank you for showing it to me," I said. "It does
help me understand."

I was not surprised at all that Catface had spoken
to me. I was in that state where I'd have been surprised at nothing.

About this time, too, I realized that the little lipping minnows were no longer bumping against my
mind. Apparently, they had finished their job, gotten
all there was to be gotten, all the flaky skin, all the
little bloody scabs, and had gone away.

"This is where you were born?" I asked.

"No," said Catface. "Not where I began. I began
on another planet, very far from here. I will show it
to you some day if you have the time to look."

"But you were here," I said.

"I came as a volunteer," he said. "Or rather, I was
summoned as a volunteer."

"Summoned? How summoned? Who would sum-
mon you? If you're summoned, you're not a volunteer."

I tried to figure out if Catface and I were actually
speaking words, and it seemed to me we weren't, although it made no difference, for we were understanding one another just as well as if we had been
speaking words.

"You have the concept of a god," said Catface.
"Through the history of your race, men have worshipped many gods."

"I understand the concept," I said. "I'm not sure I

worship any god. Not the way most men would mean if they said they worshipped a god."

"Nor I," said Catface. "But if you saw who summoned me, and not only me, but many other creatures, you'd be convinced that they are gods. Which they are not, of course, although there are those who think they are. They are simply a life form, biological or otherwise—of that I can't be certain—that got an early start at intelligence and over millions of years were wise enough or lucky enough to avoid those catastrophic events that so often cause the downfall and decay of intelligence. They may have been biological at one time; certainly, they must have been. I'm not certain what they are now; over the long millennia, they may have changed themselves. . . ."

"Then you have seen them? Met them?"

"No one ever meets them. They are above all mingling with other creatures. They disdain us, or they may fear us, an unworthy thought that I had at one time. I must have been the only one, for no other has ever spoken to me of such a thing. But I saw one once, or think I saw one once, although I could not see him clearly. To impress the volunteers, they afford them all this glimpse—although care is taken not to let volunteers see too clearly—either through a veil of some sort or a shadow of one of them, I have no idea which."

"And you were not impressed?"

"At the time, I may have been. It was so long ago, it is difficult to remember. In your numerology, perhaps a million years ago. But I have thought about it since and have concluded that if I was impressed, I should not have been."

"This is their city? The so-called gods' city?"

"If you want to think of it that way. It was planned by them, although it was not built by them. It is not a city, really. It is a planet covered by buildings and installations. If that's a city, then it is a city."

"You said a galactic headquarters."

"That is right. A galactic headquarters, not the galactic headquarters. There may be others we do not know about. Other gods we do not know about. It seems credible to me that there may be other galactic groups that function exactly as this city does, but without the benefit of a central headquarters. Nothing nearly so formal as a headquarters, but perhaps some other plan that may perform much better."

"You're just guessing there may be another headquarters. You don't know."

"A galaxy is large. I don't know."

"These people, these gods, take over planets and exploit them?"

"Exploit? I snare the meaning, but the concept is hazy. You mean own? Use?"

"Yes."

"Not that," said Catface. "Information only. The knowing, that's the thing."

"Gathering knowledge, you mean?"

"That is right. Your comprehension amazes me. They send out ships, with many study groups. Drop one study group here, another there. Later, another ship comes and picks them up, each one in turn. I was of one study group, the last one. We had dropped four others."

"Then your ship crashed?"

"Yes. I do not understand how it could have happened. Each of us is a specialist. Knows his job, nothing else. The creatures that operated the ship were also specialists. They should have known, should have foreseen. The crash should not have happened."

"You told Hiram, or was it Rila, you told one of them that you do not know the location of this planet that you came from. That's why you don't know; it was not your specialty to know. Only the pilot or the pilots knew."

"My specialty was only to go into time. To observe and record the past of the planet under study."

"You mean your planetary surveys not only included what the planet was at the present moment, but what it had been in the past. You studied each planet's evolution."

"Must do so. The present is only a part of it. How the present came to be is important, too."

"The others were killed when the ship crashed. But you . . ."

"I was lucky," said Catface.

"But once you got here, you did not study the past. You stayed in Willow Bend, or what was about to become Willow Bend."

"I made a few excursions only. My observations alone would have been worthless. I made the way for others. And something else—I knew another ship would come to pick us up. They would not know of the crash; they would come expecting to find us. And I told myself if the ship should come, I must be here to meet it. I could not leave. If I went into the past, there would not be others here to call me if the ship should come. The ship would have found evidence of the crash, would assume that all were dead, would not wait. To be picked up, to be rescued as you call it, I knew I must stay close to the crash site so I could be found."

"But you opened roads for Bowser, roads for us."

"If I cannot use roads myself, why not let others use them? Why not let my friends use them?"

"You thought of us as friends?"

"Bowser first," he said, "then the rest of you."

"Now you are concerned there'll be no ship to pick you up."

"Long," said Catface. "Too long. And yet, they may look. Not many of my kind. We are valuable. They would not lightly give us up."

"You still have hope?"

"Very feeble hope."

"That is why you spend so much time in the old home orchard? So you will be there if they come to pick you up."

"That is why," said Catface.

"You are happy here?"

"What is happy? Yes, I suppose I'm happy."

What is happy? he had asked, making out that he did not know what happiness might be. But he knew all right. At one time, he had been happy, exalted, overawed—on that day, when on summons, he had come to that great galactic headquarters, joining the elite company that was legend through those parts of the star system touched by the great confederation.

Unquestionably, not asking how it could be so, I moved with him through that fantastic city, fresh from a backwoods planet, agape at all I saw, filled with wonderment not only at what I saw, but at the fact I should be there at all. And I went with him to other planets as well, catching only glimpses of them, burrowing briefly into the kinds of places they had been in ages past. I stood before glories that put a pang into my heart, glimpsed miseries that engulfed my soul in sadness, worried over mysteries as a dog would worry an ancient bone, grasped frantically at sciences and cultures that were beyond my capacity to understand.

Then, quite suddenly, it was all gone, and I was back in the crab-apple patch, face to face with Catface. My mind still seethed with wonder and I had lost all track of time.

"Hiram?" I asked. "Did Hiram . . ."

"No," said Catface. "Hiram could not understand."

And that was right, of course. Hiram could not have understood. He had complained, I remembered, that Catface had said many things he could not understand.

"No one else," said Catface. "No one else but you."

"But I'm confused," I said. "Many things I do not understand."

"Your understanding," he said, "is greater than you know."

"I'll be back again," I said. "We will talk again."

I went up the hillside, and when I got back to the mobile home, there was no one there. I wondered if that last safari might have come out while I had been with Catface. I had not worried about it when I'd left because I felt that if they came out, most certainly I'd hear them. But during my conversation with Catface, I doubted I'd have heard anything at all. So I went down to the mouth of time road number one and there were no tracks coming out. That meant they were two days overdue. If they didn't come out tomorrow, I told myself, Ben and I probably should go in to see what was delaying them. Not that I was worried. Percy Aspinwall had struck me as a man who was entirely competent. Yet I found myself uneasy.

I went back to the mobile home and sat on the steps. Bowser crawled from underneath the house and clambered up the steps to sit beside me, plastered close against me. It was almost like the old days, before Rila had arrived and all this business of time travel had started.

I had been half numbed at first after what had happened with Catface, but now I could begin to think about it. At first, while it had been happening, the whole thing had seemed almost routine, nothing to be greatly astounded at, the sort of circumstance that one could confidently have anticipated. But now, with time to think about it, I began to feel cold spider feet walking up and down my spine, and while I knew that it had really happened, I began to feel a flood of denial welling up in me. The old human game of saying that something had not happened so that it would not have happened.

But despite the automatic denial, I knew damn well that it had happened, and I sat there on the steps trying to get it straight in my mind. But I didn't have the chance to do much straightening out because just when I had got settled down to it, Rila came driving up the ridge and beside her sat Hiram.

Hiram leaped down as soon as the car had stopped and made straight for Bowser. He didn't waste any words on me; I'm not sure he even saw me. Bowser came down off the steps at the sight of him and Hiram went down on his knees, throwing his arms around the dog, while Bowser, whimpering and whining in his happiness, washed Hiram's face with a busy tongue.

Rila rushed up to me and threw her arms around me and there were the four of us, Hiram hugging Bowser and Rila hugging me.

"Isn't it nice to have Hiram back?" she asked. "The hospital said it was all right for him to leave, but that he had to take it easy and build up his strength. It seems he lost a lot of strength. He's not to do much work and he . . . "

"That's all right," I said. "Hiram never was what you might call addicted to work."

"He should take some exercise every day," she said. "Walking is the best. And he should have a high-protein diet and there is some medicine that he has to take. He doesn't like the medicine. Says it tastes awful bad. But he promised to take it if they let him leave. And, oh, Asa, you should see the kind of house we're going to build. I haven't got the plans as yet, but I can draw you a rough sketch of it. All fieldstone and lots of big chimneys—there'll be fireplaces in almost every room. And a lot of glass. Entire walls of thermoglass so that we can look out on this world of ours. Just like we were sitting outdoors. There will be a patio and an outdoor broiler, built of stone just like the house and a stone chimney to carry off the smoke and a swimming pool if it's something that you'd like. I think that I would like it. Water from the spring to fill it and that water's awfully cold, but the contractor said that in a day or two, the sun will warm it and then there's . . . "

I saw Hiram and Bowser walking off, heading down the ridge, and they either didn't hear me shout at them or paid no attention, so I went running after them.

I caught Hiram by the shoulder and turned him around.

"Where do you think you're going?" I asked. "Rila says you have to take it easy, not too much exertion."

"But Mr. Steele," said Hiram, in all reasonableness, "I just have to see how Stiffy is getting along. I have to let him know I'm back."

"Not today," I said. "Tomorrow, maybe. We'll take a car and see if we can find him."

I herded the two of them back, Hiram protesting all the way.

"And you," said Rila, "how did you spend your day?"

"Talking with Catface," I said.

She laughed gaily. "What did you find to talk about?"

"Quite a lot," I said.

Then she was off on the matter of the house and I never got a word in edgewise. She talked about it until we went to bed. I'd never seen her so happy and excited.

I told myself that I'd tell her about Catface in the morning, but it didn't work out that way. Ben got me out of bed, pounding on the door and yelling for me to get out of there.

I staggered out bias-eyed, not dressed.

"What the hell is going on?" I asked. "What is it that can't wait?"

"The Safari bunch is on the prod," he said. "They are getting nervous. They want us to go in and see what is holding up Aspinwall and his outfit."

TWENTY-EIGHT

Ben had more to worry about than the overdue safari. He told me about it as we got ready for the trip.

"That goddamn Hotchkiss," he said, "opened up a can of worms. Churches and church organizations are lining up. One newspaper writer the other day said there's been nothing like it since the Reformation. The Vatican is expected to make a statement in another week or two. I meant to bring you this morning's paper, but I got busy with other things and forgot it. Petitions are being circulated to ask Congress to pass a law about going back into the early Christian era. The congressmen are running for cover. They want no part of it. They cite the separation of church and state; because of that, they say, they have no authority to pass any kind of law bearing on the matter. A couple of them pointed out, too, that we are the only ones who can send anyone into time and they have no authority here, either, because Mastodonia is not a part of the United States. I'm afraid there'll be an argument over that, too, if this controversy keeps on. I think everyone's confused. They don't know if we're part of the USA or not."

"We can make as good an argument against being part of the country," I said, "as anyone can claiming we are."

"I know," said Ben, "but if that gets to be a part of general argument in this church uproar, it is going to strike pretty close to home. I don't like it, Asa. I don't like any of it."

I didn't like it either, but right at the time, I wasn't as upset about it as he was.

Rila was determined to go into the Cretaceous with us, and it took us quite a while to convince her she'd better stay behind. She was all burned up at not being allowed to go along. She was outraged; she said she had the right to go.

"Not a chance," I told her. "You risked your neck once and that's enough. That time we had to go for broke, but this time, it's different. We'll be back in a little while."

It developed that during all the ruckus, Hiram had sneaked off to go hunting Stiffy. Rila wanted me to go after him, but I said to hell with him; I said that if, right at that moment, I did go after him, I'd most likely shoot him and have it over with.

So Ben and I started out in something of a foul mood. When we hit the Cretaceous, the local weather didn't help us any. It was hot and stormy and the landscape steamed. A high, hot wind was blowing; the touch of it almost burned you. Great cloud masses, torn apart, raced across the sky, and every once in a while one of the clouds would pull itself together and deliver a five-minute downpour of rain so warm that it seemed to be scalding. Underfoot, the ground was greasy from being soaked by the intermittent downpours, but Ben's four-wheel drive was a good mudder and we didn't have too much trouble with it.

The vile weather apparently had tamed down the fauna. Most of them, perhaps, were hiding out in groves of trees. Those that we did disturb went racing away from us, including one small tyrannosaur. We had to drive around a herd of triceratops, who stood with their heads drooping, not bothering to graze, just waiting for the weather to get decent.

The track made by the safari was fairly easy to follow, the wheels of the heavy trucks leaving deep depressions in the soil. In a few places, recent rains had either filled the tracks or washed them out, but where they were missing, it was no great problem to pick them up again.

We found the first campsite about five miles down the river valley. It seemed the safari had stayed there for several days. The campfire locations were thick with ash and there had been a lot of traffic out and back. After some looking, we found the trail the outfit had made in moving out: west over the ridge across the river, then across a prairie for twenty miles or so.

At the end of that twenty miles, the country broke suddenly, plunging down into the valley of the Raccoon River. The trail that we were following snaked crookedly down the hills. As we rounded the sharp angle of a ridge, we came upon the camp. Ben braked the car to a halt and for a moment we sat there, saying nothing. Tents, many of them down, fluttered in the wind. One truck was tipped over on its side. The other was in a ditch, one of those deep gullies so characteristic of the Cretaceous, its nose buried against one wall of the gully, its back canted up at a steep angle.

Nothing moved except the fluttering fabric of the tents. There was no smoke; the campfires had burned out. Here and there were clutters of scattered whiteness lying on the ground.

"For the love of God!" said Ben.

Slowly, he took his foot off the brake and let the car ease forward. We crept down the slope and into the camp. The place was littered with debris. Cooking utensils were scattered about the dead fires. Torn clothing was tramped into the ground. Dropped rifles lay here and there. The scattered whitenesses were bones—human bones polished clean by scavengers.

Ben braked the car to a halt and I got out, cradling the heavy rifle in the crook of my arm. For a long time I stood there, looking around, trying to absorb the enormity of what I saw, my mind stubbornly refusing to accept the full impact of the evidence. I heard Ben get out on the other side of the car. His feet crunched as he walked around the vehicle to stand beside me.

He spoke harshly, as if he were fighting to keep his voice level. "It must have happened a week or more ago. Probably only a day or so after their arrival here. Look at those bones. Stripped clean. It took a while to do that."

I tried to answer, but I couldn't. I found that I had my teeth clenched hard to keep them from chattering.

"None got away," said Ben. "How come none got away?"

I forced myself to speak. "Maybe some of them did. Out in the hills."

Ben shook his head. "If they had been able, they would have tried to follow the trail back home. We would have found them coming in. A man alone, or an injured man, would have no chance. If something didn't snap him up on the first day, they would have on the next, certainly the next after that."

Ben left me and walked out into the campsite. After a minute or so, I trailed after him.

"Asa," Ben said. He had stopped and was staring at something on the ground. "Look at that. Look at that track."

It had been blurred by rain. Little pools of water stood in the deep imprints left by the claws. It was huge. The blurring might have enlarged it or given the impression that it was larger than it actually was, but the print appeared to measure two feet or more across at its breadth. Beyond it and slightly to the left was another similar footprint.

"Not rex," said Ben. "Bigger than rex. Bigger than anything we know. And look over there. There are more tracks."

Now that Ben had found the first track, we could see that the area was covered with them.

"Three-toed," said Ben. "Reptilian. Two-legged, I'd guess."

"From the looks of the evidence," I said, "a pack of them. One, or even two, couldn't make that many tracks. Remember our pair of tyrannosaurs? We thought they hunted in pairs. Before that, the impression was they hunted alone. Maybe they hunt in packs. Sweeping across the country like a pack of wolves, grabbing everything they can find. A pack would pick up more prey than a lone hunter or even a pair of them."

"If that is the case," said Ben, "if they hunt in packs, Aspinwall and the others didn't have a prayer."

We walked across the campsite, trying hard not to look too closely at some of the things we saw. The four-wheel drives, curiously, stood where they had been parked. Only one of them had been knocked over. Cartridge cases gleamed dully in the half-light of the cloudy day. Rifles lay here and there. And everywhere, the marks of those huge, three-clawed footprints.

The wind whined and moaned in the hollows and across the ridges that ran down to the river valley. The sky of torn and racing clouds boiled like a cauldron. From far off came the rumble of thunder.

Leering out of a small thicket at me was a skull, tattered bits of hairy scalp still clinging to it, a patch of beard adhering to the jawbone. Gagging, I turned back to the car. I'd had enough.

Ben's bellow stopped me. When I looked back, I saw him standing at the edge of a deep gully that ran down the southern edge of the campsite.

"Asa, over here!" he yelled.

I staggered back to where he stood. In the gully lay a pile of massive bones. Bits of scaly hide fluttered from some of them. A rib cage lay gaping, a clawed foot thrust upward, a skull with the jawbone still attached had the look of being interrupted in executing a mangling snap.

"That foot," said Ben. "The one sticking up. That's a forefoot. Well developed, strong, not like the forelimb of a rex."

"An allosaur," I told him. "It has to be an allosaur. One grown to gigantic size, its fossilized bones never found by anyone."

"Well, at least we know our people got one of them."

"They may have gotten others. If we looked around . . . "

"No," said Ben. "I've seen enough. Let's get out of here."

TWENTY-NINE

Ben phoned Courtney, while Rila and I listened in on other phones. We were a fairly sober lot.

"Court, we have bad news," said Ben when Courtney came on the line.

"I welcome you to the club," said Courtney. "This Hotchkiss business is getting out of hand. It could cause us trouble. The whole damn country's upset. Everyone is getting into the act."

"I don't like it either," said Ben, "but that's not what we are calling you about. You know one of the safaris is overdue."

"Yes, a couple of days or so. Nothing to worry about. Found better hunting than they expected. Or drove farther than they realized. Maybe vehicle breakdown."

"We thought the same," said Ben, "but this morning I got a call from Safari in New York. They were a little nervous. Asked if we could check. So Asa and I went in. Asa's on the phone with me now. So is Rila."

Suddenly, Courtney's voice took on a note of worry. "You found everything all right, of course."

"No, we didn't," said Ben. "The expedition was wiped out. All of them dead. . . ."

"Dead? All of them?"

"Asa and I found no survivors. We didn't try to count the bodies. Not bodies, really—skeletons. It was pretty horrible. We got out of there."

"But dead! What could . . . "

"Courtney," I said, "the evidence is they were attacked by a pack of carnosaurs."

"I didn't know carnosaurs ran in packs."

"Neither did I. Neither did anyone. But the evi-

202

dence is they do. More footprints than would be made by just two or three . . . "

"Footprints?"

"Not only footprints. We found the skeleton of a large carnosaur. Not a tyrannosaur. An allosaur, more than likely. Quite a bit bigger than rex."

"You talk about skeletons. Not bodies, but skeletons."

"Court, it must have happened quite a while ago," said Ben. "Maybe shortly after they went in. Looks as if the scavengers had a while to work on them."

"What we want to know," said Rila, "is where we stand legally. And what do we do next?"

There was a long silence on the other end, then Courtney said, "Legally, we are blameless. Safari signed a waiver to cover each group that went in. The contract also makes it clear we are not responsible for anything that happens. If you're wondering if they can sue us, I don't think they can. There are no grounds."

"How about the clients they took along?"

"Same thing. Safari is responsible if anyone is. I suppose the clients also signed waivers, holding Safari blameless. I would think it would be regular procedure. What we have to worry about is the impact on Safari's business. Once this is known, will clients cancel out? What will be the impact on public opinion? Will some damn fool come out screaming that safaris into the past must be stopped? You must remember, too, that Safari has paid only half of the contract fee. The other half is due in six months. They could hold up payment, or refuse payment on the second half."

"It all depends," said Ben, "on how Safari takes this news."

"They're hard-headed businessmen," said Courtney. "Sure, this is a tragic thing, but tragedies do happen. Miners are killed in mines, but mining still goes on. If too many clients cancel, if others don't come in and sign up for the hunts, then they will be concerned."

"Some may cancel," said Ben. "Not many. I know the breed. This will only make it more zestful. Something big back there, something dangerous, let us go and get it. A bigger trophy than anyone has ever dreamed."

"I hope you're right," said Courtney. "Safari is the only deal, so far, that we have going for us. It does beat hell. We thought there'd be other big deals knocking at our door, but they're slow developing. The same with things we worried about. We figured the IRS would hassle us. They did come sniffing around, but that is all, so far."

"Maybe they're lying low," said Ben, "trying to figure out a line of approach."

"Maybe so," said Courtney.

"How about the movie people?" Rila asked. "Is this lost safari going to scare them off?"

"I doubt it," Courtney said. "All of the periods are not as dangerous as the Cretaceous, are they, Asa?"

"The Jurassic could be hairy," I told him. "Those two would be the worst. Every period would have its dangers if you don't watch your step. It's all unknown country."

"The immediate question is how to let Safari know," said Ben. "I can phone them. But I thought we should fill you in before we did anything."

"Why don't you let me phone them, Ben? I know them a little better than the rest of you. Except Rila, perhaps. How about it, Rila?"

"You go ahead," said Rila. "You'll do a good job of it. Better than any of the rest of us."

"They may want to call you back. Will you be there?"

"I'll be here," said Ben.

THIRTY

Late in the afternoon, Safari phoned Ben. They would send in an expedition, they said, to visit the scene of the disaster and bring out what remained of the victims.

Rila and I went back to Mastodonia. Neither of us had much to say on the trip; both of us were depressed.

Hiram and Bowser were waiting for us, perched on the steps. Hiram was bubbling with talk. He had found Stiffy and had a good talk with him; he had hunted up Catface and talked with him as well. Both had been glad to see him, and he had told them all about his stay in the hospital. Bowser, he said, had found a woodchuck, run him into a hole and tried to dig him out. Hiram had hauled him from the hole and rebuked him. Bowser, he said, was ashamed of himself. Hiram had fried some eggs for lunch, but Bowser, he reminded us severely, did not care for eggs. We should always plan to leave some cold roast for Bowser.

After dinner, Rila and I sat out on the patio. Bowser and Hiram, tired out with their day, went to bed.

"I'm worried, Asa," Rila said. "If Safari has paid us only half of the contract, we may be running low on funds. We gave Ben his commission on the Safari deal even though he had nothing to do with it."

"He had it coming," I said. "Maybe he had nothing to do with the Safari contract, but he worked his tail off for us."

"I'm not complaining about it," said Rila. "I don't begrudge it to him. But it all adds up. The fence cost us a fortune and the office building didn't come cheap. The salaries for the guards run to several hundred dollars a day. We still have money, but it's being eaten up. If Safari should pull out, if the movie people decide to wait, we could be in trouble."

"Safari won't pull out," I said. "They may mark time for a while until this blows over. But Ben is right. The more dangerous the situation, the more anxious your hunting type will be to have a shot at it. The movie company I don't know about, but they had dollar signs in their eyes. They won't pass it by."

"Another thing," said Rila. "Courtney doesn't work cheap. God knows what kind of bill he is piling up."

"Let's not get upset right yet," I said. "It will all work out."

"You think I'm greedy, don't you, Asa?"

"Greedy? I don't know. You're a businesswoman. You spent all those years in business."

"It's not business," she said. "It's not greed. It's security. Even more than a man, a woman needs to feel secure. Most women can feel secure in a family, but I didn't have a family. I had to look for some other basis for security and I came up with money. Money seemed the answer. If I could pile up enough money, then I'd be secure. That's why I am so grabby. That's why I latched onto the time-travel idea so fast. I saw big possibilities in it."

"There are still big possibilities."

"There are also headaches. And our base is so slight. Catface and Hiram. If either of them fails us . . ."

"We managed without Hiram."

"Yes, I suppose so. But it was awfully awkward."

"Not any more," I said. "I've been trying to tell you for a couple of days, but I never had the chance. First, there was the house, then Hiram coming back, and after that, what happened to the Safari people. What I wanted to tell you is that I can talk with Catface."

She looked at me in surprise. "You mean, really talk to him? Just like Hiram?"

"Better than Hiram," I said. Then I went ahead and told her, while she watched me closely, with a faint tinge of disbelief.

"What a spooky business," she said. "I would have been scared."

"I wasn't scared. I was too numb to be scared."

"Why do you think he tried so hard? To fix it so he could talk with you?"

"He ached to talk to someone."

"But he could talk with Hiram."

"Hiram wasn't here, remember? He hadn't been for days. I don't think Catface understood what had happened to him. And Hiram would not have been the most satisfactory person to talk to. He would have understood very little of what Catface showed to me. Catface is a human sort of being."

"Human?"

"Yes, human. An alien, sure. But with certain human characteristics you'd not expect to find. Perhaps he hid his alien characteristics from me, accentuated what you might call his human streak. . . . "

"In which case," said Rila, "he is a very clever creature. And sophisticated."

"Anything that has lived for a million years would have to be sophisticated."

"Once he told us he was immortal."

"We didn't talk about that. Not a great deal, actually, about himself."

"You're fascinated by him," Rila said.

"Yes, I suppose I am. Funny thing about it is that I have talked with an alien intelligence. That's the kind of thing a newspaper would blow into big headlines. A sensational story. Rightly sensational, I suppose, for it is something that has been written about and talked about for years. Are there other intelligences in the universe? What would happen if a human met an alien? All the wonder about that first contact. But to me it doesn't seem sensational at all. It all seems friendly and quite ordinary."

"You're a strange man, Asa," Rila said. "You always were a strange man. I think that's why I love you. What other people think makes no mark upon you. You think for yourself alone."

"Thank you, my dear," I said.

And I sat there, thinking about Catface, wondering about him. He was out there now in the gathering dusk, perhaps in the crab-apple patch, perhaps in the old home orchard. And I found, as I thought about him, that I knew much more about him than he had told me. The knowledge, for example, that he was not biological, but some strange combination of electronic-molecular life that I could not understand. Perhaps, I thought, an electronics engineer might be able to understand it, but not in its entirety. The knowledge, too, that he thought of time not as a part of the space-time continuum, not as a glue that held the universe together, but as an independent factor that could be explained by certain equations, which I could neither recognize nor make any sense of (for no equation made any sense to me) and that it could be regulated or manipulated if one had an understanding of the equations. And the knowledge that while he had said he was immortal, he still held a faith and a hope of afterlife—which seemed to be an extremely strange idea, for to an immortal, there should be no need of such faith or hope.

How was it, I asked myself, that I should know such things about him? I was certain he had not told me, but it was, I admitted, possible that he had, for during much of the time that he had talked to me, I had been confused and perhaps not as sharp as I should have been.

Rila got up. "Let's be off to bed," she said. "Maybe tomorrow will be a better day."

It turned out to be not a bad day, not a good day; actually, nothing much happened.

Late in the morning, Rila and I drove to Willow Bend. Hiram had already disappeared somewhere, leaving with Bowser shortly after breakfast. We didn't try to hunt them down and herd them home. We couldn't spend all our spare time playing nursemaid to Hiram. He'd been told at the hospital to take it easy, but the only way to make him take it easy was to hogtie him.

Ben had got word that the Safari people would arrive the next day. There were no indications, how-ever, when, or if, other safaris would be coming in.

The newspapers had given a lot of space to the Cretaceous disaster. According to the stories, Safari,

Inc., had made an almost immediate disclosure of the incident. There had been no attempt to soft-pedal the horror of it, but Safari officials were quoted as saying that over the years many people had died while on safari—that this was different only in that the entire party had been wiped out.

With the disaster taking up a good part of the front pages of the papers we saw, the Hotchkiss story had been shoved onto inside pages, but it was still there, many columns of it. The wrangling over whether it was proper to travel into the past to study the life of Jesus was still going full blast. It had been a long day since the news editors had been given a chance at so large and wide a controversy, and they were making the most of it.

Rila stayed at the office to talk with Ben and Herb, but I cut out, after a short time, to see if Catface might be in the orchard. He did happen to be there.

I didn't tell him anything of what had happened. I was not sure he'd be much interested and, besides, there were a lot of other matters we could talk about.

We settled down to talk and spent a couple of hours at it. It was not so much talking as showing. As had happened before, I found myself sort of tucked into Catface, as if I were part of him, seeing through his eyes.

He showed me more of the headquarters city and some of the specialists who worked there: the insect-like race that were trained historians, paying attention not so much to the events of history as to trends and development, treating history as a science rather than a mere progression of happenings; the globe-shaped creatures who specialized as sociologists, working to identify the racial characteristics and the historical trends that made intelligent beings what they were; the snaky whitherers, who dealt not so much in prediction as in scientifically attempting to extrapolate the future trends of civilization, trying in the course of their studies to pinpoint possible future crisis points.

He also tried to show me how he employed certain equations and manipulated certain forces (all of which were beyond my understanding) to construct the time roads. I asked him a lot of questions, but it appeared that my questions were so wide of the mark that they did no more than confuse him. When he did try to explain, his explanations confused me more than ever.

Knowing that Rila probably was wondering where I'd gone, I broke off the talk and went back to the office. Rila, Ben and Herb were still deep in conversation and seemed not to have noticed my absence.

Early the next morning, the Safari expedition showed up. Ben and I went into the Cretaceous with them and this time, Rila went along.

It was a grisly business. I did none of the work, but only stood around and watched. The crew put the stripped human skeletons into plastic bags, making the best guesses they could as to which bones belonged to which skeletons. In some cases, however, the bones had been dragged around a bit and I'm not sure the effort was successful. In a few instances, where ID bracelets or chains were still in place, some identification was possible, but most of the bags were anonymous.

The skeleton of the huge allosaur, if that was what it was, also was loaded on one of the trucks. A Harvard paleontologist had asked that it be brought back.

In a couple or three hours time, the campsite was cleared of all bones, guns, ammunition, tents and other supplies, and we returned. I don't mind admitting I was glad once we were back in Mastodonia.

Ten days went past. The newspapers were hammering away at both the stories—the Cretaceous disaster and the Jesus uproar. A couple of suits were filed against Safari. Several members of Congress made speeches calling for governmental regulation of time travel. The Justice Department called a press conference to explain that regulation would be difficult since Time Associates were operating in what amounted to a foreign nation, although it was stressed that the status of Mastodonia under international law was far from clear. The number of newsmen and camera crews who had been standing watch at the gate in Willow Bend shrank considerably.

Stiffy came up the ridge several times to visit us, and after paying him off with carrots, we shagged him out of there. Hiram was outraged that we didn't want him around. Bowser got into a fight with a badger and was soundly whipped. Hiram spent two days holding his paw until his lacerations began to heal. The crowd of tourists fell off slightly, but Ben's parking lot and motel were still doing a good business. Ben drove Rila to Lancaster; she hid in the back of the car until they were out of Willow Bend. She talked with the contractor and came home with a set of preliminary blueprints. We spent several nights with the plans spread out on the kitchen table, talking over what we wanted modified or changed.

"It will cost us a lot," she told me. "Twice as much as I had expected. But I think, even at the worst, there'll be enough money to build it. And I want it so badly, Asa. I want to live in Mastodonia and have a good house to live in."

"So do I," I said. "One of the nice things about it is that we won't have to pay taxes on it."

I had several conversations with Catface. When Hiram found out that I could talk with Catface, his nose got slightly out of joint, but in a day or two, he got over it.

Ben had some good news. Courtney phoned to say the movie people were negotiating again. Safari announced that it would be sending out more safaris in a week or ten days.

Then the bottom fell out of everything.

Courtney phoned Ben to say that he was flying to Lancaster, asking to be picked up there. "I'll tell you what it's all about," he had said, "when I get there." Herb drove in to tell us and we were waiting in Ben's office when Courtney and Ben arrived.

Ben got out a bottle and paper cups.

"That's a good idea," Courtney said. "We all better have a stiff drink to brace ourselves. This time we really are in trouble."

We sat and waited for the word.

"I don't know all the details yet," said Courtney, "but I wanted to talk with you to get an idea of what you may want to do. You've been placed under quarantine. The State Department issued an order this morning barring American citizens from entering Mastodonia."

"But they can't do that," said Rila.

"I'm not sure whether they can or not," said Courtney. "I think, perhaps, they can. The fact is that they have. No reason given. I assume they might not have to cite a reason. As a matter of fact, it is within their power to do this anywhere in the world simply by specifying countries to which a citizen may not travel."

"Why should they want to do it?" asked Ben.

"I'm not sure. Perhaps this Jesus business. The Cretaceous disaster may have something to do with it as well; Mastodonia opens the gate to places where it isn't safe for a citizen to travel. But I would suspect the other matter. It is causing worldwide ruckuses. It is tearing this country apart. There was a lot of wailing in Congress that the issue was ever allowed to arise. Terrific pressure groups are developing. It is the hottest potato Washington has ever fielded, or tried to field. The answer, of course, is to strike at Mastodonia and time travel. If you can't get to Mastodonia, you can't travel in time. And if you can't travel in time, the Jesus issue becomes moot."

"This means that Safari can't use the time roads," said Ben. "That nobody can use the time roads. This probably kills the talks with the movie people. This action could put us out of business."

"At the moment, it does," said Courtney. "We can move for a temporary injunction. If the injunction is granted by the court, then we'll be back in business until the merits of the case can be adjudicated. The court then could make the injunction permanent, which would mean we'd be back in business for good, or it could deny the injunction, which would mean that the order would stand and we'd be out of business for good."

"Or we could move the operation to some other country," said Rila.

"I suppose that could be done," Courtney told her. "But it would involve negotiations with the country you wanted to move to and that might take considerable time. I wouldn't be surprised if it also would require substantial payments of monies."

"Bribes," said Ben.

"They'd probably call it something else. Most nations, in the face of what our government has done, would be reluctant to let us in. First, you'd have to find a country. I warn you it would not be one of the better countries, probably a dictatorship. Once you were there, you might find the officials difficult to get along with. There is one good thing about the State Department order. It tacitly admits that Mastodonia is another country and that spikes the guns of the IRS."

"You'll file for the injunction soon," said Ben.

"Immediately," said Courtney. "I think it likely I can convince Safari and the movie people to join us in the action. They can claim unfair restraint of trade. There probably are a lot of other arguments we can cite. I'll have to think about that."

"It looks as if we'll just have to hunker down and weather the storm," said Ben. "How certain are you that you will get an injunction?"

"I honestly don't know. Ordinarily, it's no great problem to get a temporary injunction. But in this case, we are bucking the State Department. That could be heavy."

He hesitated for a moment and then said, "I don't know if I should mention this right now, but I suppose I may as well. There may be another out. I'm not sure. I may have my signals wrong. But the CIA has been in to talk with me. Hinting about cooperation and our patriotic duties. Trying to make it off the record, but I never told them it was off the record—although if I were you, I'd not talk about it. I gained the impression they'd like to use time travel to get some of their men into position ahead of time in some sticky situations. They didn't say so, but that's one way they could use time travel. I played stupid, but I don't think I fooled them."

"You mean that if we'd let them use time travel," said Ben, "the State Department might lift the order. That the order may be no more than a pressure tactic."

"I can't be sure," said Courtney. "The signal's not strong enough. If I signaled back to the CIA we were willing, there might suddenly be a lot of pressure on the State Department."

"Well, why don't we try it," said Ben. "It's no skin off our noses who uses time travel, or for what."

"No," said Rila.

"Why not?" asked Ben.

"Once you give the government a foot in the door, they begin taking over," she said.

"I'm inclined to agree," said Courtney. "My advice, for what it's worth, is to save the CIA for future consideration. We might want to make that last desperate deal to save ourselves."

"Okay," said Ben. "I guess that makes sense."

"Understand, I'm not even sure how the CIA ties into this," said Courtney. "I'm just guessing."

He rose and said, "Ben, if you'd drive me back. I have work to do."

Rila and I headed for home. As we drove into Mastodonia, we saw at once something was wrong. The mobile home had been tipped over. Standing beside it was Stiffy. Bowser stood a little way off, barking fiercely. Hiram was belaboring Stiffy with a stick, but the old mastodon was paying no attention to him.

I speeded up the car.

"He's after those goddamn carrots," I said. "We never should have fed them to him."

I saw as we drove nearer that he was not only after the carrots; he already had them. He had smashed the kitchen end of the home, had somehow gotten the refrigerator open, and was contentedly munching carrots.

I skidded the car to a halt and the two of us jumped out. I started forward, but Rila grabbed me and held on.

"What are you going to do?" she asked. "If you try to drive him off . . . "

"Drive him off, hell," I yelled. "I'm going to get a rifle and shoot the son-of-a-bitch. I should have done it long ago."

"No," she shouted. "No, not Stiffy. He is such a nice old guy."

Hiram was yelling at him, one word over and over: "Naughty, naughty, naughty."

And, as he yelled at Stiffy, he beat him with the stick. Stiffy went on eating carrots.

"You can't get a gun, anyhow," said Rila.

"If I can clamber up there and get the door open, I can. The rack is just inside."

Hiram yelled and beat at Stiffy. Stiffy switched his tail, leisurely and happily. He was having a good time.

As I stood there, I found the anger draining out of me and I began to laugh. It was ridiculous—Hiram yelling and wailing away at Stiffy and Stiffy paying no attention whatsoever.

Rila was weeping. She had let go of me and her arms hung at her side. She stood erect, too stiffly erect, while she was racked by sobs. Tears ran down her cheeks. In a few more minutes, I realized, she could become hysterical.

I put an arm around her and got her turned around and urged her back toward the car.

"Asa," she gasped between her sobs, "it's awful. Nothing has gone right today."

I got her in the car, then went back to collect Hiram. I grabbed him by the arm that held the stick and took it away from him.

"Cut out that yelling," I told him sternly. "It's not doing any good."

He looked at me, blinking, surprised to see me there.

"But, Mr. Steele," he said, "I told him and I told him. I told him not to do it, but he did it just the same."

"Get in the car," I said.

Obediently, he shuffled toward the car.

"Come on," I said to Bowser. Bowser, no fool, glad

to get off the hook, stopped his barking and trotted at my heels.

"In the car," I told him and he jumped in back with Hiram.

"What are we going to do?" asked Rila wildly. "What can we do?"

"We're going back to the farm," I told her. "We can stay there for a while."

That night, in my arms, she cried herself to sleep.

"Asa," she said, "I love Mastodonia. I want to have a house there."

"You will," I said. "You will. One too big and strong for Stiffy to tip over."

"And, Asa, I so wanted to be rich."

I had no assurances on that.

THIRTY-ONE

Ben and Herb went back to Mastodonia with us. We used a block and tackle to tip the home upright. It took us the better part of the day, once that was done, to repair the structural damage. Once we were through, the place was livable. Despite Stiffy's messing around to get it open, the refrigerator had not been damaged.

The next day, over the protests of both Hiram and Rila, we took two four-wheel drives and went looking for Stiffy. We found him in the valley and herded him down it. He got irate at the treatment and several times threatened to charge. We made discreet use of shotguns loaded with birdshot, which would sting but do no damage, to keep him on the move. He protested, grumbling and groaning every foot of the way. We shagged him about twenty miles before we turned back home.

A few days later, he was back in his old stamping ground, but from then on, despite whatever memory he might have had of carrots, he did not bother us. I gave Hiram strict orders to leave him alone and, for once, Hiram paid some attention to what I told him.

We had not heard from Courtney for several days. When he finally got in touch with us, I was in the office talking with Ben. Ben signaled me to pick up another phone.

Courtney said he had moved for a temporary injunction, joined by Safari and the movie people. But the proceedings, he said, were going to take longer than he had thought because of the number of complex arguments cited by both sides. He was particularly incensed by one allegation put forth in defense of the State Department ban—that traveling into time presented a health hazard. He would, he said, be quite willing to agree that travel into more recent, historic times might present such a danger, but the government brief had extended the claim to include time brackets millions of years into the past, postulating that bacteria and viruses that had existed in those times might be able to adapt to the human organism and bring about plagues that could become pandemic.

There had been, Courtney reported, no further word from the CIA.

"Maybe State has called them off," he said.

Senator Freemore had been in to tell him that bills would be introduced in both houses of Congress to implement emigration of the disadvantaged population (or such of them as might want to go) into prehistoric periods. Freemore, he said, wanted to know what period would be best.

"Asa is on the line with us," said Ben. "He can tell you about that."

"Okay," said Courtney. "How about it, Asa?"

"The Miocene," I said.

"What about Mastodonia? It would seem ideal to me."

"There's not enough time span," I told him. "If you are going to establish a human population sometime in the past, you have to be sure there is enough time margin so it doesn't collide with the rise of the human race."

"Mastodonia is pretty far back, isn't it?"

"No, it's not. We're only a little more than one hundred fifty thousand years back in time. You could go back three hundred thousand and still be in the Sangamon, but even that's not far enough. There were men on Earth then, primitive men, but still men. We can't afford a collision with them."

"But you and Rila?"

"Just the two of us. We're not going to introduce anyone else into the era. Just transitory people who come in to use the time roads. And there will be no men in America for at least a hundred thousand years."

"I see. And the Miocene? How far back is that?"

"Twenty-five million years."

"You judge that's deep enough into the past?"

"It gives us better than twenty million years before there could be anything even resembling man. Twenty million years from now, when the first possible collision could take place, there probably will be no humans left on Earth. Either in our present time span or twenty million years into our past."

"You mean we'll be extinct by that time."

"Extinct or gone somewhere else."

"Yes," said Courtney, "I suppose so."

He waited for a moment, then asked, "Asa, why the Miocene? Why not earlier? Why not a little later?"

"There'll be grass in the Miocene. Grass like we have now, very similar to it. Grass is necessary if you are going to raise livestock. Also, grass makes possible the existence of wild game herds. It would be important for settlers to have game herds; in the early days of settlement, they would supply food. And in the Miocene, the climate would be better."

"How so?"

"A long rain cycle would be coming to an end. The climate would be drier, but probably still sufficiently rainy for agriculture. The big forests that covered most of the land area would be dying out, giving way to grassland. Settlers wouldn't have to clear forests to make farmland, but there'd still be plenty of wood for them to use. No really vicious animal life, or, at least, none that we know of. Nothing like the dinosaurs in the Cretaceous. Some titanotheres, giant pigs, early elephants, but nothing that a big rifle couldn't handle."

"Okay, you've sold me. I'll tell the senator. And Asa . . ."

"Yes?"

"What do you think of the idea? Of sending these people back?"

"It wouldn't work," I said. "Not many of them

would want to go. They're not pioneers; they don't
want to be."

"You figure they'd rather stay right here, on welfare the rest of their lives? For that is what it amounts
to. They're in a poverty trap and they can't get out."

"I think most of them would stay right here," I
said. "They know what they're facing here. Back there,
they wouldn't know."

Courtney said, "I'm afraid you're right. I was in
hopes that if our injunction move fails, Freemore's
plan might bail us out—if it passes, that is."

"Don't count on it," I said.

Courtney and Ben talked only a short time longer.
There wasn't much to talk about.

As I sat there, listening to Ben's parting words,
I thought about the brightness of the promise that had
so quickly darkened. A few weeks ago, it had seemed
that nothing could interfere with us; we had the Safari
contract, the movie deal was moving forward, and we
were confident that other business would be shaping
up. But now, unless Courtney could prevail against
the State Department's order, we were out of business.

Personally, I did not mind too much—oh, of course,
I wouldn't have minded becoming a millionaire, but
money and success in business never had mattered too
much to me. For Rila, however, it was quite a different story, and while Ben said but little about it, I
knew that it meant a lot to him as well. My disappointment, I realized, was not so much for what I had lost
as for what the other two had lost.

When I left Ben's office, I went out into the orchard and found Catface there. We settled down to
talk. He did most of the talking. This time, he told
me about and showed me his home planet. It was an
entirely different place than the headquarters planet,
an outback world that had a poor economic basis.
Its land was thin for farming, it had few natural resources, no great cities had arisen. Its people dragged
out a dismal existence and they were different from
Catface—definitely biological, although there was
about them a puzzling ephemeral tendency, as if they
hovered indecisively between groundlings and sprites.

Catface must have sensed my surprise at this, for he said to me, "I was a freak. What would you call it? Perhaps a mutant. I was unlike the rest of them. I changed and they were puzzled at me and ashamed of me and perhaps even a little frightened of me. My beginning was unhappy."

His beginning—not his childhood, not his boyhood. I pondered over that.

"But headquarters took you," I said. "Perhaps that's why they took you. They were on the lookout, probably, for people just like you—people who could change."

"I'm sure of it," said Catface.

"You say you are immortal. Were the other people of your home planet immortal as well?"

"No, they were not. That is one of the measures of the differentness in me."

"Tell me, Catface, how do you know? How can you be sure that you are immortal?"

"I know, that's all," said Catface. "I know inside of me."

Which was good enough, I thought. If he knew inside of him, he probably was right.

I left him more puzzled than I had ever been before. Each time I talked with him, it seemed I grew more puzzled. For while I felt, for some strange reason, that I knew him more thoroughly than I'd ever known any other being, increasingly I sensed depths in him that seemed forever out of reach. I was puzzled, too, by the illogical feeling that I knew him well. I had talked with him, really talked with him, not more than a dozen times, and yet I had the impression that he was a lifelong friend. I knew things about him, I felt sure, that we had never talked about. I wondered if this could be attributed to the fact that on many occasions he had taken me inside of him, had made me, for a moment, one with him, in order that I might see with him certain concepts that he could not put in words I would understand. Was it possible that in these times of oneness with him I had absorbed some of his personality, becoming privy to thoughts and purposes that he may not have intended to convey?

By now, most of the newspapermen and camera crews had deserted Willow Bend. Some days, there were none at all, then at times a few would show up and stay for a day or two. We were still occasionally in the news, but the magic had left us. Our story had run out.

The tourists fell off. Usually, there were a few cars in Ben's parking lot, but nothing like the number that once had been there. Ben's motel now had vacancies—at times, a number of vacancies. Unless there was a turn in events, Ben stood to lose a lot of money. We still maintained the guards and turned on the floodlights at night, but this began to seem a little foolish. We were guarding something that perhaps no longer needed guarding. It was costing us a pile of money and we talked, off and on, of dismissing the guards and not turning on the lights. But we hesitated to do it—principally, I think, because doing it would seem an admission of defeat. As yet, we were not ready to give up.

The debate on the emigration issue raged on in Congress. One side charged the proposal meant abandonment of the disadvantaged; the other side claimed it was a move to offer them the advantages of a fresh start in a new environment not subject to all the stresses of their present one. Arguments thundered over the economics of the issue—the cost of giving the emigrants a fresh start in a new and virgin land as opposed to the yearly cost of welfare. Welfare recipients now and then raised voices that were submerged in the din; no one listened to them. Newspapers published Sunday features and TV networks staged specials explaining and illustrating the situation that would be found in the Miocene. The capitol was picketed by contending groups of citizens.

At Willow Bend, a few bands of cultists showed up. They carried banners and made speeches that favored abandonment of the present society and a retreat into the Miocene, or if not into the Miocene, into any place at all to get away from the callous injustices and inequities of the present system. They paraded back and forth in front of the gate and set up camp in Ben's parking lot. Herb went out to talk with them. They didn't stay long. There were no newspapermen to interview them, no photographers to take their pictures, no crowds to jeer them, no police to hassle them. So they went away.

The two houses of Congress passed the emigration bill. The president vetoed it; it was passed over his veto. But the State Department ban still held.

Then, the next day, the court made its decision. The ruling went against us. The injunction was denied; the ban on travel to Mastodonia stood and we were out of business.

THIRTY-TWO

A day later, the riots broke out. As if on signal (and perhaps on signal, for we never knew how they came about), the ghettos flared—in Washington, New York, Baltimore, Chicago, Minneapolis, St. Louis, the West Coast, everywhere. Mobs invaded the glittering downtown business areas and now, unlike the situation in 1968, it was not the ghettos that burned. The great plate-glass windows of the downtown stores were shattered, the stores were looted and fires were set. Police and, in some cases, the National Guard, fired on the rioters; the rioters fired back. The placards that said: GIVE US THE MIOCENE; that said: LET US GO; that said: WE WANT ANOTHER CHANCE, lay scattered in the streets, soaked in rain and, at times, stained with blood.

It went on for five days. The dead, on both sides, ran into the thousands, and business came to a standstill. Then, at the end of the fifth day, the violence dwindled to a halt. The two sides, the side of law and order and the side of outraged protest, drew apart. Slowly, haltingly, fumblingly, the talks began.

At Willow Bend, we were isolated. For the most part, intercontinental phone lines were out of order. The television stations, as a rule, continued in operation, although in a few instances, they, too, were silenced. We had one phone call from Courtney, but after that we heard nothing more from him. Attempts to reach him failed. In his one call, he had said that he was considering the possibility of appealing the court's action, but there were some situations he would have to study first.

Night after night, sometimes during the day, we gathered in Ben's office and watched the television

224

screen. At all times of the day or night, whenever there was a new bit of news about the riots, reports were put out, so that, in effect, television became an almost continuous news program.

It was a numbing thing to watch. In 1968 we had sometimes wondered if the republic would stand; now there were times when we were sure it wouldn't. Personally, and I suppose this also applied to the rest of us, I felt a sense of guilt, although we never talked about it. The thought kept hammering through my head: If we had not developed time travel, none of this would have come to pass.

We did talk about how we could have been so blind, so complacent in believing that the emigration law was simply an empty political gesture, that few of the underprivileged to whom it would apply had any wish to become pioneers in an unknown land. I felt especially remiss on this, for I had been the one, from the very first, who had said the entire proposal was senseless. The fury of the riots seemed to demonstrate that the ghettos did want the second chance the legislation offered. But it was difficult to judge how much of the violence was keyed to a desire for this second chance, and how much might have been caused by ancient, suppressed hatred and bitterness, cleverly touched off by those who led and directed the rioting.

There was a rumor that an army of rioters from the Twin Cities was moving on Willow Bend, perhaps with a view to taking over the time-travel operation. The sheriff hastily put out a call for volunteers to block the march, but, as it turned out, there had been no march. It was just another of the many ugly rumors that at times crept even into the news reports. Why the rioters did not think of taking us over, I will never figure out. From their point of view, it would have been a logical move, although, in all likelihood, it would not have worked out as they might have thought it would. If they thought of it at all, they probably envisioned a time machine of some sort that could be physically taken over and which they probably could operate. But, apparently, no one thought of it. Perhaps the leaders of the operation were concentrating on a violent confrontation that would bring the federal establishment to its knees.

The Five Days passed and relative calm fell over the battered, blackened cities. Talks began, but who was talking and where and what they might be talking about was not disclosed. The newsmen and the networks were unable to penetrate the silence. We tried to reach Courtney, but the long-distance lines were still out.

Then, late one afternoon, Courtney came walking through the gate.

"I didn't phone from Lancaster," he said, "because it was quicker to grab a cab and come." He took the drink that Ben offered him and sank into a chair. The man looked tired and harried.

"Day and night," he said, "for the last three days. Christ, I hope I never live through anything like this again."

"You were sitting in on the negotiations?" asked Ben.

"That's right. And I think we have it all worked out. I never saw such stubborn sons-of-bitches in all my life —both sides, the government and the rioters. I had to fight off both of them. Over and over, I had to explain to them that Time Associates had a big stake in the matter, that we had to protect our interests and that without us, no one could get anywhere."

He drained the paper cup he'd been given and held it out. Ben slopped more liquor into it.

"But now," he said, "I think we have it. The documents are being drawn up. As it stands, if none of the bastards changes his mind, we'll supply a time road into the Miocene without charge. I had to make that concession. The government points out that the program will cost so much that any fee to us would wreck it. I don't believe this, but there was nothing much that I could do. If I'd refused, the talks would have collapsed; the government, I think, was looking for some reason to walk out of them. We only furnish the time road, that is all. We say to them, here it is, and then it's their headache. In exchange for that, the State Department ban is removed and stays removed and there will be no effort, ever, to impose any kind of governmental regulations, state, federal or otherwise. And, furthermore—and this one, once again, almost wrecked the talks—Mastodonia is accorded recognition as an independent state."

I looked across the room at Rila and she was smiling—it was the first time she had smiled for days. And, somehow, I knew what she was thinking—that now, we could go ahead with that house in Mastodonia.

"I think," said Ben, "that is good enough. You did a good job, Court. We'd probably have trouble, anyhow, collecting any fees from the government."

The door opened and Hiram came into the room. We all turned to look at him.

He shuffled a few feet forward. "Mr. Steele," he said, "Catface would like for you to come. He wants to see you. He says it is important."

I rose and Rila said, "I'll come with you."

"Thanks," I said, "but no. I'd better see what this is about myself. It's probably nothing. It won't take too long."

But I had a horrible feeling it would be more than nothing. Never before had Catface sent for me.

Outside the building, Hiram said, "He's down near the chicken house."

"You stay here," I said. "I'll go alone."

I went down across the yard and around the chicken house and there was Catface, in one of the apple trees. As I walked toward the tree, I felt him reach out for me. When he did that, it seemed to me that we were in a place together, just the two of us, with all the rest of it shut out.

"I am glad you came," he said. "I wanted to see you before I left. I wanted to tell you . . . "

"Leave!" I shouted at him. "Catface, you can't leave. Not now. What are you leaving for?"

"I cannot help myself," said Catface. "I am changing once again. I told you how I changed before, back on my home planet after my beginning. . . . "

"But change?" I asked. "What kind of change? Why should you change?"

"Because I cannot help myself. It comes on me. It's no doing of my own."

"Catface, is this a change you want?"

"I think so. I have not asked myself yet. And yet, I feel happy at it. For I am going home."

"Home? Back to the planet of your birth?"

"No. To headquarters planet. Now I know that that is home. Asa, do you know what I think?"

I felt cold inside. I felt limp and beaten and suddenly, bereft. "No, I don't," I said.

"I think that I am becoming a god. When I go back, I will be one of them. I think this is how they come about. They evolve from other forms of life. Maybe only from my form of life. Maybe from other forms of life as well. I don't know. I think some day, I will know. I have served my apprenticeship. I have grown up."

I was in an emptiness, a black abyss of emptiness and the thing that rasped across my soul was the realization that it was not the loss of Catface's ability to construct time roads for us, but the loss of Catface himself that made the emptiness.

"Asa," he said, "I am going home. I had lost the way, but now I know the way and I am going home."

I said nothing. There was nothing I could say. I was lost in the emptiness.

"My friend," he said, "please wish me well. I must have that to carry with me."

I said the words, wrenched out of me as if they were dripping gobbets of flesh wrenched from my body; I wanted to say them, I had to say them, and yet they hurt to say: "Catface, I wish you well. Most sincerely, I do wish you well. I shall miss you, Catface."

He was gone. I did not see him go, but I knew that he was gone. There was a chill wind blowing out of nowhere and the black of the emptiness turned to gray and then it changed to nothing and I was standing in the orchard, at the corner of the hen house, looking at an empty apple tree.

Dusk had come across the land and any minute now, the floodlights would turn on automatically and the homestead would change into a garish nightmare, with the uniformed guards tramping up and down the fence. But, mercifully, for a few moments, I had the dusk and I needed it.

Then, the lights snapped on and I turned about to head for the office building. I was afraid that I would stagger, but I didn't. I walked stiff and straight, like a wound-up toy. Hiram was nowhere around and Bowser, more than likely, was somewhere hunting woodchucks, although it was a little late for woodchucks. Usually, they went to ground shortly after sundown.

I walked into the office. When I came through the door, they stopped their talking and sat there looking at me.

"Well?" asked Rila.

"Catface is gone," I said.

Ben came to his feet in a single surge.

"Gone!" he shouted. "Where has he gone?"

"He's gone home," I said. "He wanted to say goodbye. That is all he wanted—just to say goodbye."

"Couldn't you have stopped him?"

"There was no way to stop him, Ben. He grew up, you see. He served his apprenticeship. . . ."

"Now, just a minute," said Courtney, trying to be calm. "He'll be back, won't he?"

"No, he won't," I said. "He changed. He changed into something else. . . . "

Ben banged his fist on the desk. "What a lousy, goddamn break! Where does this leave us? I'll tell you where it leaves us. It leaves us up the creek."

"Not too fast," said Courtney. "Let's not go too fast. Let us not close out our options. There may be something left. We may salvage something."

"What do you mean?" asked Ben. "You and your lawyer talk . . . "

"We could save what we have," said Courtney. "The Safari contract and that's a cool two million bucks a year."

"But the Miocene. What about the Miocene?"

"Not the Miocene, Ben. Mastodonia."

Rila cried, "Not Mastodonia! I'll not have them in

Mastodonia. They would foul it up. Mastodonia is Asa's and mine."

"With Catface gone and no more time roads," said Courtney, his voice sharp and cold, "you'll have them in Mastodonia or you will have nothing at all." He said to me, "You're sure that Catface is gone, that he won't be back?"

"That is right."

"No more time roads?"

"No," I said. "There'll be no more time roads."

"You are sure of that?"

"Positive," I said. "Why the hell should I lie to you? You think this is a joke? I tell you, it's no joke. And I'll tell you something else. You're sending no one into Mastodonia. I explained to you the other day. There's not enough of a time margin. In the time of Mastodonia, there are already men. Hunting mastodons in Spain. Chipping flints in France."

"You're crazy!" Ben shouted. "You'd lose the little that we have . . . "

"Yes, by God," I yelled at him, "I'd lose it. To hell with the cool two million. To hell with the government and the rioters."

"And to hell with us?" asked Courtney gently, far too gently.

"Yes," I said, "to hell with you. By sending those mobs into Mastodonia, we could wreck all we have right now—all the human race may have right now."

"You know he's right," said Rila softly. "He's right on one premise and I'm right on another. Mastodonia belongs to the two of us and no one else can have it. Right now, it's clean; we can't make it dirty. And there's something more . . . "

I didn't wait to hear what more she had to say. I turned and stumbled out the door. I went down the hall, scarcely knowing where I was going, and out the front door to the gate. I said to the guard who stood by the gate, "Let me out," and he let me out.

The dusk had deepened and it was almost night. I could just make out the dark loom of a clump of trees across the road that ran into Willow Bend. Ben's big parking lot was empty and I moved toward it. I didn't know where I was going. And I didn't really care. All I wanted was to get away.

Because I knew that no matter what Rila and I did or said, we would lose; that under the pressure that would build up, we'd be forced to let the hordes into Mastodonia. The thing that hurt the most was that Ben and Courtney would be among those who pressured us.

I walked out quite a ways into the parking lot and then I turned around. And there, looming against the lights that shone upon it, was the fence. I'd not seen it from the outside except for that time I'd come home from Europe, and on that occasion, there'd been so much else to see—the crowds of people, the jam-packed parking lot, the hot dog stands and the man who was selling balloons—that I'd scarcely noticed the fence. But now I saw it in all its grotesqueness and otherworldliness, and its being there made me remember how it had been before—before there was a fence. Standing there, I felt the lostness and the loneliness of one who's lost his home—not only the old farm, but Mastodonia, as well. For I knew it was only a matter of time until Mastodonia would be gone. And gone with it, the fieldstone house with its many chimneys, the house that Rila had planned and of which we'd talked so many nights.

Rila, I thought—Rila, the self-styled pushy bitch who wanted to be rich—and yet, only a little while ago, she had made her choice, without any hesitation, between Mastodonia and a cool two million bucks a year.

You're a fraud, I told her. It had all been a pose, the bitchy business side of her. When it had come down to the final mark, she had dropped the pose and made her choice. She was still, no matter how you cut it, no matter all the growing up, that girl I'd loved back at the dig in the Middle East, the one whose face had been burned by the relentless sun, the one who always had a dirty face because she had to rub her itchy, sunburned, peeling nose with a dirty hand.

The Miocene, I thought, why couldn't we have reached the Miocene? Why didn't I think to have

Catface engineer a road into the Miocene days ago, so it would be ready if we needed it? If we had the Miocene, even with Catface gone, we could still save Mastodonia.

And Catface? A memory now. No longer grinning from a tree. Finally knowing what he was and would be.

Catface, I said to him, so long, old friend. I wish you well; I will miss you sorely.

It seemed in the instant of that thought that I was with him once again, that I had become one with him as I had so many times before, when he'd taken me in with him to see as he saw, to know what he knew.

To know what he knew.

To know, even if I did not entirely understand them, the things he had never told me; to be aware of, even if I could not understand them, the things that he had shown me.

Like the time equations, for example.

Suddenly, thinking of them, the time equations were there again, exactly as he had shown them to me, and looking at them, through his eyes from inside himself, I saw how they fit together neatly and how they could be used.

The Miocene, I thought, twenty-five million years into the past, and the equations fit together and I did other things that were necessary and I engineered a time road.

I receded out of him and he went away. I was inside of him no longer. I was not seeing through his eyes. And the equations . . . the equations . . . they had meant . . . but I'd lost the equations, the feel and shape of them, the knowing how to use them. If I had ever known. I was just a stupid human being now, one who had dared to dream he'd engineered a time road, using the information and the knowledge that had been fed into him, that had been given him without conscious telling, the gift of a being that was now a so-called god far among the stars.

I found that I was shaking. I hunched up my shoulders and clasped my hands together, hard, to try to stop the shaking. You goddamn fool, I told myself, you've psyched yourself into a classic state of jitters. Pull yourself together, fool; know yourself for what you are.

And yet . . . and yet . . . and yet . . .

Go ahead, I raged at myself, walk those few feet forward, tread that silly time road. You'll see. There is no Miocene.

I walked the few feet forward and there was a Miocene. The sun was halfway down the western sky and a stiff breeze from the north was billowing the lushness of the grass. Down the ridge, a quarter-mile away, a titanothere, an ungainly beast with a ridiculous flaring horn set upon his nose raised his head from grazing and let out a bellow at me.

Carefully, I turned about and stepped back down the road, walking back into the parking lot. Stooping, I took off my shoes and set them precisely, one ahead of the other, to mark the entrance to the road. Then, in my stocking feet, I walked down the lot to pull up an armload of the numbered stakes that had been driven into the ground to mark the stalls where cars should park. Along the way, I picked up a fist-sized stone and used it to drive in the stakes to mark the way into the Miocene.

Having done this, I sat down, flat upon the ground, to put on my shoes. Suddenly, I was tired and drained. I sought for triumph and found little of it in me. I just felt a sort of thankful peace. And I knew that everything would be all right now, for if I could engineer a road into the Miocene, I could engineer other roads as well. Not by myself, I couldn't. Not as I was now, I couldn't. But once I stepped inside of Catface . . .

It took quite a while to put on my shoes, for I seemed to be extraordinarily fumble-fingered. But I finally got them on and stood up, then headed for the gate. There was something very urgent that I must do. I must, as soon as possible, tell Rila that the two of us could keep Mastodonia.

KOPEKT A
EINLEIN

ABOUT THE AUTHOR

Clifford D. Simak is a newspaperman, only recently retired. Over the years he has written more than 25 books and has some 200 short stories to his credit. In 1977 he received the Nebula Grand Master award of the Science Fiction Writers of America and has won several other awards for his writing.

He was born and raised in southwestern Wisconsin, a land of wooded hills and deep ravines, and often uses this locale for his stories. A number of critics have cited him as the pastoralist of science fiction.

Perhaps the best known of his work is *City*, which has become a science-fiction classic.

He and his wife Kay have been happily married for almost 50 years. They have two children—a daughter, Shelley Ellen, a magazine editor, and Richard Scott, a chemical engineer.